Don't Ever Wonder

also by Darren Coleman

Before I Let Go
Do or Die

also by Darren Coleman

Before I Let Go
Do or Die

Don't Ever Wonder

The sequel to *Before I Let Go*

Darren Coleman

 Amistad *An Imprint of* HarperCollins*Publishers*

Designed by Chris Welch

ISBN 0-7394-5476-5

For Monica Allen, Derek Lowe, and Chad Cunningham

You three spoiled me by *always* taking time out of your busy days at work to read my manuscript chapter by chapter. Your encouragement meant the world to me! That is the only exclamation point you will see in my whole book, so recognize that I mean that from the bottom of my heart. I can't count the number of times that I got sidetracked and lost focus, starting five other books, at least, while trying to complete this one. You all kept asking for more and more until one day I messed around and finished a book. I love ya'll and I hope that I have touched your lives the way you've touched mine.

Special thanks . . . Kelli Martin and Rockelle Henderson. You both believed in me from the start, and I want to thank you for your hard work and dedication. You've lived this book and helped me breathe life into it. This is *our* book and *our* success is forthcoming.

Your background, it ain't squeaky clean,
Shit, sometimes we all gotta' swim upstream,
You ain't no saint. We all are sinners,
but you put your good foot down and make your soul a winner.
                                        —*Jill Scott*

Once Upon a Time

Aubette was already packed at seven p.m. People piled in for happy hour after work, and on the weekends they stayed until three in the morning once the party started. I hadn't come for mingling or party atmosphere this time though. I came for one quick drink and a little conversation. On my cab ride over to 27th Street, my fingers were crossed that my meeting wouldn't turn ugly, even though I had been assured that we were adult enough to handle this.

Once inside I made my way past the bar and headed toward the rear of the lounge. Aubette was filled with a mix of folks dressed in business attire and around-the-way girls already dressed for the club. As Twista's "Slow Jams" was coming to an end, I had to weave through a few dancing couples to get to the table. I looked over to my left and spoke to my favorite bartender, Terri. She waved and shot me a smile. As soon as I cleared the bar I saw her sitting at a small table off to my right. A mix of emotions flared up and I swallowed hard as I made my way to her. Our eyes were locked and she stood up as I reached the table. She extended her arms and gave me a tight hug. The warmth was familiar and when she pulled away she was sporting a smile as wide as the Hudson River.

"Mr. Dandridge. How nice to see you after all this time," she said both sarcastically and seductively. Anthony Hamilton's "Float" was coming through the speakers and for a second I remembered our first dance together. It was hard to believe that one innocent dance could have led to all of this.

I smiled at her. "It's good to see you too. You look lovely." I couldn't help but notice that she was looking exceptionally beautiful. Not that I had expected anything less from her, but when you don't see someone for a while you tend to forget some of what you loved about them. She was wearing a copper strapless dress that showed off some serious tan lines and had on the necklace that I had gotten her from Tiffany. She had obviously been on vacation. "Nice necklace." I mentioned and then added, "Nice tan too."

"Oh thanks." She was grinning. "An old friend picked it up for me a while back. As for the tan, I picked that up in Puerto Rico at my family reunion."

I knew about the reunion because my wife, Shelly, had contemplated for weeks whether or not to attend. She had decided not to go once her mother had confirmed that Nina would be there. We sat and the waitress came back for our orders. I pointed at Nina and asked the waitress to take her order first. "I'll take a glass of white zinfandel and the adobo-roasted chicken for my entrée."

"I'll take a vodka martini and the shrimp dish right here," I said, pointing to the menu.

The waitress took the menus and headed off. There was a moment of uncomfortable silence that I tried to fill by observing my surroundings. I was interrupted with, "Cory, are you okay?" My hands were on the table and she reached for them. "If you are uncomfortable, we don't have to do this. You can leave."

I lied. "No I'm fine. I was just thinking about work. I have to stop doing that." I paused. "So what did you want to talk about?"

"Whoa. I wanted to have a drink and chill with you first, been a long time, right?" She released my hands. Her touch had been so subtle I had forgotten that she was holding them. "I must admit that I am surprised that you even agreed to meet me."

I nodded my head in agreement because I was surprised as well and it *had* been a long time. But I guess that deep down inside I had wanted to see her months ago just to be sure she was okay. I granted her request and relaxed a bit while we ate and ordered our second and third drinks. It was a quarter past eight when my phone rang. I excused myself and went down the steps and into the restroom.

"Hey, sweetie." I said to my wife on the other end.

"Hey, do you think you can pick up Amani from the sitter's? I told Mrs. Lamar that I would be there by eight and Rockelle and I are still out trying to pick up a few things for Christina's baby shower tomorrow." Shelly had been planning a baby shower for her college roommate, who lived in Brooklyn.

"Why don't you call and ask Mrs. Lamar if she can stay a little later. I am in the middle of something and probably won't make it there for at least two more hours. I have a really important assignment and this deadline . . ."

"Fine." I heard the disgust in her voice as she cut me off. Then she hung up. Shelly's combative behavior whenever she didn't get her way, or if I didn't jump through hoops, was becoming a routine. If I went to the gym, or, heaven forbid, got a drink before coming home, she bitched. I was getting so sick of it that the makeup sex no longer seemed worth it. I knew I was headed for attitude city by the time we met up at home, so I decided to loosen up and enjoy my time with Nina.

Nina's face looked a little flushed from the wine when I got back to the table. All my apprehensions had faded and now I wanted nothing more than to sit and talk for at least another hour with my sister-in-law, who happened to be my ex-fiancée. As a matter of fact, I was feeling way too relaxed for my own good. I was relaxed enough to give my wife the impression that I was probably still working on some important project. And thanks to the alcohol, I was relaxed enough to let the truth come out of my mouth: "Nina you are so beautiful. I am so sorry for hurting you the way I did. If I could take it all back I would."

After coming out of left field with the first statement, I began rambling. "I didn't even realize how much I loved you. I have to admit that I think I made the biggest mistake of my life." She looked down at the table for a second, dodging my eyes. "I don't expect you to forgive me, I just want you to know that . . ." I shook my head in disgust at myself for spilling my guts like a loser. I went on. "I just want you to know that I am sorry and have been miserable without you."

While I spoke I hadn't noticed that her eyebrows had raised and that her lips had parted, exposing her shock. She would have interrupted me if she could have but I had stunned her with my confession. She placed her hands over her face, stood up, and rushed off to the bathroom.

I waited in confusion for about ten minutes, wondering what was going through her mind. Was she embarrassed, angry, or was she feeling the same way? While she was in the restroom the waitress came back and I paid the bill and continued to sit patiently waiting for her. Feeling drained, I closed my eyes and tried to tune out the crowd's chatter.

"How much do I owe you for the bill?" I looked up and saw her standing right next to me.

"C'mon now. You know better than that." I motioned for her to sit down and she shook her head no. My heart was sinking fast as I asked, "Are you are ready to leave?"

"Yes." Her demeanor had changed. Her body language communicated that she was no longer relaxed. Her arms were folded and she was clutching her purse as if I was going to steal it and she looked like she had been crying.

"Let's walk then." I said as I led her toward the door. The spot had gotten packed. Everyone was piling in trying to get the last taste of summer before September and the fall weather rolled in. We hit the street and moved toward the curb. "I'll get you a cab."

"No, wait. Walk a little up the block with me. I want to respond to what you said in there." We started walking. The air was warm and people were moving about on both sides of the street. We made it halfway down the block before she turned and said. "Cory." I was still. Hands in my pockets. My heart began pumping wildly. I looked directly at her. "I want you to know something."

"I'm listening."

"I was wrong too. Not just you . . . the whole thing was wrong. I should have never dated you. A crush is one thing because believe me, brother, you are *fine*." She punched me in the chest softly and laughed. "What we did though was wrong. You and my sister were together and made a child. I still think that she is ignorant as all hell for keeping you in the dark for five years about the child you two had together. That will never make sense to me and I hope that it never makes sense to you either."

I digested what she had said but wasn't sure if she wanted a reply. It was obvious she didn't because she went right on. "But two wrongs don't make a right. I should have been better than that and so should you."

I cut her off. ". . . But baby girl . . . *you* are so damned fine. How could I resist you?" I pinched her cheek, lightening the mood, and we both laughed. "You're right. No doubt about it. I have lost many nights of sleep over the way I have handled things."

"As well you should have."

"But what does it mean to be here now? Everything that has happened can't be undone. These feelings can't be turned off." I looked down at the sidewalk. "I do still love you though." The words just slipped off of my lips.

I felt her fingers touch my chin. "Poor Cory," she said. "You'll love me today, then Shelly tomorrow. Whoever ain't there . . . that is who you will love, Papi. With you it's never the here and now. You are a faraway love."

"What?"

"You're a faraway love. No good at loving up close and in the present. That's the funny thing about men. Something most women will never understand." She sensed that I was all ears. "When a sistah leaves your ass, you all of a sudden gain all this clarity. But by then it's too late. She has picked up the shattered pieces of her heart and moved on."

"So it's too late." At that moment I was thinking that I could end my marriage to Shelly and make everything right. Thoughts of my life as it was cruised through my mind. Not many people get a chance to go back and try to re-create a magical feeling that once meant everything. I had taken that chance with Shelly and found out that sometimes the past is better left right there, in the past. She still found it necessary to argue over small things and hold grudges. As far as I was concerned Shelly was still spoiled, and to listen to her tell it, I was still selfish.

Looking deep into her eyes and almost through her, I was half-listening and half-wishing that Nina and I could move somewhere far away and be happy, never worrying about anyone judging us because we fell in love. The idea of it sent a wave of happiness through me. Realizing though that Nina would have probably figured me crazy, I didn't share my thoughts and instead remained silent.

"It's way too late," she said, backing toward the curb. She turned and hailed a cab.

"So how long are you in town for?"

"I leave on Sunday."

I pulled out a card and wrote my cell number on the back of it. "Call me tomorrow. The afternoon will be best."

"I'll think about it." A cab stopped and she opened the door. "I won't make any promises," she said nonchalantly. Her tone stung a bit.

"Hey."

She looked back. No smile.

I couldn't believe myself as the words slipped off of my lips. "Do you still love me?"

As she backed into the cab she said, "Once upon a time." The door shut . . . and just like that Nina was gone again.

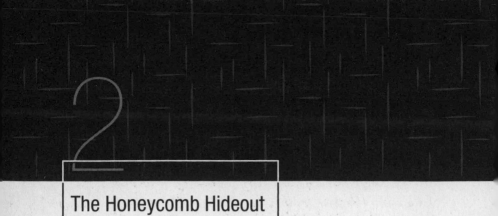

The Honeycomb Hideout

He was in the fetal position, sleeping like a baby. The sheets were all twisted up between his chocolate legs and saliva dripped slowly out the corner of his mouth. As usual only the aroma of bacon, eggs, and fried potatoes were enough to stir him from his slumber. Like clockwork Janette came into her bedroom with breakfast on a tray.

"Wake up, baby." She nudged his slow-moving body so that he could sit up.

"I'm up." Nate stretched and propped the pillows behind his back. "Where is the remote?" Janette pointed to the covers next to him and he nodded his head, letting her know he wanted her to hand it to him.

"So are you going to come down to the office today and join me for lunch." Every day she asked and every day he gave her the same answer.

"We'll see." Nate flipped the channel to ESPN. "I told you I was going to go down to Run n' Shoot today to renew my membership. While hiding out in Charlotte he had gained

fifteen pounds. He seemed to meet one great cook after another, but Janette was a triple threat. She fried, broiled, and
baked her thick ass off. Although he would never admit it
she was the only woman whose cooking topped his grandmother's.

"You said the same thing last week and the week before."
Janette was in the closet deciding which shirt to put on. "I
don't know why you think you need to go to the gym. No
woman wants a man that is skin and bones. You look great."

Compared to you I look great, he thought to himself. "Nah,
this isn't me. I don't feel right. I have never weighed over two
hundred pounds." He had a mouth full of food and was talking at the same time. "And you *are* going to stop making me
all this fattening food. I know what you are trying to do."

"And what is that?" Janette said, sticking her head out of
the closet.

"You want me all fat so nobody else will want me." He was
spreading Country Crock on his toast.

"Negro, please. I'm a thick sistah and brothers are constantly pushing up on me."

"Yeah, that's because you are a two-hundred-pound god-
dess." He puckered his lips up to get a kiss. Janette walked
toward him and gave him a smooch on the lips and turned
away to continue getting ready for work. "And that CL600
you pushing don't hurt either." He started laughing. Janette
walked back over toward Nate and punched him softly in the
arm and snatched a piece of bacon off his tray. "Hey, now.
Don't mess with a dog's food while he's eatin," Nate growled.

"And don't bite the hand that feeds you."

"Speaking of biting, come here." Nate placed the breakfast
tray on the floor. He reached for Janette and his hands caught
hold of her waist.

"No, sweetie. I am going to be late for work. We don't have time." She didn't try hard enough to pull away.

"Work. I got all the work you need right here." Nate slid his Calvin Klein boxer briefs down to his ankles and kicked them off. His dick was halfway hard and when Janette took a look she couldn't fight the arousal that washed over her body. From the first time she had laid her hazel eyes on Nate she had wanted him. The tricky part had been getting him to do more than sex her. Her weight was distributed mostly on her hips and ass. Although they sagged a little, her 40DD breasts made most men drool and she kept them encased in the most beautiful brassieres money could buy. All of this is to say that Janette had no problem with her size, nor any problem enticing men with her appearance. She did however harbor deep fears of a man straying and wanting a smaller woman once she had become attached and decided she wanted him all to herself.

Nate had noticed Janette heading to her car after a jazz concert at Marshall Park on a Sunday afternoon. He had been intrigued with her walk. He had never seen a full-figured woman move with the grace of a runway model. He had no intention of stopping to talk to her until he moved past her car and saw her smile at him. He smiled back at her and then he heard her laugh and ask him if he was scared to stop and talk. Janette was confident and beautiful. Her hair, nails, and feet were always done. She was showing off at the concert with a tight pair of capri pants and a linen shirt with no bra underneath it. He had ended up standing at her car talking and putting his mack down until every car had emptied from the parking lot.

They had spent the next few days talking on the phone before Nate had decided to give thick loving a try. He had not regretted it. Janette ended up breaking him down with a massage that left him weak as a lamb. Before he met her he hadn't slept soundly since leaving D.C., almost a year back. After Kim's suicide Nate had succumbed to guilt and shame to the point that he had nightmares and anxiety attacks that left him short of breath. Eventually the cooking and pampering that Janette provided softened Nate, and he was able to fight off the guilt and depression that haunted him almost every night. As time wore on he became dependent on Janette and had all but abandoned his old ways of womanizing and running the streets. Although he was officially living in his Aunt Marion's basement, he slept at Janette's almost nightly. He'd put on weight like a pregnant woman and had stopped getting his hair cut regularly. It was as if he simply no longer cared about his appearance. The stress of Kim's death and the guilt for his role in it had begun to wear him down. He was lost in feelings of regret for his treatment of her. Secretly he longed for some relief from the despair, but he'd never had to ask anyone for help. He didn't know how, and now it was beginning to cost him. The man he'd always been was fading into something far less appealing. It would have been apparent that he was a broken man to anyone who truly knew him. But to Janette, he was a cuddly dream come true.

She took a glimpse at her clock and knew she would be late for her first patient. Still she leaned over and took him in her mouth. As she began sucking Nate, she thought long and hard about getting married one day. She had an idea what it would take to keep a husband happy and this was her version of it. Nate's head instantly fell back and his mouth dropped open. She was sucking him so good. He knew that she was trying to take him out fast so that she could get to work. He wanted to slow her down so that he could show her that he was the boss. He attempted to pull himself up but her hands slid up his chest and pressed him back into the bed. With the other hand she began to pump his shaft while making loud slurping and purring noises with her mouth wrapped around the tip of his manhood.

"Oh, Nett. Oh, Nett." He moaned out. "No, baby, not like this."

She knew she had him. She started bobbing her head up and down using her tongue and the roof of her mouth to drive him over the edge. She had one hand on his nipples, pulling and caressing them. With the other hand she gripped his balls and massaged them, never stopping the suction she had going on.

The room began spinning. Nate was flat on his back trying to watch in amazement as Janette used her tongue like a weapon of mass destruction. Just as Nate was about to reach his orgasm, he regained his composure and caught her head on the upstroke. He pushed her head back and rolled away.

"Take those pants off," he demanded. Her face showed disappointment that she hadn't made him erupt but she knew her body was in for a delightful pounding. She grabbed her Nextel and smashed a button.

"Liza," she said into the phone.

"Hey, Janette. What's up?"

"Are you at the office?" Nate was standing behind her sliding her pants off. She stepped out of them. He then grabbed her thong and began sliding it down as well.

"I just got in."

"Okay, I am running about a half hour late. Call Mrs. Tucker and see if we can push her down to three-thirty. What is she getting anyway?"

"Fillings. Two of them."

"If she can't make it then . . ." Janette stopped when Nate's fingers found her button and penetrated her at the same time. "Whoo." She said aloud. She mouthed "stop" to Nate but didn't mean it. "Just do what you got to do. S . . . s . . . see you in a little bit."

"Girl, you all right over there?" Liza had a feeling what was going on. Liza was Janette's first and only receptionist and she noticed that Janette had been running late more in the last three months than she had in the previous four years combined since she had been practicing dentistry.

The phone was already on the floor and Janette had leaned over the bed. Nate had slipped on a condom and was entering Janette an inch at a time. "Mmmm," he said. "Slippery when wet."

Janette's breathing quickened as Nate locked onto her hips and began banging away. Sometimes he hit it slow but that was more for him than her. She loved to be licked slow but fucked hard and fast. "That's right, daddy. Bang it. Bang it."

The bed was shaking as Janette used it to hold herself up. "You like that? You want it harder?" Nate quickened his pace and was pulling all the way out and slamming back into her. He worked nonstop on her, hitting it from the back like a madman for five minutes straight as sweat began pouring off of his chest.

Janette's eyes rolled up into her head and she thought about how lovely life had been since Nate had been around. Any women who said size didn't matter obviously had never been hit by a Mandingo like Nathan Montgomery. She was bouncing back against him, enjoying the feeling of him thoroughly working her middle. "Ooohhh, baby. Don't stop." She felt electric sparks start in her toes and creep slowly up past her ankles. Her thighs began to tremble to the point that she feared she wouldn't be able to keep her balance.

Nate felt her orgasm nearing and decided to send her over the edge. He took the thumb that was gripping her right cheek and let is slip into her ass. When he did this Janette growled like a grizzly that had been shot with a dart gun. She tried to stand as the tides of her orgasm crashed through her body but she was too weak. "Are you cumming, Nett?"

Why he had to ask she never knew. "Yes. Yes. Yessss." And she let out a series of short screams. His breath quickened and she knew what to do. She summoned all the energy in her body and pulled away from him, spun around, and dropped to her knees. In one motion she had the condom off and Nate in her mouth.

"Oh yes." His body stiffened and the veins in his neck seemed to pop out at the same time he released into her mouth. She took him all in until she was sure he was finished. *This is how to get a man and that food I cook is how to keep one,* she thought as she swallowed his juices. "Girl, you so nasty," Nate said as a smile slowly formed out of the fuck face he sported moments earlier.

Janette wiped the drops that had run on her chin and licked her fingers clean. "You love it. You love it." She repeated.

"I can't get enough of it." He began laughing. He pointed down to his penis, which was still hard. He walked into the bathroom singing, "It's the remix to ignition coming hot out the kitchen. . . ."

He could see that Janette had picked up her cell. "Liza. Cancel and reschedule all my appointments. I'll work late all next week." He stood in the door of the bathroom and shook his head.

"Girl, you are crazy."

"Nasty, crazy, whatever. Just come eat me."

3

It Takes a Fool to Learn

Of all the people Brendan expected or wanted to bump into in Dr. Carson's office, he would have been close to last. When Brendan saw his face he wished he could turn around and walk right back out the door. Mr. Shoreham put the *Black Enterprise* magazine down and immediately noticed Brendan.

"Hey fella," Mr. Shoreham said. Brendan was surprised that there wasn't even the slightest hint of hostility. He leaned across the magazine table to give Brendan a handshake. "Where you been? Just because Renée moved out of town doesn't mean you can't stop through and say hello once in a while."

Brendan swallowed hard and tried to digest what Mr. Shoreham had just said. "Oh. I have just been working hard, you know trying to put those hours in." Sensing that he needed to keep the conversation moving, he added, "I will try to get by there one day to see you and the missus." Brendan was stunned that Renée had moved out of town and not so much as said good-bye.

"You need to do that. How is your family?" Before Brendan

could answer, Mr. Shoreham went on. "As a matter of fact I saw your mom a few weeks back out at Arundel Mills."

"Everyone is fine." Brendan shot him few questions about his grandson, followed by a couple of comments about the weather, before he came up with a way to ask him about Renée. It was obvious that she hadn't told her parents about the way that they had fallen out. If he had known Brendan had broken his beloved baby girl's heart, Mr. Shoreham might have tried to put a chokehold on Brendan right there in the waiting room. "So how does Renée like it down there . . ." Brendan faked a yawn. "Excuse me."

"No problem. She said she loves it in Houston. She complains about the heat but it's Texas. I mean what did she expect?" Mr. Shoreham laughed. "I think I am going to make it down there this fall. You ought to come with me."

Brendan imagined himself showing up at Renée's door. His face tightened when he thought of the drama that might unfold. "Yeah I might do that," he said, knowing full well there was no chance of it.

"Yeah, her fiancé is a really nice guy. He reminds me of you, to be honest. Just a clean-cut, decent guy. Just like you, as a matter of fact." He patted Brendan on the shoulder. "When I met him on Easter, I joked with her. I said you didn't have to go all the way to Houston to marry Brendan." He burst into laughter and Brendan's face had the kind of look you get when you pass gas out loud in a crowded elevator.

"Wow, that's really something." Is all he said in a low tone, but really wanting to scream out, *That's some bullshit.*

The receptionist called Mr. Shoreham up to the counter and gave him a prescription. He gave Brendan a handshake as he was on the way out. "Don't be a stranger, son. I mean that." Brendan nodded and Dr. Carson came out and told him to come to the room in the back. His mind was racing with thoughts from all the news that he'd just gotten. His best friend since middle school had cut him off. He had played with her emotions. Unintentional as his actions had been, a lifelong friendship had been ruined by passions gone awry. Now she had left town, which seemed to be a new trend for everyone he knew. Brendan wondered about her getting engaged so soon after leaving and assumed she was on the rebound. His mind was completely blown by it all.

As he sat on the examining table he tried not to wrinkle the white paper on the table. He thought about calling Cory from his cell to tell him about what he'd heard but decided to wait until his appointment was over. Dr. Carson walked back into the office. "Hey, Dude. How are you?"

Brendan considered telling him the truth but instead gave the traditional, "Fine."

"Great. Listen, I called you back in for two reasons." Dr. Carson was looking at his charts. "Like Yvonne told you, your sodium levels were a little abnormal but that is nothing to really worry about. Just start drinking some more water and I will check it for you in two weeks." He placed the chart down on the table.

"Okay. But what was the other thing?" he asked, thinking he'd heard the worst.

Dr. Carson took a deep breath that Brendan realized couldn't be anything good. "My friend, from looking at your culture, it, seems that you may have contracted a case of chlamydia."

"Say what?" Brendan shot back.

"I can't say one hundred percent without blood work, but I tested you for everything in your physical." Dr. Carson picked up the file and started scribbling. "I don't want to say it's no big deal, but it is easily treated. I will get you a quick shot and a prescription." He grabbed a needle and told Brendan to drop his pants. A few seconds later and the needle was pulled from his hip.

"So what does this mean?" Brendan was trying to make sense of it all. "Has my girlfriend been cheating?"

Dr. Carson smiled. As far as Brendan was concerned there wasn't anything to smile about. "Not necessarily." He handed Brendan the cotton ball doused with alcohol and a Band-Aid. "You may have contracted this anytime after your last checkup which was . . ."

"Seven months ago, and, Doc, I haven't had sex with anyone except her since then."

A frown came over the doctor's face. He nodded his head to show that his heart went out to Brendan. "Then there's a pretty good chance she has some explaining to do." He scribbled on his prescription pad. "Tell her she needs to get checked out. Also, I would advise that you don't have unprotected sex." He handed Brendan the prescription. "Two a day for ten days. Take care of yourself." He shook Brendan's hand and headed out the door.

Brendan moved up the short hallway, through the lobby, and out of the office building. When he walked outside, he was blasted by the heat. Instead of lifting him up, the sun felt like the decisive blow in a heavyweight fight. As he moved toward his car he thought, *Some days it doesn't even pay to get out of the bed.*

Brendan exited the parking lot and put on a Kindred CD as he tried to pull himself together. As he drove toward the CVS he contemplated all the possible outcomes to his situation. Trina would be coming home from work in a couple of hours and had no idea how angry he was. Renée was two thousand miles away and engaged to some clown who was "a lot like him." He wondered if he would have been happier if he and Renée had tried to work things out.

Wondering about it now was pointless. It was water under the bridge as far as he and Renée were concerned. Right now he needed to focus on his and Trina's problems and he needed a plan. He would have a better shot at hitting the lottery than he would at getting an honest answer out of Trina. She had come a long way since they had gotten back together, but she had a history of cheating and lying. It was apparent that she still wasn't playing fair. This time, though, Brendan was determined to beat her at her own game and make her pay.

4

Yearnin' for Your Love

I came home from work to a darkened house. The only light was coming from the tea light candles that were flickering in their holders, placed strategically around the apartment. The stereo was on and an oldies CD was playing. Ron Isley before he was Mr. Biggs was softly crooning that he was "drifting on a memory, ain't no place that I rather be than with you." I was feeling his sentiments exactly as I was caught up in feelings of excitement and surprise. "Day will make a way for night, all we need is candle light and a song."

I had expected to come home to a major attitude but instead my wife had given me romance. For a moment, I felt some measure of guilt for having met up with Nina. It wasn't as if I didn't love Shelly. I just didn't think that we had *enough* of what it took to make it for the long haul. This may have been a good start at fixing things, and the romance with my wife could help me forget about Nina.

I followed the candlelight past the living room toward the hallway that led to the master bedroom. I walked through the

French doors and saw the comforter pulled back off the bed revealing a fine set of gold satin sheets. There was a small pot-pourri holder burning on the nightstand and the room smelled like the majestic place that the Ojays were singing about on "Stairway to Heaven," which was now playing.

I could hear the streams of the shower and see the steam flowing out of the bathroom door, which was ajar. "Don't you want to go, don't you want to go," the chorus rang out. I made my way to the door of the bathroom and watched my wife as she was washing herself with a Victoria's Secret body wash. I stood there for a moment, as she lathered up and began to delicately sponge every inch of her body. I loved watching her shower. Something in the way the water ran over her face and off her chin. The way it formed a small river and found it's way between her breasts. It turned me on, and this time was no different. When she noticed I was standing there she invited me to join her. I kicked off my shoes and my pants fell to my feet. Once my shirt was unbuttoned she could see my excitement as my penis had already began to fight to get through the hole of my boxers.

"Lets get it on," Marvin was singing. I guess I was moving too slowly because before I could get my shirt off she had stepped out of the shower and pulled me in with my wife-beater still on. My underwear was at my ankles and I almost tripped as I stepped into the shower. The water was hot but her kisses were hotter. She pushed my back to the rear wall of the shower and forced her tongue into my mouth. After a few seconds of kissing she pulled back and with a hungry look in her eyes she reached out and grabbed my T-shirt with her fin-gernails and ripped it off. She came back to me and placed her mouth on my chest and began licking and biting at my nip-ples. Her hands were at my manhood and I could feel the lather of soap lubricating me. She began stroking it as she kissed me on the neck. I was getting high from the sensations as she tickled the head just the right way.

The candle on the counter flickered and created a dizzying effect. At least I thought it was from the candles. It was more likely the combination of the steam and the fact that all the blood in my body was rushing to my pelvic area. I was panting, trying to catch my breath, and felt my body about to erupt when she stopped. "Rinse off, I want you in the bed. I have a surprise for you," Shelly whispered into my ear.

I struggled to regain my composure and made my way out of the shower. I didn't take the time to dry off thoroughly as I couldn't wait to get into the bed and enjoy her. I sat on the edge of the bed with my towel underneath me. She walked out of the bathroom, body glistening from a quick rubdown with her scented oil, and I looked at her standing before me. I was wondering what she was going to do next when she knelt down in front of me. She never broke eye contact as she eased toward my center with her mouth wide open. I was shocked because she hadn't gone down on me without me asking for it since we had been married.

"Love them and leeeeeaaave them," Rick James belted out. "That's what I used to do." Shelly's head was bobbing up and down as she gave me the head of my lifetime, and with the hand that she wasn't using, she pushed me back so that I was now flat on the bed. I didn't know how her technique had improved so much. She was gliding up and down so quickly that the sensations were mixed together and my body felt like a firecracker ready to pop. Once again, when I almost reached my peak, she stopped. This time she climbed up onto the bed and rocked onto my chest placing her ass in the air long enough to position the head of my dick at her entrance. In one smooth motion she had me inside of her and she was grinding her bottom on me trying to get every inch.

She looked like a porn star as she stared into my eyes, licking her lips. "You love this pussy don't you, daddy?" she asked.

"Yeah, you know I do." I replied in hurried breath.

"Then tell me, Cory." She was bouncing up and down, pulling on her nipples. "Tell me you love it."

"Oh, I love it."

"Say it again."

"I love it." She was wet as a waterfall and her flower was opening wider, taking me all in.

"Call my name." My eyes opened and my head was thrashing back and forth. She yelled it a second time. "Call my name, baby. Who's your bitch?" I loved it when she talked foul during sex. *"Qué es mi nombre?"* She said in her native tongue.

In that instant I lost control and yelled out, "Nina."

Instantly the room froze and a smile formed on Shelly's face. I looked at her and then back to the door of our bedroom. "Nina, what the hell are you doing here?"

Shelly was still on top of me and made no attempt to move or cover herself. "Cory, I invited her. I figured that it was time that Nina and I made up. No man is worth losing a sister over." I looked at Nina in disbelief.

Nina finally spoke. "Listen, Cory. It's obvious that you love us both and there's no fighting it. Shelly and I decided that we would do anything to make you happy and now we're going to give you what you want. I just hope you can handle us both." Once she said that, she opened her three-quarter-length jacket, revealing what she was wearing underneath. Nothing.

I watched her approach the bed as she dropped her jacket to the floor. Shelly climbed off me and got down on all fours. I immediately entered her from behind.

Nina walked up and placed her hand on the small of my back and her other hand on my chest. She then pulled my face to hers and she began to kiss me. I had never been with two women at one time and the experience had my heart beating so fast that I felt like I might pass out. "Here, lil' sis, your turn," Shelly said. She moved away from me and guided Nina to the bed. She pulled Nina's legs apart and guided me into her. On one hand I was so shocked that Shelly was allowing this, but on the other I was so overjoyed and turned on that I was working myself into a frenzy.

I was pounding Nina the same way I had the entire year before Shelly and I got married. Nina and I had enjoyed some hot sex. While Nina was a little more reserved than Shelly in the beginning, I had gotten her to open up as time went on. Now she was beneath me humping me back as if her life depended on it. "Papi, I missed you so. Ahhhh," she moaned out.

"I missed you too, baby." I felt myself on the brink of my orgasm when Shelly grabbed my shoulder and yelled.

"Who the hell do you miss?" she said angrily as I opened my eyes. She startled me so much that I rolled out of Nina and felt myself falling. In the next instant I hit the hardwood floor with a thud.

I opened my eyes to the sunlight bursting through the windows. I came to and realized that I was lying on my back. Shelly was looking over the edge of the bed at me. "No more Domino's Pizza for you in the middle of the night. You must have had a hellified dream."

When I realized that it was all a dream, I felt a sense of relief and disappointment at the same time. "Yeah, I must have been having a nightmare." I climbed up off the floor and headed for the bathroom to try to get rid of the hard-on that I had. A few splashes of cold water and a morning piss would do the trick.

I ran cold water on my washcloth and scrubbed my eyes as I stared at myself in the mirror. I thought back on my dream and wondered if I had slipped up and said Nina's name.

"So you don't remember your dream, Cory?" Shelly said as I climbed back into the bed.

I slid underneath the covers and the scene came back to me. I was inside Nina with Shelly watching. I closed my eyes and said. "I almost never do."

"Mmm hmm," she purred. I felt her fumble for the remote to the radio. A few seconds later Rick James and Teena Marie were singing "Fire and Desire." My eyes opened wide and I knew that going back to sleep was going to be hard.

Mrs. Lamar showed up at one thirty as she did every Saturday. She worked for us Tuesday through Saturday. On Saturdays she would bring her granddaughter with her to play with Amani. They were both six going on sixteen and would take turns doing each other's hair. They would see who could outdo the other's Powerpuff Girls drawings and then sing on the karaoke machine for another hour or two. I often used the opportunity to escape and do a little shopping or meet up with one of the guys from work at a bar. Shelly was almost never home on Saturdays. She had several college friends in the area and had really embraced the whole idea of being a New Yorker.

Amani and I were still bonding. Meeting your daughter for the first time when she is already five years old can make it tough turning mommy's princess into a daddy's girl, which is what I was trying to do. Up until I came around, Shelly's whole life had centered around Amani and vice versa. Most of the time I felt more like her buddy than her father.

Shelly had left earlier for Christina's baby shower. I had mentioned the possibility of going into the office and was about to do so when my cell rang. "Hello."

"Good afternoon, Mr. Dandridge, are you busy?"

"Is this who I think it is?" I asked.

"Perhaps. This is Elena in shipping. Mr. Hakito told me that you'd be expecting my call."

My heart sank. "Oh, okay," I said, my tone shifting from playful to business, "So I'm assuming you all have the Winthrop order ready to ship to Phoenix?"

"Actually we do. All we need are the final approval forms. That's why I was calling to see if you could fax them over. Mr. Hakito is in Orlando and he said that you had the authority sign off on it."

"Okay. I was headed to the office anyway. I'll have them to you within the hour." I took down her fax number and headed out the door. I was a little disappointed. Elena was Dominican, and her accent threw me off for a moment. I honestly thought that it was Nina calling to tell me that she would see me after all before she left. She stayed on my mind the entire time as I left my Gramercy Park neighborhood and headed up Madison Avenue to the office.

I faxed Elena the documents and went over the agenda for a meeting that I was holding on Monday morning. I decided to head home and catch the Sixers and Spurs game and let Mrs. Lamar leave early. She usually stayed until seven or so, but I figured that she would appreciate a short workday.

As I rode home I noticed that a light drizzle had begun to fall. I remembered a time when I welcomed the rain because it provided an excuse to fall back into bed with a lover and snuggle up. I passed the driver a ten and hopped out the cab. I was headed for my building when I heard my name called. "Cory."

I stopped dead in my tracks when I saw Nina standing there in the rain. I tried to keep it in, but the joy that captured me at that moment brought a smile to my face. She smiled back and said, "Coffee. Nothing more."

"Yeah, I'd like that." I said. "I'd like that a lot."

How Sweet the Sound

While having sex with Janette one night Nate looked down at his own stomach and couldn't believe the condition he was allowing his body to slip into. He had never been so out of shape in his life. Lying in the aftermath of lovemaking, he ran his hands over his stomach and sides and felt the love handles that were beginning to form at his midsection. He was disgusted. Then he looked over at Janette, dozing off, happy and confident with her ample size, and decided that he could never be all right with his pudginess. While he still longed for control over his up and down emotional state, he knew that his physical condition was one thing that he could control. That night's self-reflection had finally prompted Nate to act.

The laps were getting easier each day for Nate. He had gotten a gym membership and was making good use of it. It was his fourth week of working out and he had shed ten pounds already. What had been a big help was that on his second day at Run n' Shoot he had met Larry Lawson. Larry was a big man; he threw the javelin at the University of North Carolina in the nineties. Now he spent his days working as a personal trainer part-time. He'd also told Nate he was active at his church.

Nate was struggling to get to his two-hundredth crunch of the afternoon when Larry came over and started barking in his ear. "Come on, Nate. Suck it up. You can do it. No pain, no gain." Painfully, he pulled it together and yanked his body up.

"Two hundred." Nate yelled and then stood up to grab his towel. He was drenched in sweat.

"Good job. You're a natural, bro." Larry said, giving Nate a pound. "You could do the same thing, you know?"

"What's that?" Nate asked.

"Train folks. You have this workout down to a science. You have more drive than anyone I've ever seen. When you first came in here you couldn't do thirty crunches. Now look at you." Nate's body had started to come back. He was working out with a vengeance. His grandmother had come to town for a visit and told him that he looked like shit. She had told him to get himself together and most importantly to get a haircut. While he had started working out, he still hadn't visited a barber. He looked a lot like R. Kelly did when he pulled his braids out. Afro Almighty.

Responding to Larry's comments, "I enjoy working out. I had gotten away from it for a while. To be honest I had been kind of depressed, but I'm starting to feel a little better."

"Of course you do. Working out allows you to release some stress and releases endorphins."

"Endorphins?"

"Yeah, those are the body's natural happy juices. Working out has been scientifically linked with the release of them endorphins in the bloodstream."

"Cool. I need all the happiness that I can get right now." Nate said.

"It's funny that you say that. I noticed from the time that we met that your heart seemed heavy. Anyone who spends any time around you can tell that you've been carrying a lot of weight on your shoulders."

"Really? It shows?"

"Yeah, it does," Larry said, peering straight into Nate's eyes. "Listen, Nate, I don't want to be pushy, but I've got a spot that I want to take you to. All I need is a couple hours of your time. I'll even feed you afterward."

Without thinking about it Nate answered, "Sure, man, where to?"

"It's a surprise. But let me get your address and I'll pick you up on Sunday morning."

Nate knew where this was headed, but it was too late to back out. "Church?" Nate asked.

"The best one in the state of North Carolina." Larry wrote down Nate's address. "So I'll see you Sunday morning." Larry was smiling ear to ear.

"No doubt." Then Nate thought about Janette. "Would it be all right if I bring along a friend?"

"Don't be silly. We always have room for more in the house of the Lord." Larry gave Nate a pound and was about to head for the locker room. "Be blessed and remember one thing."

"What's that?"

"Between now and Sunday you are going to find ten reasons why you shouldn't come to church, and if you fight the spirit of doubt off, then be ready for the devil to throw five more obstacles in your way." He placed his hand on Nate's shoulder and added, "Just keep bobbing and weaving. Just don't give up the fight. I have a feeling that this could change your life."

Larry's words rang through Nate's head and in that instant

he was determined to make it. He hadn't been to a church in almost ten years. The closest he had come to attending church were the Sundays that he had to drive his grandmother to church. She was the one person who commanded his respect but even her request for him to attend had fallen on deaf ears. With the life that he had lived, getting up on Sundays had never been a consideration.

For a couple of reasons, Nate felt compelled to accept Larry's invite. Though he had tried to fight admitting it, there was no denying that Nate wanted to atone for his part in Kim's death. He also felt that something was missing in his life and deep down he held some hope that there might be an answer for him in church, but most of all he appreciated Larry's help as a workout partner and didn't want to offend him. As soon as Larry left, Nate decided to find a barbershop and headed to Southpoint Mall to hit Belk's and Nordstrom's to find a suit. He had left his entire wardrobe behind and only shopped on an as-needed basis. Up to this point he'd had no use for a suit.

Janette had been up since seven thirty. She'd been to the grocery store and back by the time Nate woke up. When he finally stirred from the bed, Janette had prepared him a plate with sliced fruit, a bagel, and turkey bacon. Janette's body cringed from desire when she saw his naked body come into the kitchen. She had asked him not to a hundred times but as usual he took the Sunny Delight from the fridge and held the bottle to his lips. Janette watched the muscles in his throat as he chugged the juice down. He had lost all the weight that she had put on him.

She placed the sports page on the table next to his breakfast. Then she pretended to be interested in the sale paper as she sat and watched him. His hair was cut close, not bald, as he had worn it when they met. His goatee was neatly trimmed and she noticed that his dark skin shone as if he had had an expensive facial. He had.

Janette didn't say anything about Nate's appearance. She had seen his rapid transformation back to a model-quality physique. She would have lied if she said she didn't feel a little insecure about him restoring his self back to optimum status. She also felt a little bad that she hadn't taken the initiative to start working out as well. It made her wonder if it was just a matter of time before he grew tired of her thick girl lovin'.

"I'm going to get dressed. I'll lay your clothes out for you," she said as she walked past him. She had on a mid-cut silk robe and her breasts were bouncing freely inside. Part of her was hoping that she would arouse him to the point where he would come and take her, but when he never looked up from the *Observer* sports section, she realized that his mind was somewhere else.

"Okay. I'm right behind you."

When Larry arrived at ten o'clock sharp, Nate was surprised to see that he was driving a burgundy twenty-passenger luxury bus with the name GREATER CHARLOTTE WORD CONGREGATION on the side of it. Nate yelled to Janette and she came to the door, purse and Bible in hand. She hadn't been to church in ages but welcomed the chance to get back into it. She'd been raised in the church and often thought about finding a new church home. She took Nate's suggestion as a sign to finally start.

"Man, you are looking cleaner than the board of health," Larry said as he greeted Nate. Nate laughed and shook Larry's hand. "And good morning to you, lovely lady."

"Good morning." Janette replied.

There were almost fifteen ladies, most of them elderly, and a couple of small children on the bus. Everyone spoke as Nate and Janette took a seat. "You two are in for a treat. My brother is preaching today. He came down from Washington, D.C. He has his own church up there, but he brought his choir down for a concert that we had last night and today he is going to bless us with a presentation of the Word. He is out of sight. I promise you won't forget it."

"Is that so?" Janette asked.

"You'll see. You won't regret coming today, not one bit." Larry said and winked at Nate.

As the bus moved up Speedway Avenue, Nate sat back, closed his eyes, and leaned his head against the window behind him. He was trying to remember the last time he had gone to church, or prayed for that matter. Thoughts of Kim slowly crept into his mind. It still bothered him that he didn't attend her funeral. There was a distinct possibility that he would have met his own death at the hands of a few of her cousins, but what weighed more in his decision not to show up was the fact that deep down, he felt responsible for her death. She was so young and beautiful, but she made one huge mistake. She fell in love with and gave her heart and soul to Nate. He swallowed hard and tried to fight back the feelings of guilt that began to consume him. Just then he felt a slap on his knee.

"Wake up, nigga."

Nate opened his eyes to see a little kid no more than eight. Shocked, he said to the kid, "Excuse me?"

"No sleeping in church. That's what my grammaw be saying." Just then an older lady called up from a few seats back.

"Boy, get your tail over here. Leave that man alone."

Nate felt compelled to interject. Though he didn't feel like being bothered with the kid, he said, "Ma'am, he's fine." Then he turned back to the boy. "So what's your name?"

The kid stared at Nate and replied, "Man, why you all up in my business?" Just that quick the kid turned and walked back to the rear of the bus to go irritate someone else.

Nate's face turned into a scowl and he made a mental note to stick his foot up the little boy's ass the first chance he got. He couldn't believe how awful these kids had gotten today.

The church was a renovated grocery store. There was still a sign out front that said Winn-Dixie and there was evidence of construction all over the grounds. Larry explained that the congregation had only been in this location for two months. His brother, Reverend Lloyd Lawson, had purchased the building for their congregation. He explained how Lloyd's church was doing really well. So well, in fact, that they had been able to build a church from the ground up near 7th Street in northeast D.C.

The space was adequate for now but wouldn't be large enough for long if the congregation continued to grow at its present rate of almost thirty new members a month. Still, it was a step up from the gymnasium and folding chairs at the high school where they had held their services prior to moving here.

"Amen." The church erupted. Every one of the four hundred people in attendance was stomping, shouting, and singing and the choir was just getting warmed up. The service hadn't even started yet. The organ was humming as Larry led Nate and Janette to their seats three rows from the altar and headed off.

After a few moments the organ faded out and only the voices of the choir echoed. There was angelic harmony as they began to sing "He Is My Rock." Two teenage boys came out. One lit candles and the other tested the microphone. Suddenly the church grew silent as everyone stood. Nate's mouth dropped open when he saw what happened next.

Larry walked out from the back door with a full minister's robe on. A second man, who was even larger than he was, followed and took a seat behind the pulpit as Larry addressed the church. "Good morning."

"Good morning," everyone said in unison.

"So blessed are we in this day that God has made. So blessed are we to be here today."

"Amen" came from all over the church.

Larry surprised Nate as he took command of his congregation. They had been working out for a month and Larry had never once mentioned that he was the pastor. Nate began thinking back, trying to recount each conversation that they'd shared. He was hoping that he hadn't insulted Larry at any point with vulgarities. In his favor was the fact that he hadn't had much to brag about the entire time he was in Charlotte. He had been a one-woman man.

It was clear that Janette was impressed that Nate was friends with a pastor. She had no idea that it was just as much of a shock to Nate. After about ten minutes Larry announced that he was going to hand the pulpit over to his brother. "This man is responsible for getting us into this building, and for buying the bus that I have been using to get so many of you here. He is more than just a pillar of our community, his community. He is someone who is worthy of the title reverend, but most importantly, folks"—the congregation's applause made it hard for him to finish. He yelled into the microphone—"Most importantly, he is my big brother. Welcome him with love. . . . All the way here from the nation's capital, Reverend Lloyd Lawson." The congregation was standing and clapping as Reverend Lawson took the podium. He waved his hand above the crowd and a calm came over them.

He took his handkerchief from his pocket and wiped his forehead. "Ohhhhhhhhhh yeah," he suddenly shouted loudly. Nate looked and saw quite a few people other than himself jump. "If you didn't come to feel the Word this morning, then you better run." He repeated himself. "I said, if you didn't come to feel it deep down in your soul then you better run."

"Amen," in unison.

"I don't need to introduce myself. Ya'll know me and you know how I do it."

"Till it can't be done no mo,'" answered someone.

"That's right," Reverend Lawson replied and he went on to offer prayers, sing a solo, and then he sang with the choir before he began his sermon.

Nate had either forgotten or never witnessed a pastor take command of the emotions and hearts of a congregation the way that Reverend Lawson did. If nothing more, he was entertained. He'd mainly come to the service out of respect for Larry, whom, up to the moment he donned the robes, Nate thought was only a personal trainer. The other part of him came out of curiosity. He wondered if he was missing something. He had known church folks all his life, folks who swore that the Word had changed their lives. His curiosity was about to be satisfied.

"Can I ask you all a question?" The church was silent. "Is it me, or is it hot as heck in here?" He laughed as he wiped his brow. "Seriously, though, I'm so happy to be here." He paused and looked over the crowd and then held up a few papers. "I was going to preach to you today from these notes. I had a nice sermon prepared for you with lots of scriptural relevance. I guarantee you would have been impressed . . . but I received a last-second order from the Father."

The church was quiet until someone yelled out, "It's all right with me."

"I'm glad to hear it," Reverend Lawson answered. "You see someone here today is in need of the healing powers, the strength, and the direction of the Kingdom. In this particular situation, there can be no mistaking. You all understand." He wiped his brow.

"Yes, sir."

"I don't need anyone"—the tone of his voice rose up—"*wondering* if in fact the message today was indeed intended for them." He shook his head no. "No, we don't need that. We need a direct hit. We need a message so clear that there will be no mistaking."

"No mistakes. Amen," came from the choir.

"Someone needs to know that it's okay to wander in from the wilderness. It doesn't matter that you've been lost all this time. We've been waiting for you. So many of our young are afraid to start where they are . . . to change a day at a time. Understand that God will accept you today as you are. The only thing that he won't supply you with is an excuse."

Nate's eyes grew blurry and he began to make eye contact with the reverend. The message was hitting home and Nate was struggling with the feelings that were coming over him. He had never felt anything like the electricity running through his body. Reverend Lawson was now talking directly to him and Nate could no longer make out any other sounds or movements around him. "Oh ye', I understand that you're still young. I'm still young myself." He stepped back and waved his hand to the drummer. The drummer kicked a quick beat and Reverend Lawson eased back from the pulpit and did the chicken-head dance that Chingy made famous, then he switched up and hit the Crip-walk across the podium to the beat.

The church erupted, especially the young members of the congregation. "That's right," a yell came.

"Do it, Rev."

Reverend Lawson continued, "I understand that it's tough to walk the right path. But have you even considered it? I ask you all to take a look at how you been living your lives, because your Creator already has. He has already forgiven you, he just wants you to take advantage of his mercy."

"Aaaaaaaamen."

"Ecclesiastes Twelve, 'Remember, now, your Grand Creator in the days of your young manhood, before the calamitous days proceed to come, or the years have arrived when you will say: "I have no delight in them." ' " His brow was sweating and he wiped only a few drops away. "Don't let it come to that, young people."

Reverend Lawson continued on, and by the time he finished his sermon, Nate was holding back the tears. The choir sang "God Can and Will" slowly in the background as Reverend Lawson rocked back and forth. His voice was soothing as he made promises to everyone in the house. He told them of the peace that God had in store for them. "One step toward him and he'll take two steps toward you," Reverend Lawson said. "Is there anyone out there who is willing to accept Jesus Christ as their savior today? Don't be afraid to start where you are. Come on up, HE has been waiting for you." One by one, a few people made their way out of their seats.

Janette was standing along with everyone else. She was

filled with joy, but she wasn't ready to make her way to the front. She was, however, shocked when Nate released her hand and walked out of the pew and up to the altar to surrender his life, his fears, and his guilt.

It was amazing. Amazing Grace.

Out of the Frying Pan

Brendan sat in the barber chair waiting for Dee to finish with a phone call so that he could resume his haircut. He didn't complain for two reasons. First, it was Freestyle Friday on BET's *106 and Park* and the entire shop, including Brendan, had their eyes glued to the set to see which amateur rapper would spit the best rhyme and win the weekly battle. Second, it did no good to complain. Dee was gonna be Dee. He was famous for running outside in the middle of a cut to talk to a honey, getting two or three phone calls, and even playing deejay by changing CDs during one of his marathon cuts. It was a wonder how he made any money cutting hair.

"Man," Dee yelled out. "I love me some Free." He smacked his lips like he was sucking barbecue sauce from his fingers. "I better not eeeever catch that ass on the street."

Mike, the owner of the shop, chimed in, "Awww, man what you gonna do. She ain't gonna hollar at your ass."

"Shit. Don't sleep. I got game like LeBron James. I will run up on her and hit her with some shit she ain't heard."

"Like what?" Brendan asked.

"Like the truth," Dee answered.

"The truth. That's right." Dee laughed and continued, "You see, a lot of niggas still stuck in the nineties with that weak-ass game. You know, lying and playing that macho role."

Brendan nodded his head. "So you saying you don't do any of that?"

"Nah," Dee answered. "I'm into telling broads the truth." He turned off his clippers that had been running for five minutes without cutting one strand of Brendan's hair. "Like if I saw Free, I would walk up to her and say to her, 'I like your work, but I love your style.' Then I would tell her that she personifies everything that is beautiful and powerful about the black woman. I would then say, 'You know I'm kinda hoping we can do something personal together, but I'm positive we can do business.'" He paused and lifted his hand up and dangled the diamond-encrusted TechnoMarine watch he was wearing, "Then I would look at my watch and say . . . 'I would love to stay and talk to you, Free, but unfortunately I have an appointment. . . .' By this point I would have her ready to hear more so I would flip open my cell and be like . . . 'Let me get that number so we talk at a later date.' The rest, folks, would be history."

"Get da fuck outta here," Mike yelled out as everyone in the shop burst into laughter.

"So you think that would work? Where is the truth in that?" Brendan asked.

"That is the truth. I would mean every word of it."

"What kind of business would you have to do with her?" Big Pete asked from the back while he was cutting.

"That's none of *your* business," Dee said and everyone laughed again.

"Don't make me hurt you," Big Pete said, cracking his knuckles, trying to hold back a laugh.

Getting back to Brendan, Dee turned the clippers on and began to give Brendan the usual. "So what's been up with you, B? How's life treatin' ya."

Brendan exhaled. "Man, don't even get me started. It's rough."

"Really, how so?" Dee asked.

Brendan's voice dropped down to a whisper so that only his barber could hear him. He began to explain the news that he had gotten from the doctor a couple days ago. He added that he hadn't had unprotected sex with anyone other than Trina in over six months.

"Damn. That's foul," was Dee's reply. "I guess you gotta' kick that ho out."

Brendan swallowed hard. "You think so? Just like that?" He asked.

"Hellllllllll yeah." Dee cut his clippers off and spun the chair around so that Brendan was facing him. "Listen, you cannot let her violate like that. You need to go home and call a locksmith first off, then pack her shit and send her on her way." He turned the chair back around and began to edge Brendan up. Then, as if he had almost forgotten the most important question, he asked, "Yo, ya'll keep your money separate right? 'Cause if you don't, you need to pull your shit out."

"Oh, nah. Everything is separate; as a matter of fact the only thing in her name is the cable bill."

"Good."

Dee finished Brendan's cut and let him out of the chair. "Don't forget what I said."

"I won't." Brendan gave Dee a twenty and headed for the exit before he shouted, "So what you getting into tonight?"

Dee handed him a flier for a party, "DJ Graham Cracker is throwing a party tonight. You ought to come on out. Get your mind off that . . ."

"Watch your mouth now . . ." Brendan shot back, halfway wondering why he was defending Trina. "Only I can call out her name."

Dee laughed. "Whatever. So you gonna roll with me tonight or not?"

"Yeah, I could use a good party."

"All right, meet me at the Jaspers over in Largo around nine. We'll have a few drinks with Shaka, Black, and Marcus before we hit the party."

"That sounds like a plan. I'll hit you up when I'm on the way."

"Peace."

Trina was on the couch watching *The E! True Hollywood Story* with her feet curled underneath her. She was so wrapped up in the trials and tribulations of Bobby Brown that she didn't notice Brendan sitting staring at her. He had gotten dressed to go out and she hadn't paid any attention to him as he showered and groomed. He was rocking a pair of Diesel jeans and purposely had thrown on the blue-and-gray Coogi sweater that she loved on him. He had even splashed on some Gucci Rush cologne.

He was staring at her face but was trying to peer into her soul. Still, her eyes were glued to the set. Brendan scanned her face and body language for some type of evidence of her betrayal, but there was none there. He wanted so badly to know who she'd been cheating on him with. Unprotected at that.

It had been a good six months since they had reconciled and moved in together. He was finding it hard to swallow that she would be willing to throw it all away after all that she had done to win him back. After ruining his friendship with Renée, his best friend, with an ill-fated sexual affair and catching his rebound-love Laney in a series of lies on top of lies, Brendan had been weak enough to give Trina another try. She had started counseling and Bible studies in an effort to prove that she wanted to change from the once-conniving person that she was into a woman whom he could trust.

Her efforts eventually paid off and Brendan let her back into his life full force. He had even gone as far as giving her an engagement ring for Christmas. Trina had complained that it was only a single karat but she wore it proudly nonetheless. Now she was apparently up to her old tricks. Brendan had caught her in enough lies to last a lifetime but this would be the last.

He had forgiven her when he found out that she screwed her personal trainer a couple years back. During a workout, Nate had overheard her trainer, David, pointing Trina out to a coworker at Bally's while he bragged about hitting it in the locker room. On another occasion Brendan ran into her salesman from the Toyota dealer as he exited her apartment half-dressed. Moments later he had found a wet spot in her bed big enough to be a birdbath. Brendan always suspected that there were others, but he had no real proof.

Things were about to change, Brendan thought. He checked his watch and said, "I'm about to head out now."

Without looking away from the set Trina replied, "Okay, have fun. I'll see you when you get back. Put the top lock on for me."

Brendan gave her the once over for the last time before rising from the couch. He grabbed his keys and headed out the door. Once on the other side he paused. He was leaning against the door, contemplating going back in to confront her when he heard her voice. "Heyyyyyy," She said. He couldn't make out her words after that but he quickly reached for his keys to get back in the door. He wanted to catch her on the phone.

He took the key to the deadbolt off of his chain and lined the keys up so that he could turn both locks at the same time and spring into the house before she could get off the phone. His hands were jittering a little as he quietly slid the keys in and turned the locks. In the next instant he sprang through the door. Trina turned around quickly to see Brendan behind her. She didn't try to hang the phone up. Instead she asked, "You forget something, sweetie?" She gave him a blank stare.

"Yeah, I think I left my . . . uh . . ."

"Uhhh, what?" She shook her head. "Boy, you crazy," she said and continued with her conversation. She was no longer paying Brendan any mind as she yelled into the phone, "I don't care what nobody says, girl, Bobby was a bad mufucka back in the day. Look at his ass go." Then she sang along as a clip of Bobby Brown performing "My Prerogative" was on the screen.

Realizing that he hadn't caught her, Brendan headed back out the door to meet Dee. For a second he wondered why he should even bother coming back home after the party. He wasn't sure if it was love, sex, or sheer habit that caused him to hang in there with Trina.

Brendan was sipping on his third cup of Armandale and cranberry juice as he swayed to the beat. Graham Cracker was playing all the right music and the women, big and small, were shaking what their momma's gave them. Dee was on the floor grinding on some girl's ass in the disguise of a dance as he waved for Brendan to join him. Brendan shook his head in disbelief as he saw Dee put the girl into what looked like a bear hug. As the vodka began to take its toll on him he began to feel himself moving toward the dance floor. It wasn't long before Brendan was dancing next to Dee and his partner. Dee motioned for Brendan to get behind her and put the girl into a sandwich. Brendan was reluctant until he felt the sudden thrust from the girl's bottom against his crotch. She was letting him know that she was ready, willing, and able to handle becoming the meat between the two of them.

"Shout out to my barber, Dee, and his man, Brendan," Graham shouted through the microphone. "And this one goes out to my pastor, Reverend Parker, in the house tonight." His reverend was actually on the dance floor dropping it like it was hot. "I see you out there getting it on." Then he switched songs and mixed in "In Da Club" by 50 Cent.

"Awwwww shiiiit. That's my jam," the girl in the middle shouted. She was obviously drunk, and Brendan backed away a little as she began dancing wildly. Her face was wet with sweat and her shoulders glistened too. She was wearing a dress that was made for a warmer month and it was clinging to her body. Although he didn't want her sweat on him, Brendan couldn't help but feel a little aroused as he saw her thong print and noticed that her ass was jiggling like Jell-O with each body thrust.

"Get up on this thing, boy," Dee shouted over the music as he began to manhandle the girl. He grabbed her waist and began to pump her like a wild animal right on the dance floor.

"That's what I'm talking about," the deejay shouted as he looked over at Dee and Brendan and gave them the thumbs-up.

Brendan was thinking that he must have been out of the loop. He loved a good party like the next man but it just wasn't his style to shake it like a Polaroid picture. When he hung out with his two best friends, Cory and Nate, they all seemed to play it real cool. Cory almost never danced, but when he did he was too reserved to get truly freaky on the floor. Nate, on the other hand, loved to dance. He was smooth enough to take a girl's panties off on the floor and no one, except the girl he was dancing with, would ever know he'd done it. As Brendan watched Dee do the ghetto Lambada with this girl, he longed for the days when he and his crew hung out.

Graham Cracker took the mike and asked, "I'm about to slow it down a little, is that all right?" He then put on R. Kelly's "Step in the Name of Love" and the entire ballroom erupted. Couples ran to the floor to get their grind on and some folks fled the floor just as quickly. Brendan turned to walk away from Dee and his dance partner and headed for the bar.

When he reached the bar he heard a voice behind him. "Are you buying me one too?"

He turned around and saw a light-skinned sistah with high cheekbones and hazel eyes staring at him. "You talking to me?"

"No, I'm talking to myself," she laughed. "Is that a problem?"

"No, it's no problem. What are you having . . . drinking?" Brendan asked with a smile on his face.

"Sex."

"Huh?"

"I said a Sex on the Beach."

"Oh, okay." He ordered their drinks and Brendan's mind slid away for a second when he'd only heard the word *sex*. "I didn't know people still drank those," he added as he looked her up and down. She was well dressed. She had on a pink cashmere sweater, a tight pair of Seven jeans, and a pair of Louis Vuitton boots.

"Well, I'm not one to switch up every time something new

...es out." She reached for her drink and said thanks and then added, "Once I get something that works for me I like to stick with it for a long time."

"I see." Brendan shot back.

"Do you want to come over and sit with me for a minute? All my girls are on the floor and I just want to chill for a few moments."

"Sure. Can I get your name?" Brendan asked.

"Tanisha. What's yours?"

"Brendan." She nodded and began to walk. Brendan followed and did what all men do when they follow a woman. His eyes locked on her behind as it switched back and forth. He had a moment to notice how her sweater cradled her body and dipped into the small of her back. She had a small waist for such a big bottom.

She turned swiftly when she reached her table and caught him staring. She responded with a smile as if she'd hoped he would have been doing just that. She took a seat and Brendan sat beside her. She spoke but he couldn't hear her so he scooted closer. "So do you hang out a lot?"

"Not like I used to. Both of my best friends moved out of town the same week and you know it's hard to replace your crew."

"Both moved away and left you behind? Poor baby." She smiled.

Feeding into her pity routine he responded, "Yeah, my man Cory got married and moved away to New York for his job, temporarily though. My other partner, Nate, he was going through some drama so he had to just get away."

"Nate?" she paused. "The name sounds familiar. I had a homegirl who used to date a Nate who moved away. Her name is India."

Brendan shrugged his shoulders to indicate he didn't know who she was.

"So who are you with tonight . . . don't tell me your lady." She smiled as she sipped her drink.

"No, I'm with another buddy of mine. Actually, my barber," he continued, "I'm real cool with him too. He hangs out with my regular crew from time to time but he's always been into some shady dealings so we kind of had to limit the contact with him. Nothing against him, just you gotta be careful out here these days."

"I understand," she said.

Brendan added, "Lately though, he's kinda chilled out and left that fast life behind so I don't mind coming out with him."

"Plus you don't have anyone else to hang with," she laughed.

Brendan smiled and laughed. "Right."

"So, Brendan, do you have a lady, a wife, or whatever?"

She caught him off guard with her question. Brendan looked into her hazel eyes and was hypnotized. Time slowed down and he took a minute to think about his life. Trina was cheating on him. Renée was about to get married. Tanisha seemed nice enough. She was definitely a cutie with Beyoncé-quality booty. He needed something to change his luck, so he replied, "No, I'm kinda between relationships." He immediately thought of how Nate always ran game on women by deceiving them so much that they wouldn't recognize the truth if it smacked them in the face. He always got what he wanted by doing just that, at least until Kim committed suicide. "What about you, do you have a man?"

Brendan was surprised when she answered, "Yeah, unfortunately. Remember I told you that I stick with something for a while. In this case though, I think that I may have stuck around a little too long." She sipped her drink and then said, "But there's always tomorrow."

They sat and finished their drinks and talked until the lights came on. Tanisha was a nurse at Southern Maryland Hospital. She owned a town house in Clinton, Maryland, which was fifteen minutes outside of D.C. Her boyfriend didn't live with her but to her dismay he spent a lot of time camped out in her crib with her remote on his lap. She told Brendan that she had been thinking of ways to get him out of her life for months. Brendan didn't give as many details of his life because he, of course, had started lying to her out of the gate. When her girl friends came to the table to get their coats she whispered into Brendan's ear, "I hope that I can see you again."

Brendan's chest poked out a bit. "No doubt. Gimme your number."

"I can only give you my work and my cell, you understand?"

"That's fine. When should I call you?"

She smiled. Brendan used a sweet and genuine approach. Even in his mack mode he still came across as a gentleman. "I'll leave that up to you, but don't make me wait too long. Good night." And she walked off to catch up with her girl friends.

Brendan stood there with the napkin in his hand that she'd written her number on. He was excited because in his opinion he had met the most gorgeous woman in the place. He caught up to Dee at the door. Dee had two honeys with him. One was his dance partner from earlier in the evening. "Yo, B, we gonna go get some breakfast and head back to my crib, or we gonna head back to my place and get some breakfast. It's whatever. Right, ladies?"

"That's right," they answered.

"B, this is Carmen and Pam." Pam was his dance partner.

"Hey, nice to meet you," Brendan replied.

"So you ready to roll?" Dee shot back.

"Honesly, Dee, I think I'm gonna take it on in. I ain't trying to start too much drama."

Dee sucked his teeth and shook his head. Brendan caught that he was disgusted with the respect that he was showing Trina. "Man, F that." He leaned over to Brendan so that the two ladies couldn't hear him. "Man, these hoes are ready to get loose. You want me to handle both of them by myself? Look at Carmen. She is tight." Brendan took a glimpse at her. She wasn't bad looking at all. Her weave could have been a little less obvious but that wasn't Brendan's reason for passing.

"Another time. But you have fun."

"Suit yourself, nigga," Dee said and backed away. He grabbed both girls by their asses and said to them, "I guess I got to handle all this coochie myself."

The girls laughed and Pam said, "Dee, you so crazy."

Carmen added, "Nigga, you better have some Viagra at the crib 'cause it's early."

"Viagra my ass. King Kong ain't got nothing on me." He shouted, imitating Denzel in *Training Day*. "You better hope your booty gets wet like the Niagara Falls, 'cause I am gonna put in work." They all laughed as if they did that sort of thing all the time and headed for the door.

Brendan headed for his car and thought about what the rest of Dee's night would be like. Dee was the closest thing to Nate that he knew. The major difference between them was that Dee focused more on quantity of women, where Nate was concerned more with quality. Dee would screw a high school senior or a senior citizen if she looked good to him. He didn't care what the woman had going for herself. Nate wanted only women he considered to be top-flight professionals and entrepreneurs. They also had to be fine but the looks weren't the only qualifier for him.

Brendan was glad that Nate had rubbed off on him in that manner. He wasn't fooling around with any chicken heads just because they came clucking in his direction. If and when he left Trina, it would be for something much better. As he drove up Pennsylvania Avenue headed toward the Beltway he thought about Tanisha. The image of her in those jeans flashed through his mind and before he knew it he had dialed her number.

Life was never supposed to be so complicated. For years after my college sweetheart Shelly and I broke up because she was going to grad school out of state, I had secretly wondered what it would be like to have her back in my life. I never told a soul. During the six years that we were apart, she often crept into my dreams, stealing my heart over and over again. Sometimes the dreams were haunting because they felt so real. I would actually see us back together doing the small things that make a couple fall so deep in love. I'd dream that I was watching her shop and try on clothes while I looked forward to the day that I would be able to afford to buy her everything her heart desired. Other times I could smell her skin and hair in my sleep. I'd reach out for her only to find an empty bed.

Sometimes we would be making the sweetest love and I would awaken with my heart beating faster than if I had run an actual sprint. Those dreams were the worst kind of torture because once I woke I'd realize that there would be no experience to equal what I felt in my imaginary paradise. Shelly's sex was the ultimate and after her, though some were great, none took me to the heights that she did.

It's crazy how life and decisions change everything. Now I was lying next to the woman whom I had dreamed about. Our daughter was in the next room, safe, healthy, and beautiful. I was set financially. Yet in my heart or my mind, I couldn't decide which, I still felt a deep emptiness almost like I was missing out on something.

It had been three weeks since Nina had left New York. Shelly and I had been fussing ever since over the smallest of things. What was for dinner, when bills were to be paid, how much money she was spending, and how much I was working all became major obstacles to our harmony. Part of our problem had to be my indecision to commit to the marriage. Like so many married couples, I had gotten married without realizing that it meant dealing with the other person as they were. I thought that we would marry and things would go back to where they were seven years ago. I only came to see that Shelly and I no longer knew each other. The other part of the problem was that I was missing Nina and taking it out on Shelly every chance I got.

I couldn't stop thinking about the coffee date Nina and I had after running into each other in the rain. During which she had admitted that she still loved me.

"But sometimes love isn't enough," she'd said. I'd listened to all her reasons why she could never take me back and why it would never work between us. Amani has been through too much already. Nina's family would never forgive her for breaking up Shelly's marriage. Finally she broke down and told me the most serious of all her reasons. "Cory," she had said, staring into my eyes, "you hurt me like I have never been hurt. You have destroyed my faith in love. Loving you like I did was supposed to be enough and yet it somehow wasn't. The one thing I'll always remember about you is the pain that I felt when you walked away with her. When you married her."

When she said those words I finally realized how bad I had hurt her. I tried to assure her that I was sorry for the hurt that she'd suffered at my hands. I told her that I would do anything to erase her pain. "There's no way you can do that, Cory."

"I can try."

"Try what? Try to rewrite the past, undo the deeds." She laughed. When she got up to leave I knew that there was no making it up. I felt so hopeless and desperate that I was afraid to even try to change her mind. I simply walked out with her and watched as she hailed a cab. In parting, she said something that stayed on my mind from that day until this moment. "Cory, have you figured out your biggest mistake?" She continued without giving me a chance to respond. Instead she took the blank look on my face as an indication that I had not. "You chose the sister who loved the *idea* of Cory Dandridge after being with the sister who loved the man."

I rolled over to look at the clock and saw that it was already ten minutes to six. Shelly would be getting up for work soon. Before she left she would make breakfast for Amani and lay her uniform out. When I got up I would only have to see her to the door. Like clockwork, Mrs. Lamar would knock at seven thirty and pick Amani up and walk the three blocks to school with her. She would be there to pick her up at three thirty as well, along with all the other day-care providers. Needing to feel close to Amani, I felt compelled to walk her to school. We headed out the door together and up the block, hand in hand.

"Cory, why are you taking me to school today?" she asked.

"I thought I asked you to call me Daddy or Papi."

"Oh yeah. You know I keep forgetting stuff all the time," she answered.

"Okay, but try."

"So why?" she asked again.

"I just wanted to. I want to spend more time with you."

"Why?"

I should have known what I was getting myself into. "Well, because you are my daughter and it's important that you and I *always* have a bond. No matter what."

I was thinking about my father saying the exact same words to me as a child. He had passed many years back and although I missed him, I liked to think that he had shown me that a father's job was to nurture as well as protect.

"Okay," she said.

"You understand that?" I asked.

"Yeah," she said.

"Good."

We crossed the street and headed into the courtyard in front of her school. The East Manhattan Primary Academy cost fourteen thousand dollars a year to send a six-year-old. There was a diverse mix of students who attended and the students had some of the highest scores in the nation on standardized tests. Amani had been introduced to French, Italian, and Japanese and could subtract and tell time with the best of them. Reading was an afterthought; she was already a grade ahead when we moved to New York, but the accelerated program at the school was pushing her even farther along.

I kissed Amani on the forehead and watched her take off when she saw one of her friends. "Kali," she screamed.

"So you're Amani's dad." I heard a voice behind me say. I turned around and saw a light-complexioned man heading my way. He extended his hand. "I'm Ricky Reyes. Kali's dad. Kali talks about Amani all the time at home."

"Oh yeah. That's great." I shook his hand. We exchanged a firm grip.

"Yeah," he laughed. I couldn't see his eyes through the dark shades he was wearing. He reminded me of Lenny Kravitz, except taller. "I met your wife a couple weeks back when she picked Amani up. She's nice. I told her that she looked like she needed to be riding in a Mercedes . . . as I tell everyone I meet." Then he pulled a card from his pocket. "I'm part owner of a Mercedes dealership on Long Island. No surprise when she told me that you already own one, but I have some outstanding values. She said *she* was interested but maybe she lost the card. I would love to put you two into a new Benz, so don't hesitate to call."

I looked him up and down. Did he just say my wife was nice? Did he say she was interested? "No, you go ahead and keep that for someone who might buy one from you," I offered as I refused to accept his business card. "We aren't in the market right now."

"Well, I also own an art gallery in SoHo and a jewelry store over in the Diamond District, so I'm sure I could interest you or your wife in one of my pieces." His hand was still out holding the card.

My cordial smile left my face and I said simply, "That's quite all right but like I said, *we* don't need any of your services." Then I turned and headed off.

As I hopped into a cab I began wondering what kind of approach he had given Shelly. He was very pushy and seemed way too arrogant for his own good.

"Where to?" I was surprised when the cabdriver asked. In New York the cabbies usually don't even say hello. They let you sit down and look at you like you're crazy if you don't immediately give your destination.

"Thirty-second and Madison."

I sat back in the cab, staring out my window, watching the people as they moved toward their jobs. It was late April and spring was in bloom, although there was still a chill in the air. I started thinking about my marriage and wondering if all this thinking about Nina was my way of fighting the adjustment to a new life filled with responsibilities. There was no denying that I did love Shelly. At the same time, it was obvious that things were different than what I had expected. I was torn between trying to have a family with someone I thought I'd be in love with forever and someone I thought I wanted to be in love with. My life was turning into a Sade record and I needed to flip it before was too late.

I pulled out my cell and called her. "Hey, babe," I said when she answered.

"Hey. You got Amani off to school okay?"

"Don't I always? As a matter of fact I walked her to school."

"Oh really? What prompted that? Was Mrs. Lamar running late?"

"Nah. I just felt like I needed a little bonding time with her. I'm feeling the same way about you right now. So what do you say we hang out tonight? We can go smoke some cigars at the 40/40 or go down to Justin's since you like that spot so much."

"Sounds great. Are you going to be getting off early tonight?" she asked.

"I will try to get out of here by five thirty at the latest. Jamison will be in the office today and we are setting up our conferences. We are bidding on three contracts in the Midwest. I may be off to Chicago in a few weeks."

"You know you have to take me if you go."

"No wives, only girlfriends and hookers on business trips."
I laughed.

She laughed back. "Cory, don't make me cut you."

We talked for a few moments more and hung up.

We decided on dinner at Justin's and drinks at a spot called
Ida Mae's. Ida Mae's had a jazz band playing, so we found
ourselves seated, drinking martinis, and swaying to the
groove. We sat talking about nothing in particular. I noticed
that our conversation seemed a lot more forced than it had
ever been in the past. On the flip side I thought of how easily
the conversation between Nina and me flowed when we were
together. I chased the thoughts of her from my mind, realizing that I could drive myself insane playing the comparison
game. As the conversation moved on I had a chance to ask her
about Kali's father. She admitted that he had been a little
pushy with her, even trying to set up a play date for the girls.
She told me that she had taken his card and tossed it almost
immediately. We went on about her job and then some of
mine before I finally looked over at Shelly and said, "You
know I think you're beautiful, right?"

She showed all her teeth. "How would I know that?"

"When a man looks at you like this"—I made a funny face
and licked my lips—"it means he thinks you are gorgeous."

"Thanks. You're not too bad yourself," she responded.

"Did I mention how hot you looked in that dress?"

"Oh, this old thing?" She was referring to a five-hundred-
dollar Christian Dior dress that I'd bought her from Bal Har-
bour Mall in Miami. "You are just full of compliments
tonight."

We ordered another round of drinks and finished them before the band finished. We were both feeling the effects of the

alcohol and decided on a fourth martini before we hit the road. As the band began to play "Anytime Anywhere" by Janet, Shelly leaned over to my ear and whispered. "These drinks have me so horny." Then she looked at me seductively as she sang the words to the song.

I peered into her eyes and saw the come-fuck-me look on her face. "We can get out of here right now."

"No. I want it right here right now." She grabbed my earlobe gently with her teeth. Then she whispered, "Did you know that I don't have any panties on?"

In that second I felt my manhood beginning to swell. "Oooohh girl, you are so bad when you wanna be. Do you want to go into the bathroom?" I looked back to see what kind of traffic was moving back and forth in the rear of the restaurant.

She shook her head no. Instead she pulled her hand up from under the table and placed her fingers to my mouth. I extended my tongue and tasted her wetness. I was now doubly intoxicated. "Pull it out right now. I want you to make yourself cum with me."

I mouthed the word *what,* but before I could protest she reached over and freed me from my pants. "Hey baby . . . make . . . sure . . ." was all I got out before I felt her stroking me. She reached into her purse, which was on her other side, and, after fumbling through it with her free hand, she reached over to me. Instantly I felt the oil that she had on her hands as she greased my dick.

"Now, Cory, I want you to stroke it as you stare into my eyes," she whispered into my ear. "I have two fingers on my clit and two more inside of myself right now." She leaned back against the cushioned seat of the booth. She didn't suspect that anyone was watching us, but I wanted to be sure. I scanned the room and didn't notice any attention on us. I looked back over at Shelly and her eyes were halfway shut and her chest heaved slightly. I read her lips as she said, "You better hurry."

I saw that her legs were spread apart and I could see the muscles in her shoulders twitching as she worked her fingers. I began stroking myself feverishly. The sensations began sweeping over me as I watched my wife finger herself into a frenzy. She loved watching me jerk myself off but usually it was after I pulled out of her vagina to keep from cumming inside of her. Even that would put her over the edge when she was close to reaching her orgasm. There was something about seeing the sperm pour out of my dick that drove her crazy. "Ohhhh." I moaned quietly as I watched her eyes rolling up into her head. I knew that she was getting close to exploding. Her back began to slide lower into the booth.

Her lips parted and I saw her teeth clenched together. She was watching me as I pumped up and down my shaft. In the next instant one of her hands clenched my thigh and her bottom began to shake. In three short bursts she began to erupt. "Damn, damn. I'm cumming, bayyybeeeee." She shook again as the words dragged slowly from her lips. This time it was too much for me.

"Fuck. I'm cumming with you." I tried to keep my cool as I began to shoot all over the tablecloth in front of me. She didn't care who was looking and quickly moved over to see the last of the liquid escape me. She grabbed it and gave it a few strokes and squeezes until the tingling was too much and I pulled her hand away.

A few seconds later and she had a smile on her face, letting me know that she was satisfied. "You know you have nut on your slacks, right?"

I looked down and I did indeed have a dark stain on my trousers. I shook my head. "C'mon, let's roll."

We climbed out of the booth and headed for the door.

On the ride home we both burst into laughter, talking about how freaky we used to be. It was nice to know that we could still walk on the wild side.

"So we gonna finish up when we get home."

"Oh, you got some gas left in the tank?" She smiled.

"Enough to put you into a deep sleep."

"Well bring it on, my nigga."

"Oh, it will be brought." We laughed some more. For the rest of the ride I filled her in on my upcoming trip to Chicago and told her that I would see how busy I would be out there. Being the head of sales and acquisitions for HE wasn't easy, I just made it look that way. At my direction, Hakito Electronics was buying up smaller companies that didn't have the assets to survive the flailing economy. Although HE's biggest profits came from manufacturing programming chips, we were expanding our services by acquiring other specialty companies, thus increasing our revenues exponentially. The acquisition of Trybe Technologies was my baby from the ground up. I was going to make a boatload of money for HE and a hefty commission for myself.

"It would be nice to spend some time being in love with my ultra-successful husband." She paused for a second then added, "Honestly, I just luuuuv the idea of it."

8

Without a Strong Rhyme to Step To

The True You salon had moved from Georgia Avenue to a bigger location down on U Street and had been packed with customers ever since. Easter had just passed and Daphne, who had two shampoo girls working for her, was still falling behind. "What's it gonna be, Tressa?" Daphne asked as she made sure her customer was comfortably seated. Then she shouted to one of her helpers, "Sweetie, check Tam's hair to see if it's dry."

"Give me some two-string twist. I'm headed out of town and I need something simple."

"You got it. As a matter of fact . . ." Daphne stopped midsentence as she faced the door of the salon. Tressa saw the expression on Daphne's face and looked to the television. Perhaps the videos had sunk to an all-new low. Then Daphne dropped her comb and her mouth twisted as she stepped out from behind her chair. "No, you didn't show your face up in here."

Nathan Montgomery was back in town for good. He stood

still at the receptionist's desk for a moment, nodded his head, and approached Daphne. "Listen, Daphne, I need to speak with you for a minute."

Daphne began to scream at the top of her lungs. "How dare you show your face up in here, you selfish son of a bitch? I hate you." Her screams turned to tears and the shop fell silent. Every one of the ten stylists stopped working and tuned into the drama. "You have the nerve to show your face around here after what you did to Kim? Who do you think you are? I'm calling Mo, John-John, and she got another cousin who just came home from jail. I'm sure they'll be real glad to know you are back in town."

Daphne was now pointing her finger in his face and the patrons grew scared that she could erupt into a rage at any minute. "Call who you like. I didn't come here for you to judge me. I came because . . ."

Nate's words were interrupted with Daphne's open-handed slap. Like a professional he turned his face with the blow, minimizing the effect but not the sound. "I don't care *what* you came here for. You are responsible for what happened." She began to cry and in the next instant she swung her hand again. This time Nate grabbed her wrist before it could make contact. He held it for a second and looked into Daphne's eyes.

"Daphne, I'm sorry for what happened. I'm sorry that my actions played a part in her death. I'm sorry that you lost your friend. I lost a friend in her as well." Then he let her hand go. "I came here only to apologize to you. I would like your forgiveness, but if you can't see clear to do that, then perhaps you could pray for me and I will do the same for you."

"What?" A look of confusion was on Daphne's face.

"Pray that my walk is completed and I will pray that your heart is softened. I came back to D.C. to make amends for my behavior. I treated Kim badly. Although no one should take their own life, I recognize that she loved me more than she should have, but that is between she and the Creator. Still, I must atone for my part in the whole thing." Daphne's expression showed the look of someone in unfamiliar territory.

"You come up here talking about praying and it's supposed to be all good," she yelled. Her client stood up and held her before she made another attempt at fighting him. "You ain't right and you *are* gonna pay for what you did."

Nate turned and began to walk away. When he reached the front door he turned back and asked, "How do you know that I haven't already paid?"

Her mouth dropped open but no words escaped. "I'm going to see her mother later today. If anyone is looking for me you can tell them that's where I'll be. But know this, my life belongs to God now and I am promised that no weapon formed against me shall prosper."

"Motherfucka, you crazy," Daphne screamed. "Get your fake holy ass out of this shop and never come back."

Nate gave her nothing but a slight smile as he headed out the door.

Forty minutes later he walked into the barbershop. "Awwww shit. Kaboom look who stepped in the room," Mike yelled out when he saw Nate.

A smile slid across Dee's face. "My Dawg is back." He stopped cutting to give Nate a handshake and a hug. "When you get back?"

"Last night, real late."

"You talk to Brendan yet?"

"No, not yet. I had a couple of runs to make this morning and then I had to help out at the church this morning, feeding the homeless."

"Church?" Dee asked. "You had to help feed the homeless?"

Nate nodded his head. "That's right."

"Getdafuck outta here." Dee laughed. When he saw the expression on Nate's face he asked. "You serious?"

"Yeah."

"That's decent, young man," Mr. Hackley, the eldest barber, chimed in. "We need more young brothers trying to do something positive."

Nate smiled. "Thank you, sir."

"There must be some freaks down at the church if Nate's ass is hanging down there," Mike said before he started laughing.

"There are some nice sistahs down there, but that's not what it's about for me right now," Nate replied.

"So what church is this?" Dee asked with his arms folded.

"The Greater D.C. Word Congregation. You ought to come visit."

"No, thanks, I can't afford to go to church, it cost too damn much. The last time I went to church they passed that plate seven times, I bullshit you not. The girl I was with was talking about, could you put a twenty in for me cause I left my wallet, I was like shiiiieeet girl, I don't have that kind of money."

Everyone in the shop erupted in laughter, some with him and some at him. "You a fool," Mike answered. "Nate, don't pay him any attention. That's good you going to church trying to get yourself together."

"Yeah, it's all good. Yo, Dee, you got anybody next or can you hit me off with an outline?"

"You know I got you. I'm almost finished, go ahead and chill for a minute, I'll have you out of here inside a half hour."

"I've heard that before," Nate said and everyone laughed.

Ten minutes later and Nate was in the chair. Dee commented on the fact that he had let his hair grow out into a shadow. He then jumped from subject to subject trying to catch up on eight months' worth of happenings. Dee stopped short of telling Nate that he missed him, but he did admit that things hadn't been the same since he left town. He told him that Brendan seemed a little lost at times without him, but what he failed to admit was that he had called Brendan and told him that Nate was sitting in his chair.

Nate had no idea until he walked out the door of the shop and heard, "So it's like that, chump. You slide back into town and don't call a brother."

Nate's face lit up when he saw Brendan. He didn't say a word, he just moved toward Brendan and embraced him, "Man, it's good to see you, B."

"You too. I didn't ever think you were coming back."

"C'mon. You knew I'd be back."

They stood in front of the shop for an entire hour catching up and finally Dee came out front. "Yo, I'm finished cutting for the day so let's go hang and get some grub or drinks."

"I'd love to but I have something to take care of," Nate responded.

"Man, you work fast. What's her name?" Brendan asked playfully.

"Actually it's not even like that. I'm practicing celibacy right now."

Brendan and Dee just looked at each other, then to Nate as if they were waiting for a punch line. Nate finally interrupted the silence with, "I'm going over to Kim's mother's house."

"Kim who?" Dee asked.

"Kim," Nate replied. They were quiet so he went on, "I need to go apologize to her mother."

"Man, do you think that's a good idea?" Brendan asked before continuing. "Maybe you ought to let it be water under the bridge."

"Yeah, cuz. Let sleeping dogs lie and shit like that," Dee added.

"I appreciate that thought but this is something I got to do. It's for my spirit as well as for her. You two might not understand but you don't have to."

Dee said what Brendan was most likely wondering. "Man, what about her crazy-ass cousins? Man, them fools been selling death since you left. It might just start some unnecessary shit."

"Don't worry about that. I'm taking backup with me."

Dee nodded. "Oh okay, so you going strapped?"

Nate just smiled. He gave them both his new cell number and hopped into his rental car. "I'll catch up with you later."

"So what's up for tomorrow?" Brendan asked.

"Church . . . you two trying to roll with me?"

Dee shook his head. "On that note . . . I'ma catch you later," he said, chuckling, and walked toward his car.

"I just might have to come along and see what has you turned inside out. I guess for the better."

"I'll call you then."

"Peace, man, be careful all right?"

"No doubt."

Nate knocked three times and there was no answer at the door. There was no car in the driveway and he feared that she wasn't home. He was about to walk back to his car and sit when Mrs. Winters arrived as the Metrobus stopped at the corner. Nate recognized her when she stepped off and headed up the block to her home. She looked a lot like her daughter except that Mrs. Winters was a couple shades darker than Kim and her cheeks were chubbier. She didn't notice that Nate was on her porch until she made it to her yard. Looking into her face rattled Nate. He had been to the home with Kim several times but had only been face-to-face with her mother once. He was feeling Kim's presence and he had to make an effort to stay composed. "May I help you?"

Nate cleared his throat. "Yes ma'am. My name is Nate Montgomery and I was dating your daughter before she died." Mrs. Winters looked Nate dead in his eyes and said nothing as she made her way past him and put her keys into the door. "I came because I wanted to express to you . . . I wanted to apologize for the way that I treated your daughter . . ."

"You waited almost nine months to come and apologize. Why bother now, son?" She placed her bag down and turned back to Nate. She didn't seem upset, merely curious.

"Well, I have been out of town for a while and I was advised by most everyone to give you time to grieve." Nate's face was full of anguish. "I didn't know how you would handle seeing me. Everyone blamed me, and I figured that you and your family would as well. I know her cousins did . . . I received a lot of threatening messages and I figured that they were basically speaking on your behalf as well."

"Well, do you feel as though you are to blame, Nate?" She stepped away from the door and took her blazer off, hanging it on a coat hook.

"Well . . . at first I did. I blamed myself for her taking her life. I blamed myself for being so immature and not being upfront about the real me. I was never any good at relationships. I wanted people near me but I always hurt everyone who got close to me, but I never intended to cause her so much pain."

"Hmmph," she said. "Well, son, that's the nature of relationships and women. Some of us love too hard to be played with." She saw the look on his face and could tell he was looking for something from her. "You can come in for a moment. I just got in from work," she said, then continued as she led him to her living room, "and now?" She offered him a seat.

"And now what?"

"Do you still blame yourself?"

Nate was shocked at how he'd been received. The best he'd hoped for was a polite acceptance of his apology, but it had become much more. A real chance to explain himself. "Honestly, no. I don't blame myself for her death. But please know that I do fully accept responsibility for treating her badly. I have found God and I have come to find his mercy and grace. I wish I could undo what has been done. I have asked for forgiveness and I have prayed for you and your family every day. I prayed that you could forgive me."

She nodded her head and a smile appeared on her face. "Nate, I forgave you a long time ago. Son, I prayed that you wouldn't blame yourself and, believe it or not, I even held out faith that you would come to see me one day so I could say these things to you. Kim's death was by design of the devil. He put that idea in her head to do something like that."

Nate was silent. He was so overtaken by her words that tears welled up in his eyes. He was about to speak when Mrs. Winters cut him off.

"Nate, not many people know this, but my daughter attempted suicide twice before this. Once in high school because she claimed that her father and I didn't understand her. A second time after a failed relationship with some guy whose name she barely remembered a year later. Kim was bipolar and suffered from severe depression as well. Her demons ran a lot deeper than being dogged out by a man . . . you understand."

"I had no idea," Nate said.

"You couldn't have." She offered him something to drink and when he accepted she brought him a glass of iced tea. "Nate, I actually owe you an apology."

"For what?"

"Well, judging from the fact that you are even here . . . you are obviously a man of some conscience. Even if you were a d-o-g then or now, it's obvious to me that you suffered behind this. I could have reached out to you, but . . ." She paused. "I actually wanted you to suffer a bit."

Nate laughed. "I understand. Truly I do and I accept your apology."

Mrs. Winters smiled. "I want you to know that I think that you are a decent man for even coming. It means a lot to me." She stood and he stood to meet her with a hug.

"Thanks. Also, Mrs. Winters, if you ever need anything, please call on me. Anything at all . . . a ride, some help around here . . . here is my new number."

"That's very sweet of you. I doubt if I will need anything. Even though we're divorced, Kim's father still comes around to maintain the house and I am saving for a new car now, but you can stop past every now and then to say hello."

"I'll do that," Nate said with a smile. He felt a hundred pounds lighter as she showed him out. As he headed out, he turned back to her and said, "God is good."

She replied, "All the time."

Nate headed down the steps and toward his car. He hit the switch to the alarm and opened the door when a silver Audi pulled up beside him. Immediately the driver and the man in the backseat jumped out. Mo, the driver, yelled to Mrs. Winters, "Go on in the house, Aunt Shirlene. You don't need to see this."

"I will not." She began, storming down the steps. "What are you doing around here? I told you and John-John a long time ago not to come around here and especially bringing your thug friends," she barked at the top of her lungs.

"Listen, Aunt Shirlene, this nigga is gonna get dealt with for what he did to Kim," the guy who had climbed out of the back replied. He was holding a gun in his hand as casually as a cigarette.

"First off, I'm not your aunt. Did you even know Kim?"

"I met her before," he replied. Realizing how stupid he sounded, he added, "but, I'm rolling with Mo. So if that's his peoples, then they my peoples."

"So, what do you plan to do to this man, Mo? What, you gonna shoot him in front of my house in broad daylight? Boy, if your momma could see you now she would be sick."

"You don't understand, Aunt Shirlene. Me and Kim were close."

"I know you were. But killing Nate isn't going to bring her back. He came here to apologize to me. I have accepted his apology and that is where it ends. There are things that you don't know about Kim, and I am not going to explain it to you. I will say this—Nate did not kill her or force her to take her life. You have no right to harm him."

Nate stood motionless as his eyes looked for a way to gain an advantage. There was a chance that he could wrestle the gun from the man standing there, but if Mo had a pistol on him too, he'd be done for. Mrs. Winters was his best and only chance. These guys were killers; they didn't bring their guns for show.

"Let me say this to you, boy. I have his number." She put her hand on his shoulder. "I am going to call him every day. The first time I don't get an answer I'm calling the police. I am going to tell them about your threats, the guns I see you with, and your motive. Then I am going to give them your government names, Social Security numbers, license plates, and descriptions. I will tell them where all your baby mothers live. Do you understand me, Maurice?"

"Yeah."

"Pardon me?"

"Yes, ma'am."

"I'm not playing. I don't want a hair harmed on his head. I will testify against you . . . make no mistake."

A grimace formed on Mo's face as he looked Nate up and down. "Your lucky day, you faggot."

"Man, I got no beef with you," Nate said humbly.

"What? Nigga, you getting smart? I will crush you out here."

Just then a voice rang out. "You all right, homey?" Dee's face appeared. He was in the passenger seat of Brendan's Corvette.

A smile appeared on Nate's face. "Yeah, I'm straight."

"Well, let's roll. We got moves to make," Dee said.

Nate turned to Mrs. Winters. "Thanks for talking to me."

She nodded. "It was my pleasure, son."

As Nate prepared to climb into his car, Mo took a swing at him. Nate saw it and ducked out of the way. In the next instant Brendan and Dee jumped out of the car. Dee held a pistol and took aim at the passenger in the backseat.

Before a shot was fired Mrs. Winters screamed and grabbed Nate.

"Hold it. Hold it," Nate yelled out at the top of his lungs. "In the name of the Father be still." Everyone halted while her arms were still around Nate. The man in the passenger seat of Mo's car climbed out. He was a mountain of a man. If he made a move, the only way that he might be stopped would be with a bullet or two. "It doesn't have to be this way. Ya'll can put the guns away." Nate pulled away from Mrs. Winters. "Ya'll are disrespecting this woman and her home." Then he turned to Mo. "If you have to work your frustrations out, then we can do it like soldiers. I'm not trying to get into that gunplay. Nobody wins with that, but if that's the only way you can express your manhood, then I'll get in that car and leave town for good. I don't want to die . . . and I don't want to kill you. But I won't walk around this town waiting for you or your partners to steal my life."

"Oh, that ain't gonna happen," Dee said. "If it does, then a lot of people gonna follow."

"Man, chill with that," Nate barked back. "Look, Mo, if you want to get it on we can put the guns away and work it out right now."

Mo stared at Nate. He really didn't want to fight Nate. He would have much preferred to shoot him. Realizing that his aunt was serious about calling the police, and that it probably wouldn't end there, as Nate had friends who had his back too, Mo said, "Fuck it. It ain't worth it." He turned to climb in the car.

The mountain laughed and said, "So you gonna let it go like that? This nigga offered you up. I know you ain't gonna shoot him, but you gonna just let it slide like that? Man, you acting like a sucka. Whoop his ass."

No one uttered a sound and Nate fought back his instincts as best he could until he said, "Big man, why don't you show him how it's done."

Brendan flinched because he felt as though Nate was preparing to bite off more than *two* men could chew. Dee showed no expression. Mrs. Winters was shocked at the display of pride but didn't want to see Nate battered.

"What?" the big man shouted. "You don't want me. I ain't never liked you anyway, you pretty mufucka."

The man in the backseat of Mo's car co-signed. "Go ahead, Byrd. Crush that nigga."

Nate stepped out from his car into the empty driveway and took his shirt off. He had on nothing but a wife-beater and his body showed that he had been working out. Brendan felt nervous and wondered if he should have been prepared to jump in. Nate's body language surprised everyone. Not only was he calm, he seemed confident and almost eager to get physical with the huge brother. Byrd moved to the driveway and never even lifted his hands. He fully expected to take Nate's head off with a haymaker and he tried. What he didn't figure was that it was damn near impossible to hit Nate. The first punch Nate ducked, the second came so slow that Nate had time to sidestep it and kick Byrd in the back when he flew past him.

Nate could see everyone in the background and even a couple of neighbors had come out onto their lawns to see if there was an actual brawl going on. After four more missed punches, Byrd was getting winded and Nate decided to give him a beating. As Byrd lunged once again with a right hook, Nate leaned back out the way, but this time he planted his right foot and fired back a left, landing on his opponent's nose. The crunch was heard by everyone. Before the pain even had a chance to set in, Nate threw two rights to his midsection and followed with one to his chin. Stunned, he tried to stop Nate's onslaught by grabbing him. Instead he was hit with another left to the eye and a hook from Nate that landed on his temple.

Byrd was at least six-four and well over two hundred and fifty pounds. When his knees buckled and he began to fall forward, Nate was surprised. No one else was after watching the display. Each punch had been precise and full of force. Nate didn't realize how much strength, anger, pain, and frustration he'd released with each blow. He stopped and looked as Byrd's eyes grew glassy and blood poured from the big man's nose. He wasn't out cold, but he was close.

Normally, Byrd would have been stomped after being floored, but Nate took one look at him and walked back toward the car. "I apologize for that, Mrs. Winters. I'll look forward to your calls," Nate said while trying hard to catch his breath.

"That's okay, baby. That's quite all right." Then she motioned for Mo and his sidekick to get Byrd and leave.

"Let's roll," Nate said to Brendan as he put his shirt back on. Mo said nothing as Nate moved past him and to his car.

Brendan nodded. "Damn, I see you're still nice with those hands."

"They're all right."

"Damnnnnnn," Dee yelled out, "somebody got knocked dafuck owwwt," doing his Chris Tucker impersonation.

They all laughed and Brendan said to Nate, "It's been a long time."

Nate chimed in like Rakim in the song, "I should'na left you . . ."

And they pulled off.

9

Sweet-and-Sour Sugar

Contrary to popular opinion, all men are not dogs. At least not naturally. Brendan was having a hard time splitting his time between two women, especially when the one he lived with had more game than he did. After meeting Tanisha at the party Brendan had been torn between following the advice of Dee versus that from the new-and-improved Nate. Dee had been urging him to put Trina out of his condo without explanation, or at the very least playing her the same way she had obviously played him. "There ain't no sense in trying to talk to her about things that you know she is going to lie about," Dee had said. "Women fuck around just like we do, the only difference is a nigga got to get up early in the morning to catch them. And know this—if you don't catch her ass red-handed, she will take that shit to her grave."

Nate, on the other hand, in light of his new spiritual consciousness, had suggested that Brendan have a serious talk with his woman. "Brendan, I'm far from a perfect example, so I can't really tell you how to live your life, but I will say that most times it's best for an honest man to stay honest. You've always treated women with respect, and I've always respected that about you. You probably never knew that, but I did. I was always so caught up in my games of deception and bullshit that I never took the time to see what open and honest communication would bring, but that's what I'm trying to do from here out."

Brendan had settled somewhere in the middle. He'd elected to spend time with Tanisha while trying his best to forget and ignore the problems with Trina.

"**Brother, you sure** have been hanging out with Dee a lot lately," Trina said while standing in the doorway of the bedroom.

Brendan said nothing in response. Instead he continued dressing. He fastened the last of the buttons on his shirt and inspected his collar in the mirror. He then slipped his foot into the Kenneth Cole loafers. He didn't want her to see him put on cologne. So he reached into his sock drawer and grabbed a sample of Gucci and put it quickly into his pocket. He went into the bathroom to take a quick leak and noticed that Trina was right behind him. Finally, he said, "Why are you following around?"

"You never minded before."

"Well, I mind today. Can I take a piss without you all up on my back?"

A surprised look came across Trina's face. "Why are you talking to me like that?"

Brendan had no response to share. *Maybe because you fucked around on me, maybe because I'm getting ready to fuck around on you,* came to mind but he gave nothing but a shake of his head. Though he would never have admitted it for fear of coming across as a punk, Brendan had an aversion to conflict. It was so deep that he chose to keep silent rather than confront Trina.

"So where are you going?"

"I'm going to the 9:30 Club."

"Oh, so is someone performing down there tonight?" Brendan was surprised that she didn't know. For years Trina and her crew had been a fixture at every hot club or nightlife event in the city.

"You mean you don't know?" Brendan asked jokingly.

"Brendan, you know I don't hang out anymore. Ever since—" She caught herself. She was about to bring up Kim's death, but knew that it would only depress her. Kim was one of Trina's best friends and it bothered her deeply that she had been the one to introduce her to Nate. "You haven't noticed that since we've been back together I have become a real homebody?"

"I guess."

"So who's performing?"

"Kenny Lattimore and Chanté Moore."

Her mouth dropped open. "Oohhhh. I want to go."

"Well, I didn't pay for the tickets. Dee got them from Kenny Lattimore himself. When he's in town Dee cuts his hair. Dee said when he went by the hotel to cut his hair earlier Kenny dropped a couple of tickets on him."

"So, why is he taking you instead of his girl?"

"What girl?"

"I thought he had a girlfriend."

"Not unless you know something that I don't. Which wouldn't really be a surprise."

"Huh?"

"Never mind," Brendan shot back, "I'm out. Don't wait up."

"What time are you coming in?"

"I don't know. Why?"

"I might want a snack."

Brendan took a look at Trina and replied, "You might want to watch the snacks. You know your metabolism starts to slow down as you approach thirty."

"Whatever. Call me when you are on the way in." Brendan turned to head out the door. "Hey," Trina called out. "A sistah can't get a little sugar before you roll out?"

Hiding his lack of enthusiasm, Brendan walked over to her and planted a kiss on her lips. When his lips touched hers, he cringed, imagining her with some other man. As the thought was eating him up inside, he concentrated on the evening ahead and stepped out to take his mind off of her.

The club was packed and Brendan had a hard time finding Dee among the crowd, but he looked over toward the bar and immediately saw Tuesday. Brendan had met Tuesday briefly on a couple of occasions, but because Dee spoke of her quite often he felt as though they were old friends. She had on a multicolored micro-mini and a fuchsia BCBG top that showed her belly button. She was the brightest thing in the place, and Dee was standing right behind her ordering drinks. Tuesday was shaped like a runway model except for the fact that she had huge breasts for a woman of her build.

Brendan walked up to them and Tuesday smiled. "Hey, Brendan, what's up?"

"Hey, Tuesday, what's up with you?"

"Not much, just chillin' up in the spot with my homey, Dee."

Then Brendan pointed to his date. "This is Tanisha. Tanisha, this is Tuesday."

The ladies exchanged pleasantries while looking each other

up and down to check each other's pedigree just as Dee turned around with drinks for himself and Tuesday. "What's good, my nigga?" Then he nodded at Tanisha. "Hey," he said, giving Brendan an approving nod.

Tanisha smiled and responded, "Hey."

Dee ordered a round of drinks for Brendan and Tanisha and the four of them stood around chatting, waiting for the show to start. The deejay was spinning some music while the band set up. The ladies were swaying to the beat as 50's "21 Questions" played. Brendan took notice of Tuesday's thong, which was showing just above her skirt. His eyes were drifting between the butterfly that she had tattooed on the small of her back and the shiny tangerine-colored material that her underwear was made from.

"You like that don't you, boy?" Dee asked Brendan when he caught him staring at her ass.

He didn't even try to lie as the smile formed on his face. "Man, she's sexy as hell."

"I'll tell her that you're feeling her."

"Nah, don't do that." Then it crossed his mind as he watched her body seductively rolling to the beat. She danced as if she were an exotic dancer and she had an imaginary customer in front of her. Brendan was mesmerized by her movement as she wound her body like a snake. "I mean . . . why would you do that?"

"She's not my girl. We're just good buddies. You remember that thing I used to do with the credit cards . . ."

"The computers?"

"Yeah, yeah."

"Tuesday, she's the connection to the cards. Nothing going on with us except an occasional business deal, and that's how I plan to keep it."

"Ohhhh snap," Brendan yelled out. "So shorty is wild, huh?"

"Wild about making dough." He laughed. "I think you got a shot."

Brendan's eyes lit up. "Seriously, even with her seeing me here with Tanisha?"

Dee looked at Brendan as if he was an idiot. "Man, don't get it twisted. She ain't gonna want to marry you." He laughed.

Brendan thought about it for a second. When he glanced at Tanisha he felt a small sense of shame. Here she was, a beautiful sister, who any man would have been satisfied to go out with, yet she was thrilled to be out with him. She'd been straight up with him from day one and hadn't played any games with him since they had met. Even though she was still dealing with her man she and Brendan had been out three times in the past couple of weeks. During dinner at Tony Roma's, Tanisha had openly told Brendan that he was the type of man she was looking for. She had gone further and confided that even though it was early in their relationship she felt as though he was providing her with the strength and desire to finally break off her dysfunctional relationship. All considered, he was still far more interested in Tuesday. She turned him on in a way he couldn't fully understand. She didn't seem like the type of girl you'd bring home to mother, yet her demeanor and sex appeal fascinated him.

The girls grew tired of dancing alone and moved back toward Brendan and Dee. Tanisha moved really close to Brendan and as she brushed up against him he felt the sudden warmth of her body as the scent from her perfume invaded his nostrils. While she leaned against his body, Brendan looked over her shoulder at Tuesday, who was standing next to Dee sipping her third drink of the night. Again he couldn't take his eyes off of her. Then, as the band took their places and began to play, it dawned on Brendan. He was actually considering acting out the exact type of behavior that he had always criticized Nate for. He had Trina at home, who unfaithfully or not, was playing the part of fiancée. He was in the club with Tanisha, who was falling for him so hard she was ready to dump her boyfriend. Even still, there was no denying that he wanted to fuck Tuesday. Right here in the club, the parking lot. It didn't really matter. He was filled with desire.

Dee caught him peeping at Tuesday once again and winked at him before he laughed. Brendan knew that Dee was inviting him into his world. He had offered Brendan women before, hook-ups that could get him into trouble, and opportunities to act foul. This time Brendan winked back and they all headed to the stage to hear Kenny and Chanté as they began to perform.

Tuesday's condo was located at the mouth of Georgetown. She had her place laid out. She gave him a tour and he took notice of the cherry hardwood floors, the expensive art hanging on the tan walls with the white crown molding. The living and dining rooms were filled with fine furniture. Brendan marveled at the stainless steel appliances in the kitchen and the fifty-two-inch plasma screen in the living room. When he reached her bedroom he remembered that Dee had told him that she ran credit card scams. She had a saltwater aquarium built into the wall, another flat-screen mounted on the wall, and a huge Victorian canopy bed.

"So you like it?" she asked as she directed him to the couch, then she went into the kitchen to fix drinks.

"Baby, your spot is all of it," he responded as he fell onto the couch. He looked at the clock and noticed it was two thirty in the morning. Tuesday had slipped Brendan her number after the show. She had scribbled on a note, "Call me when you drop Mary Poppins off if you're up for the challenge 202–777–3667." He barely had time to get Tanisha to her car at the meeting spot before he called Tuesday. Tanisha had to work in the morning and was still hesitant to take Brendan to her place. Tuesday gave him directions and told him don't stop until he hit the parking lot.

"So, Brendan, Dee tells me that you live with someone," she said as she handed him a glass of Rémy and orange juice.

He swallowed quickly and almost stuttered. "I . . . well . . ."

"No, don't trip. It's cool with me. I just think you're a handsome brother and Dee speaks highly of you. I finally got a chance to meet you and I'm feeling your vibe. As a matter of fact, why don't you call her and tell her you got too drunk to drive and you're with Dee?"

Brendan couldn't believe she'd just said that. He thought about it for a second and said, "Nah, she might ask where Dee is or something. I'll just head home in an hour or so."

"You think so?"

He didn't know how to take that, so he just nodded. They finished the first, second, and third drinks while talking and listening to slow music on WHUR. Brendan was amazed to hear that Tuesday had a degree in economics from N.C. State. He was even more shocked when she reached into her Dior bag and pulled out a makeup case filled with joints and fired one up. She passed it to Brendan, "No, thanks, I don't get down."

"Oh, my bad. Do they drug test at your gig?" Tuesday took a pull and then lit an incense.

"Nah, I work at Nordstrom." Tuesday's eyebrows raised. "I'm the manager of women's shoes." He laughed. "No need to drug test up in that camp."

"So what's up? Get high with me." She laughed out, "You afraid I'm gonna take advantage of you?"

He laughed back. "I wish you would, but . . ."

"But nothing," she said seductively. "Hit this and then maybe you can hit *this*," she arched her back poking her breasts out and sticking her rear end out.

Brendan was never into smoking but like most men, he was one to be led around by his penis. She extended her hand with the lit joint and he accepted, with thoughts of having his way with Tuesday. He took a long hard drag. The smoke hit his lungs and burned his throat and he choked and began to cough. Tuesday fell out laughing at him. "Got-damn," he said as his eyes began to water uncontrollably.

Still laughing, she said, "You got to slow down, cowboy. This here is some serious Hydro." She took another toke and blew the smoke out her nose. "I see a sistah is gonna have to teach you how to smoke."

Brendan didn't want to admit that he hadn't smoked since college. A half hour and two j's later Brendan was higher than a kite. His head was light and he was looking around the room trying to remember exactly where he was and wondering how he got there. Tuesday had turned down the dimmer and there were candles lit all over the room. He was staring at the flames as if he had never seen anything so remarkable in his entire life. When Tuesday came out of the room she was naked except for her socks. "Those are soooooo nice," Brendan said as she stood in front of him.

Taken aback, she cupped her breasts and responded with, "My titties?"

"Nooo, those candles. They smell soooo good."

A smile slid across her face and she responded, "Mufucka, you high."

A grin erupted on his face, "Helllll yeah."

With that, Tuesday leaned over the table and lit the last joint. They smoked it together and Brendan got even higher. At this point he could have fallen over and went to sleep for two days, but Tuesday went to work on him. She unbuttoned his shirt and unfastened his pants. What Brendan didn't know was that when she smoked and drank she could go all night. It was already four in the morning and if he didn't make it home in the next hour he was as good as fucked at home, and not in a good way.

Once she had his clothes off she straddled him and kissed him as if he was the man of her dreams. He wasn't responding aggressively enough for her so she began to run her fingers through his hair, gripping the back of his head and pulling his mouth to hers. She began gyrating on top of him, making contact between her clit and his penis. Finally his arousal began to catch up with hers and he wound up in a new place somewhere way past drunk, high, and freaky.

Tuesday began to get wet and her juices were getting all over Brendan's midsection. "I need you inside me right now," she growled out. She reached back onto the coffee table and grabbed a condom out of her purse. She quickly tore it open with her teeth as she slid down to her knees in front of him. She wrapped her lips around his manhood and began to tease the head of his dick while gripping it with her hand. She was making more growling and purring sounds amid the slurping and sucking. He grew rock hard and she slid the condom down on him.

Brendan was turned on but too out of it to take any control. "You want me to sit on it?"

Brendan just nodded his head yes and leaned back. Tuesday turned her back to him and gripped him with her right hand. She guided him in as she sat down on him. Even with the condom he could feel her wetness. She wasn't tight at all and he wondered for a minute if he was big enough for her. She let him know that he was just perfect as she began to moan.

"Ohhhh shit, Brendan." She was bouncing up and down.

"You like it?" he shot back as he was now staring at her back. She was bouncing up and down fast. "You like it?" he repeated.

"Oh, yeah, daddy. I love it." She began grinding and bucking uncontrollably.

Brendan was staring at the tattoos on her back. A lunging black panther, some Greek letters from her sorority, a cross with roses on it, and a design at the small of her back just above the butterfly that looked like a something a Harley-Davidson rider would have. He focused on them as she bounced up and down. She bounced until they became a blur. Soon all he could see was her brown body as she leaned forward. She began to moan loudly as he gripped her ankles. He could feel the familiar sensations of an orgasm as he started breathing heavy. "Ahhh," he panted. "Yessss."

"Cum for me, Brendan," she said as she leaned back and turned her face back toward him and kept humping him. Her back was arched and she was throwing the ass at him in perfect rhythm. "Oh, I feel it too. It's so deep." She began rubbing herself and Brendan went over the edge.

"Oh . . . yeah . . . oh . . . yeah . . . aaaahhh . . . damn." He began to ejaculate and was now lifting himself up off the couch banging into her.

"That's right. Bang me. Bang me." With that she let out a scream and started her own orgasm. "Don't . . . stop . . . fucking . . . me . . . in . . . the . . . ass."

"What?" Brendan asked.

Tuesday paid him no attention as she wound up her orgasm and jumped up off of him. When her bottom released him he heard a plop and looked down to see that he had been in her butt and not her vagina. He was stunned. He never thought that he would enjoy anal sex, but he hadn't even known the difference. She walked off to the bathroom and started the shower.

She called a still-stunned Brendan in to join her and when he climbed in she scrubbed his body from head to toe. Once they finished she led him into the room where she proceeded to fuck him in more ways than one.

At eight thirty he struggled to open his eyes as his phone began vibrating. Tuesday was still sleeping as he got up and got dressed. She barely woke up as he headed out of her place. He remembered the night and was shocked at the things that he'd done with Tuesday. She was wild, but he had to admit that he liked it. He had truly enjoyed himself, at least what he could remember.

With a smile Brendan did recall his unwitting anal experience, the handcuffs, and the pounding he had given her as she shouted sexually explicit commands at him. What he didn't remember was that during the heated sex, Tuesday had shown him why she was nicknamed Panther Girl as she scratched his back unmercifully.

10

Can't See the Forest for the Trees

Friday nights in D.C. are off the hook in the springtime. People have been cooped up all winter and are pressed to get out to see and be seen. Every restaurant, bar, and club is making money. From Georgetown, to downtown, to the suburbs of Maryland and Virginia, people are out partying and trying to mingle. Now we were back on the scene as if we never left. When I got a phone call from Nate letting me know he was back home, there was no question that a trip from New York was mandatory. He'd called the night after he left Kim's mother's house and a week later I was home. Shelly elected to stay back in New York because she had already planned a shopping trip to Woodbury Commons, so my weekend with the fellas would have no constraints.

Nate gave me the biggest bear hug in the world in the parking lot of the Jasper's over in Largo not caring how weird it might have looked.

"Man, it's good to see you," he said as we broke our embrace.

"You too." I returned, smiling at my friend. "You looking good, bro. You been taking care of yourself I see."

"Actually I had put on some weight but I got it back together and I've been working out like crazy."

"So where is Brendan?"

"He and Dee are on the way now."

"Oh, Dee is coming too? I'm going to need an appointment tomorrow," I said lifting my cap off my head.

"Yeah, you know he and Brendan have been hanging tough since we left."

"Yeah, I know and honestly I think that Dee has been a negative influence on that man."

Nate laughed. "Yeah, you might need to talk to him. He doesn't want to hear anything that I have to tell him right now."

"Why's that?"

"I told him that he needs to come to church with me."

I laughed. "So you were telling me that you found God. That's a beautiful thing. I need to come along with you myself while I'm here." I paused and tried to remember the last time I went to church. "So where are you going to go?"

"Well, the church I went to in Charlotte was actually started by a brother who has a church right here in D.C. Lloyd Lawson."

"The name sounds familiar."

"Yeah, he's really a dynamic brother. This Sunday will be my first time attending his church, but I did hear him preach in Charlotte a couple times. He's the reason why I'm back in D.C."

"How's that?"

"Well, his words motivated me to face my fears and guilt. I put it all in God's hands and here I am. I'm not running anymore not even from my own habits."

"That's deep." I said and then saw Brendan pull up with Dee following.

We greeted each other and headed inside to get a table. Just like old times, Nate rolled up on the hostess and spoke to her for a few moments. A minute later the manager, Roy, came to the lobby and greeted Nate. They shook hands and laughed before he waved for us to follow him to our table.

"Thanks, Roy." Nate said.

"No thang. It's good to see you again. Don't be a stranger."

"Some things never change, huh?" I asked, amazed at how Nate still had so much pull.

We ordered drinks and appetizers and kicked it like old times. I let them know that my time in New York was coming to a conclusion. After my meetings with a company we were trying to acquire in Chicago I would be back in the D.C. area to stay. I tried to explain to them what the married life was like and conveyed all the joy that I experienced getting to know my daughter. Then Dee asked a question out of the blue that hit me in the face like a ton of bricks.

"So, Cory, do you think that you made the right choice dropping Nina and getting back with Shelly just because you two had a kid?"

I paused and the table was silent. The thought went down like a cup of hot water burning my insides and before I could answer, Brendan jumped in. "Of course, he did. Dee, you just don't know how much this nigga always loved Shelly, 'cause if you did—"

Then I interrupted him. "No. I didn't." Every one paused again and I looked down at the table and quietly reiterated, "Damn, I didn't." It wasn't the first time that I'd admitted to myself that I should have never married Shelly. I had already told Nina that I felt that way. But saying it aloud to my friends for the first time, I realized that I needed to do something about my situation. "But you know what, fellas?"

"What's that?" they said in unison.

"At the end of the day, I'm gonna make it right."

"That's cool," Brendan responded in a low tone. Dee simply nodded and Nate's eyebrows went up to show his curiosity.

Eventually the conversation regained its pace. More drinks came between the people-watching and the laughing. The Soundstage was getting more packed by the minute. There was an assortment of professional women and men who had come in at happy hour who were blending in with the wannabe thugs and hoochies who were crowding the bar. As we laughed, talking about which summer events we were going to attend, a girl walked past our table. She was wearing a pair of Apple Bottom jeans and a handmade pink knit sweater. Her rear end was perfectly shaped and caught the eyes of everyone at our table. I watched as Nate amazingly returned his focus back to his entrée. Dee predictably said, "Damnnnn." But I was amazed at what I saw next.

Brendan stood up and moved quickly toward her and grabbed her arm. She stopped a few yards past our table and he was all over her. It was like watching a flashback of the old Nate. He said something to her and she began smiling. A few seconds later and he had his cell in his hand putting her number into it.

Once he sat back down I commented, "So it's like that now?"

He was grinning ear to ear. "What was I supposed to do?" He laughed. "You saw the ass on her, right?"

"Cory, this dude is off the chain right now," Dee said approvingly.

"You mean this dog, right?"

"Gimme a break, man," Brendan replied.

"Looks like you making your own breaks." Nate laughed, shaking his head. "You got both feet in the game now, bruh."

Dee chimed in and began to tell the story of Brendan's new and improved attitude. It was like Dee was proud of his new Frankenstein's monster. "B, tell them about Tuesday." Then he laughed out. "Ya'll, this guy is unbelievable."

Brendan, with no shame, told the story of his night with his new sex partner. Nate's mouth dropped open when Brendan explained how Tuesday had sexed him all night and scratched his back up. When he finally made it home, luckily Trina had already left for work. Just thinking of how he nearly got busted made him take a deep breath. It wasn't until the hot water and soap hit his back in the shower that he realized he had been carved up like a turkey.

When I asked how he kept Trina from noticing during sex, he answered, "We haven't had it in weeks. I think she gave me an infection and all of a sudden her sex drive has fallen off. It don't take a scientist to figure out that she must be doing her own thing. I guess a leopard never really does change its spots. The hell with it."

Nate joined in, "Why don't you be a man about it and confront her? Why play games with her?"

Every time he spoke like that it shocked us all. He was a brand-new man. Brendan shot back, "No use. Her days are numbered. I'm waiting for the right time to get rid of her, but right now she is paying half my mortgage. She doesn't give me much fuss about what I'm doing. Shit, most of the time when I get in she's asleep already." He laughed.

"So you're cool living like that?" I asked.

He smiled and looked at his ringing cell phone. "For now," he said, nodding slowly. "Hello." He answered. "Oh, what's up

Tanisha?" Dee grinned from ear to ear as if to say look at how I've helped him.

When it came to Brendan and Dee, it was a case of a lost soul following a blind man. Wherever Dee was leading him, it was sure to be uncharted territory. He had unleashed the player in Brendan and at this point there was nothing Nate or I could offer that could compare to the sense of self-worth that he had now with his new identity. We did what men do in these situations. We decided to live and let live.

We left the bar and headed downtown to my favorite club, Dream. I loved the spot because it was a place where you could see a thousand black folks together looking good and partying, and almost never a fight. There were fine women everywhere, even if half of them were looking for ballers, the other half came to play and have a good time. The warm night had the spot jumping and there was a line down the block. We valet parked and this time Dee knew a bouncer at the door, so Nate didn't even have to ask for Marc, the owner, to get us into VIP. We were inside in no time and were enjoying the atmosphere. OutKast and Sleepy Brown were scheduled to perform, so we made our way upstairs to the stage area.

We stepped in and took notice of the jam-packed room. Nate decided to play the back, so we followed suit. Soon the group came on and had the place rocking. When they performed "I Like the Way You Move" all the women who were dancing near the back rushed the crowded floor and suddenly there was a little breathing room. I prepared to take a seat and it was déjà vu all over again when I saw her standing in the back sipping a drink. I didn't say anything to Nate as I strolled over to her.

"What's a girl like you doing in a place like this?"

Paula's eyes lit up when she saw me and she beamed with affection. "Well, if it isn't Cory Dandridge."

The embrace was genuine and lasted a little longer than it should have. She smelled like a dream and was dressed to kill. She was wearing leather pants and a tight-fitting cashmere sweater that showed her cleavage. We began talking and she explained that she was in town for a conference and was staying with one of her sorors. I was so caught up in the shock of seeing her again after all this time that it never even registered that she was in my hometown and in a nightclub of all places. I asked her a series of questions but never got around to asking about her husband. The last I'd heard from her she was going to give her marriage the old college try. Our affair had ended when I left Atlanta to move back north. Months later on a trip back to Atlanta for a wedding I made an attempt to see her again. She agreed to see me but at the last minute, instead of showing, she wrote me a letter telling me that she wouldn't be seeing me in my hotel. I understood that she wanted to do right by her husband but her letter had stung me nonetheless.

"I'm headed back to Atlanta on Sunday," she said.

I nodded in response.

"I'd like to see you before I leave," she said matter-of-factly.

I felt a sense of pride and my chest swelled a bit with her offer and I replied, "I would like nothing more but . . ."

"But what?"

I held my hand up showing her my wedding band. Then all of a sudden she covered her mouth and her eyes showed both hurt and shock. When I reached for her she attempted to shove me away and I dropped my drink causing it to splash all over my shoes and pants leg. "How could you?" she screamed and stormed off.

I was in shock, and within seconds Nate had come to my side. "Yo, what the hell did you do to her?"

"Huh." I was still in shock.

"Who was that?" Nate asked as we watched her head down the steps making a getaway.

When I explained to Nate who she was, he shook his head and like a true friend he tried to hold back his laughter. He bought me another drink, a coke with no liquor in it, and we sat and talked. I was as confused as I was upset when he made sense of it for me.

"Cory, if that's the worst that ever happens to you for messing with a married woman, then consider yourself lucky. You were in a situation that was in no way sanctioned or blessed by God. It was chaos and we know who the author of chaos is."

"Yeah, I feel you."

"When you step out there like that, things become unpredictable. You may think that you're in control but in all actuality you're nothing more than a pawn." He paused, "Now what do you think would have happened if you had tried to shove her the way she did you?" He burst out laughing and I laughed too.

"They would have locked my ass up tonight."

"You know it."

"Come on. You ready to bounce up out of here?" I asked.

"Ready when you are."

The club was too crowded to look for Brendan, but since he was riding with Dee we figured he'd do exactly what he wanted to and make his way home eventually. We headed down the steps and toward the exit. As soon as we walked out the front door and headed toward the car, Nate tapped me on the shoulder and said, "Brother, for you tonight is like that old show *This Is Your Life*. The one where you meet up with everybody from your past."

"How so?" I asked just in time to see Nina standing in front of me waiting for someone. As I moved past her our eyes met and the connection that we shared made it hard to breathe.

He smiled and said, "I'm going to get the car, man." Then he spoke to Nina briefly and kept moving.

The night was getting weirder and weirder. "So what brings you to town?" Nina asked.

"I came home to see Nate."

"Is she here with you?"

"No."

There was silence and a black BMW pulled up to the curb. "Keep this." She slipped me her cell phone. "I'll call you in an hour from my house. Don't answer it unless you see the word *home* appear on that screen, brother." She had a smirk on her face. "Unless you want to get your feelings hurt."

I nodded and watched her jump into the passenger seat of the Beemer. The windows were tinted and I couldn't make out the driver's face. She pulled off and Nate pulled up.

He drove. We hit New York Avenue and headed toward 395 toward Crystal City. He didn't ask me any questions about Nina. He did tell me that he wanted me to take him to get his Lexus out of my mother's garage in the morning. "Ready to put the top down on it?" I asked.

"Nah, I'm getting rid of it tomorrow."

The car was practically brand new but nothing surprised me about the way he spent money. I figured he was trading it in even though he hadn't had much of a chance to enjoy it. I probably would have asked about it if my mind hadn't been preoccupied with the phone in my pants pocket. We drove straight to the hotel and both went to our rooms. I looked down at my slacks and shoes and thought about Paula. She was a nut. As crazy as she had acted I had to admit that I was glad to have run into her. Some part of me even felt good about rejecting her advance. After all, she had done the exact same thing to me one year earlier. I laughed aloud as I began to get undressed.

I called Shelly to say good night but she must have been asleep because there was no answer at the house. I put on ESPN and plopped onto the bed. I was excited and nervous about going to see Nina at least once before I went home. She had to get her phone. My mind began to drift back to the summer day when Shelly told me that she was pregnant. I was truly happy that day. I couldn't quite remember where we got off track. It dawned on me that we never really did. I got caught wondering about whether Shelly and I still had the magic. When Nina's phone rang and I saw *home* appear on the screen, I realized once and for all that we didn't.

If Heaven's Missing an Angel

Sitting through church sermons was a new experience for Nate. Although he was extremely attentive to the messages that Reverend Lawson delivered, he sometimes caught his mind drifting. Reverend Lawson looked like a dark-skinned version of Suge Knight except that his goatee was salt and pepper and his cheeks a little chubbier. His voice echoed through the entire church as he roused the congregation with colorful analogies and inspirational scripture. Today he preached about the spirit of second chances.

The words were extremely timely for Nate. He fully recognized that he'd been given one. Through all the sinning, deceit, and abuse he'd committed he was still here. He thought about the women who would have loved to have ended his life for the heartache he'd given them. Then there were the many boyfriends and husbands who had sat up waiting for their women to come in from the clubs or girls' night out only to have to wait until the next day or whenever Nate was done with them. His life had been filled with self-indulgence and reckless abandon when it came to the feelings of anyone else.

"Be mindful, folks, that some of you are walking around so high and mighty that you don't feel that you don't need to, or want to, give anyone . . . your husband, your wife, your children, or your friends second chances. You don't even realize that God gives you second *second* chances daily. Shucks, sometimes you need a third *second* chance before you even make it to lunchtime. I know I do." The church erupted in low laughter. "So make it a point to show that humility. That's why we have erasers on pencils . . . we all make mistakes." He quoted a few more scriptures, led the congregation in a closing prayer, and directed the choir to end the service with a song.

One thing that Nate loved about church was that everyone whom he came in contact with seemed so eager to fellowship and encourage him. Without noticing, it seemed as though Nate sought out forgiveness for his past from everyone he met. He'd become extremely humble and his demeanor had changed. It was as if a part of him had died right along with Kim. He was thinking of her as he exited the pew and headed up the aisle toward the doors of the church.

As he made his way down the steps he noticed a woman pointing at him. She was standing with two other women. Nate pretended not to notice and kept moving until she shouted his name. "Nate. Nate Montgomery." He glanced over and she shouted, "I thought that was you in the church."

He looked over and made eye contact this time and recognized her face. It was Erika. He hadn't seen her since he had thrown her and her cousin out of his apartment after sleeping with them both. He wasn't sure if he should stop and say hello or wave and keep moving. As he was thinking it over, he found himself right in front of her. She was still looking good and he wondered for a moment why he had never taken her seriously. "Hey, Erika. It's nice to see you."

She rolled her eyes. "Nice to see me?"

Nate released an uncomfortable chuckle. "Yeah. Nice to see you." He decided to play dumb. "Why wouldn't it be?"

Her eyes narrowed and her lips got tight. "Oh, I see you're still a real jackass, huh?"

"Erika," one of her friends said, trying to quell an outburst.

Nate shook his head. He wasn't disgusted at her behavior but a little shocked that she was about to take it there in front of the church. He understood why she would still be angry. She was really digging him for a while. The last time he had seen her he'd made love to her all night long and probably promised her the world. The next morning, though, instead of breakfast in bed, he served her the shock of her life. After sleeping like a baby she was awakened by a thumping sound. When she realized she was in Nate's bed alone she got up to find him. Moments later, she walked in on him banging her cousin, Jay, who had slept in the next room. A horrible scene unfolded and he, of course, had sent them both packing. Erika had never enjoyed a worse Thanksgiving, thanks to Nate.

"Hey listen E—"

She cut him off and pointed her finger into his face. "My name is Erika and—"

"Erika, I'm sorry," Nate said calmly, interrupting her before she started her tirade. "I was in a really bad place then. I behaved ya'know . . . real foul back then. I know I hurt you and I know what I did was worse than *just* wrong. So from the bottom of my heart I want you to know that I truly apologize." Erika was silent. An apology was the last thing she expected. It was evident that she had long awaited the chance to confront him and to blast him. Now here she was looking deep into the eyes of a sincere man. "Even if you can't forgive me, then at least accept my apology."

A few seconds and she nodded her head. Her friends were silent as well. One of them was looking Nate up and down. He was wearing a dark brown Helmut Lang suit and a five-hundred-dollar pair of Polo loafers. It wasn't until he had spoken so gently that they noticed how appealing he was. "O . . . okay . . . I accept your apology." Nate extended his hand to shake hers and was surprised when she reached out and pulled him in for a hug. He was even more surprised when during the embrace she whispered into his ear, "I have missed you soooooo much. No one ever made me feel like you did."

When Nate pulled away he immediately felt uncomfortable. Before he had to come up with a response, he heard a welcome voice. "Nathan. Come here for a second." He looked over and saw Reverend Lawson waving him over.

"E . . . I mean Erika, it was good seeing you again," he said. She nodded in agreement.

"You too. Do you come here every week?" She asked.

"Well I just moved back in town and . . ."

"Nathan," Reverend Lawson called again.

"Let me run. Maybe I'll see you again," he said and walked off toward his pastor, glad that he didn't' have to tell a lie to avoid seeing her again.

He walked up on the reverend and shook his hand. "How'd you like that message today?"

"It was great. I enjoyed it thoroughly."

"That's good." He laughed. "Listen, Nate, I have someone I want you to meet." He spun his big body and pulled a sister from a group of ladies behind him. He led her lightly by the arm and placed her in front of Nate. "Charley, this is the young man I was telling you about. Nathan Montgomery." Then he patted Nate on the shoulder. "Nate, I present to you my lovely sister-in-law. She is single and ready to mingle, or should I say ready to meet a fine young man like yourself." He laughed.

"Hi Nate, I'm Charlene." She extended her hand and they shook as they exchanged pleasantries. Nate noticed that Charlene had a really firm grip. Her build was like Angela Bassett's when she played the role of Tina Turner. His mind immediately took him back to the fluffy body of Janette in Charlotte. He had grown used to the soft curves of a larger woman and though he was focused on remaining celibate, when he had broken down and masturbated images of Janette and other full-figured women were always flooding his mind. Charlene was pretty enough and her smile was bright, but Nate felt no connection to her.

"Nate, I want you to come to the house for lunch. We're having some people over and I would love for you to meet my wife."

Nate knew that it was a setup. The good reverend was trying to play matchmaker and it was obvious. "Rev, I really have a lot to do this afternoon."

"Nathan, I would take it as a personal insult if you didn't come and join me."

Nate shook his head and a cordial grin appeared on his face hiding the pressure he was feeling. "Well, since you put it like that I don't see how I could refuse."

They both laughed and Charlene smiled and winked at Nate.

The church parking lot cleared and a half hour later Nate followed the pastor and ten carloads of church members into

a gated community out in Mitchellville, Maryland. Lloyd
Lawson had a seven-thousand-square-foot home in a community reserved for the area's elite. Nate remembered coming
into the community for a party at Chris Webber's house when
he played for the Wizards a few years back. It was strange to
imagine that a man working for a church could afford such a
house. The thought crossed his mind that a good portion of
the collections must have gone into paying the mortgage on
this place.

Lloyd's Mercedes disappeared into the garage and everyone
else parked in the driveway and gravel next to it. He exited his
car and followed the other members of the congregation
toward the front door. "Hey, Nathan," Charlene said as she appeared.

"Hey again."

She led him into a family room big enough for ten families
and offered him a drink. As she went off to get it Nate was approached by members wanting to make his acquaintance.
Some came off as nosy while a few seemed genuine.

"Nice to meet you."

"Let me know if there's anything I can do to make you feel
more welcome."

"So how did you find out about the Word Church and Reverend Lawson?"

"You look really familiar."

"So what kind of work do you do?"

"Are you married?"

When Charlene failed to come back with his drink he decided to wander off. When he reached the punch bowl in the
kitchen he saw an older lady sitting in a motorized wheelchair
watching the Home Shopping Network. She had on an
almond-colored dress with flower prints on it. Nate spoke to

her and her eyes never left the screen. As he filled his cup the old lady said, "Doctor Baines, don't you turn that channel I'm looking for something."

"Excuse me," Nate said as he looked around to see if she could have been speaking to anyone else.

"You heard me. Don't make me tell my son. He will kick your ass and good. You always change the got-damned channel when something comes on that I want to buy."

Nate was confused and before he could respond a woman entered the kitchen. "Miss Bethany, what are you in here fussing for?" She flipped back into silent mode and resumed watching the television. "You'll have to excuse Mrs. Lawson. This is Lloyd's grandmother. She gets a little confused at times . . . you understand?"

"Oh, of course. I just hope I didn't upset her."

"No, she's fine. I've been looking after her for the past few months and she gets like that from time to time. Whatever you do, just don't turn that shopping network off." Then she laughed, showing a smile as bright as snow in the sunshine. Nate took a look at her as he laughed with her. As he took in the sight of her he couldn't believe his eyes. He couldn't believe that he was seeing the personification of perfection. She wasn't the cliché ideal of beauty. She wasn't fair-skinned, and her hair wasn't straight. She didn't have hazel eyes and she wasn't tall. Instead her skin was the color of a Hershey bar, her eyes were slightly slanted, and the skin overlapped like a Chinese person's. Her lips were full and she had on red lipstick, which he usually found tacky. She had a perfect face, high cheekbones, long lashes, and the whitest teeth. Her body, however, was a different level of excellent. She was shaped remarkably close to Ki Toy, the girl from the OutKast video with the prototype body. Nate tried to compose himself when she turned and opened the refrigerator. With her back to him he gazed at her and took her image in and felt the air escaping his body.

The linen cargo pants that she wore did nothing to disguise the contours of her rear end. She had on a snug-fitting Chanel T-shirt and when she reached up to the top shelf of the fridge to grab a tray of cold cuts, there was a slight jiggle in her breasts, which were the size of grapefruits, and only visible to someone staring beyond the point of reason. When she turned around she caught Nate's stare and the smile she had worn quickly disappeared.

"So, what's your name? I haven't seen you around before."

"My name is Nate and I'm new to the church."

"Oh, okay, yeah, I've heard about you. Larry talked a lot about you before you moved back to D.C."

Nate had assumed that she was either a nurse for Reverend Lawson's mother or a housekeeper so he asked, "So how do you know Larry?"

She looked at him strangely. "Larry is my brother-in-law. I'm Anita Lawson, Lloyd's wife."

With her response Nate almost lost his breath. In that moment it came to him that he'd been slipping as he hadn't in months. He was lusting for this woman. Not only in a sexual manner, though. In the few moments since she had come into the kitchen, Nate had fostered a desire to get to know this woman. Something in her energy made him want to know what was behind her beauty and her body. It was all out the window now as he realized that she belonged to his pastor, of all people. Anita couldn't have been a day over thirty he guessed and Lloyd looked to be at least forty-five. Nate couldn't see the matchup as hard as he tried.

They made small talk while she grabbed some plastic ware.

Miss Bethany interrupted them, "Doctor Baines," she yelled, "take a look at this pen." She was pointing at the television. "Hurry up, they only have a hundred and fifty left. You could use this with all those prescriptions you write."

As Nate move toward Miss Bethany, Anita smiled at him. "I'll see you in a bit, Doctor Baines."

As she headed out Nate mouthed. "Who is Doctor Baines?"

"Just be glad you aren't him," she responded in a whisper. "He's been dead for twenty years."

Nate sat and talked with Miss Bethany for a good half hour. Never mind that she thought he was her doctor from some years back. She just smiled and laughed and when she told him it was time for her nap she asked him to open the door to her room.

After rejoining the crowd in the family room, Nate was cornered by Charlene. It took only twenty minutes of conversation for him to realize that Charlene was looking for a husband. He quickly escaped to the deck where he found Lloyd entertaining a group of deacons. He was surprised when he saw the reverend with a glass of Rémy Martin in his hand. Nate simply never imagined that a pastor would drink hard liquor.

"Nathan, come on and join us. Don't be shy."

Nate walked out onto the deck and took a seat as he listened to the men talk about how bad their golf games were, how poorly their stocks were performing, and about how crooked the world of politics had become. After another half hour Nate excused himself and insisted he had to run. Had to go work out and get some shopping done. In reality he was so wound up that he was thinking of taking a ride down to Charlotte to pay his dentist a visit. He was horny as hell and thought only a moment about his commitment to celibacy.

On his way out the door Anita caught him. "Leaving already?"

"Yeah, I have to go work out, do some shopping . . ."

"Shopping sounds like fun." She smiled. "As a matter of fact that's my favorite way to spend an afternoon."

"I'll bet." Trying to find a way to sound cordial, he was going to tell her that she had a lovely home and thanks for having him. Instead he came out with, "So why don't I ever see you in church?"

"Well, as you saw earlier, Miss Bethany suffers from Alzheimer's disease and she has to be under supervision at all times. We had a nurse up until a few months back, but she had to move when her husband was called up from the reserves to fight in Iraq. So until we find a suitable replacement, there's only me. I get a break every now and then but because Lloyd is so busy with the church, I'm here with her about ninety percent of the time."

"Oh, I see. Well, I'm sure she appreciates what you do for her."

"Not really, but we all do some things in life not because we *like* to but because we *have* to. But one of these days . . ." Anita laughed out.

"Well, I think it's admirable." Nate smiled. "Take care and maybe I'll see you soon."

"Maybe," she replied, sounding almost flirtatious.

Already finding her exceptionally fine, her tone nearly caused his old instincts to ignite and send him into mack mode. As he made his exit he almost broke into a stride heading for his car. He needed to get as far away from Anita as possible because what he was feeling for her at that moment was the possible prelude to disaster.

He looked back at the door to see if she was still watching

him. On the one hand, he was slightly disappointed when he saw that she wasn't, but relieved on the other.

Anita had gotten him so horny that he was prepared to break his vow of celibacy. He pulled off, headed toward the hotel he was staying in until he could find an apartment, preparing to stay only long enough to grab a change of clothes. Nate wrestled with breaking his vow for the entire ride, but when he couldn't clear his mind of the thoughts of Anita, he came to the realization that only a release would satisfy his urges. With luck and light traffic he'd be in Charlotte and inside Janette by eight. Though contact between Nate and Janette had dissipated with his move back home to D.C., there were no hard feelings on Janette's part. In addition to making the breakup a nonissue, she'd claimed to understand and support Nate's decision to give his life to God.

That being said, it took less than three minutes of conversation in Nate's moment of weakness before she'd offered her body and bed to him for comfort. It seemed old habits would die hard.

"So what is it that you needed to tell me that you couldn't tell me over the phone?"

"Nigga, we live together. Why shouldn't I have a talk with you face-to-face?" Trina shot back. Brendan placed his cell phone on the counter and took a seat on the ottoman. Brendan's body language showed that he wasn't eager to have a talk. Trina sensed it and she immediately caught an attitude. "I mean, it's not like we do much else together these days. All you do is work and keep your nose up Dee's ass the rest of the time."

"Whatever."

"Whatever, my ass. It's true and I'm sick of it."

"So what you wanna do about it?"

"I want you to do better. Be more attentive." Brendan paused before responding. The first thing that came to his mind was a conversation he'd heard in the barbershop. *It doesn't matter if you're Donald Trump and have a dick made of gold. A woman is but so patient. They want to be paid attention to. You snooze, you lose.* He couldn't remember who had said it but he never forgot the words. As of late he had stopped paying attention to Trina. It was a strange gamble since she had a history of cheating, even when he was doing right, showering her with affection, gifts, and attention. Brendan rationalized that perhaps he was ready for her to drift away, even if it was into the arms of another, or maybe he was beginning to enjoy his new lifestyle of womanizing.

"Trina, you're never satisfied," he finally responded.

"That is not true. I have been so happy since we moved in together. I thought that maybe we would be farther along toward getting married by now, but instead . . . it's like we're moving farther apart." She put her hands over her face then ran her fingers through her hair.

"Well, I don't know what to say. Just 'cause I been hanging out a little with Dee you wanna give me this drama. It's not like you haven't been having your fun."

"What's that supposed to mean?"

"You know what the hell it means." He was finally going to let her have it. In all probability, she had given him chlamydia and had never had the decency to tell him. "Why is it you think that we haven't had sex in a month?" Her face showed the look of puzzlement. It was obvious that she hadn't realized how long it had been until he'd said something. She began to count back on her fingers and Brendan finally became disgusted. "Oh, bitch, don't play dumb," he finally shouted.

"Who the hell are you talking to?" Trina stood up from the couch.

"You'd better sit your ass back down."

"You don't tell me what to do."

"Trina, sit down," he said, trying to calm the situation. "I should be the one going off."

"No, nigga, you *don't* disrespect me like that. I will lose it and whoop your ass up in here."

"You know what? I won't entertain that bullshit. You are the one who gave me a fucking disease."

"WHAT?" she yelled. "I know you have lost your mind now."

"Say what you will, but I went to the doctor's last month because my shit wasn't right."

She folded her arms and a smirk showing disbelief was on her face. "And he told you that you had a disease, huh?" With her finger pointing into his face, she said, "If you did get one, it must have come from one of those dirty bitches that you and Dee have been running around with."

"I hadn't been with anyone else."

"What the fuck do you mean *hadn't?*"

"Until you fucked around and gave me this shit I was faithful. And once again I got burned by you, but in a different way this time. So I figured what the hell, two can play that game."

Trina's face showed no emotion. She got up and walked into the bedroom and came back out holding a prescription bag. "Last month I went to the doctor's too and had an abnormal Pap smear." She threw the bag. "One of those is for a yeast infection, which I never get. The second one is for prenatal vitamins."

Brendan didn't catch on.

"Don't sit there looking stupid," she said, but he did. "The reason I had a yeast infection was because of a hormonal imbalance caused by pregnancy. Now, if your doctor says that you definitely had a disease . . . then you got it from someone else."

"Well, he didn't say a hundred percent but . . .."

Before he could finish, she screamed out, "But you started fucking around on me because you thought I did something. You are such a little boy. Why wouldn't you talk to me?" Trina collapsed onto the couch and the first tear fell.

"Trina, it was just your past . . . it was easy to see you doing the same thing that you did in the past."

The next second, she was on top of him swinging wildly. "I hate you," she was screaming. Brendan tried to cover up as she threw punch after punch. He finally escaped from underneath her and jumped up from the couch.

"Baby, calm down."

She reached for the first thing she could find. Instantly the universal remote flew toward him striking him in the forehead like a pitch from a major leaguer. Next she yanked a candle from the coffee table and slung it it his direction. It missed and hit a picture on the wall, shattering it as it fell. "I'm gonna kill you, motherfucker."

"Listen, I'm sorry, baby," Brendan begged. He was in a defensive stance.

She charged him and with a move from her tae kwon do class lunged foot first into his groin. Brendan wasn't prepared and when she connected, he screamed at the top of his lungs. "Ohhhhh, bitch, I am going to kill you." He clenched his fist, but before he could react the effect of being kicked in his nuts took over. He dropped to his knees and a look of anguish appeared on his face. "Arrrgggghhh." He rolled on the floor trying to stop the pain. His jewels felt like they were in his chest and his breathing became labored. He forgot everything that was going on at that point. He wanted to make her pay. Trina knew that by kicking him in the nuts all bets were off. There was no turning back at this point, so she stood over him, "How you like that? I told you I would whip your ass, you punk. You gonna cheat on a bitch, huh? Well, you shoulda asked somebody, 'cause you picked the wrong one this time. Brendan, I can promise you one thing. I am going to make your life miserable. I'm having this baby and you are going to pay through the nose." She was ranting and he was in too much pain to pay her any attention. The only thing he could feel was anger as the pain began to slowly lose its grip. "The only way you are going to be able to afford to eat when I finish with you is by having to rob Nordstrom's blind. In case you forgot," she said as she swung her foot, "size seven, nigga." She kicked him in the back. "Michael Kors, nigga."

Her anger was at the boiling point as she spit on Brendan. He felt the cold wetness of her saliva on the back of his neck and lost it. As she backed away he reached out and grabbed her ankle. She underestimated his strength and tried to pull away. He yanked her ankle as if he was pulling the emergency brake on a train headed for a cliff. When she stumbled he pushed with all his might. Trina quickly lost her balance and fell backward into the CD rack. When she hit it and slid to the floor the rack came tumbling down on her. She gave a new meaning to nonstop music as five hundred discs hit her right in the face seconds before the wooden rack landed on top of her. Her head was banging with pain and the weight of the rack hurt her to the point that she became fearful for her unborn child. She had put her arms over her belly to protect it. Just as her tears erupted, a hard knock came at the door. "Open up, police."

Nate was in Charlotte for a couple of days, and Dee wasn't answering his phone. When Brendan called her she had shown up immediately. As they left the county lockup in Upper Marlboro, Tanisha asked him, "Are you going to be okay?"

He didn't know the answer to that one yet. He was facing charges for aggravated assault, resisting arrest, and for battery as well. When Brendan let the officers in, Trina was the one looking like the victim of an attack. A couple of CDs had scratched her face and she was moving around as frantically as if a pit bull had bitten her. The officers had taken Trina's side completely and looked at Brendan with disgust once she told them that she had just told him about her pregnancy. They took it almost as if he tried to cause a miscarriage. His complaint on the way down the steps about the cuffs being too tight led to rougher treatment and a trumped-up charge of resisting arrest. He was feeling royally screwed.

As they drove up Brown Station Road Brendan decided to explain the entire situation to Tanisha, everything except the pregnancy. She was silent and listened quietly. Finally she said, "Listen, if you want to chill at my spot for a couple of days, it's fine."

He thought about her offer and it didn't take long to see that his options were limited. Nate wasn't settled yet and he didn't want his parents to know what was going on. Dee might have agreed to let him stay but Brendan needed to be somewhere where he could get his emotions in check. "I'd appreciate that."

"Don't mention it. Stay as long as you need." Tanisha was sweet.

"What about your boyfriend slash situation?"

She tuned the radio station. "Oh him, I ended that once and for all."

Brendan was silent and satisfied for the time being. "Hey, I want you to drop me past my crib so I can grab my car and pick up a few items. Make the second right."

Tanisha followed his directions until Brendan told her to park. "Do you want me to wait?" she asked.

"No, I might be about an hour getting some stuff together. I may even get a locksmith to come and change the locks," he said. "I mean this is *my* crib," he added boastfully. Just then he turned and headed toward his condo and caught a glimpse of his car. "Oh, shit, no," he screamed. "Awwwwww fuuuuckkk," he was repeating as he ran toward his Corvette. Every window was smashed out of it and instead of keyed up, it looked like Freddy Krueger had gone to work on it and scraped the car from front to back. At that point the slashed tires were an afterthought. Brendan fell to his knees right there in the parking lot.

He was in such a state of shock that he didn't notice Tanisha standing next to him. There wasn't anything that she could say to make him feel any better, so she just pulled out her cell and dialed the police. "Someone will be here in the next half an hour they said."

"Thanks," escaped his lips.

"Maybe you should go take a look inside."

They headed toward his place and when he reached his front door he tried to put his key into the lock and noticed the lock had a broken key in it. "I don't believe this shit."

He tried unsuccessfully for twenty minutes to get the key out of the lock before calling a locksmith. When he finally came forty-five minutes later, he charged Brendan ninety dollars to bang the doorknob off, ruining his door. His problems were only getting worse. Once inside he was amazed to find that Trina had gone psycho. His couches were cut open, things were thrown everywhere, and to top it off, his fish tank was filled with purple water, and all of his fish were dead, floating at the top.

Tanisha was standing behind him in shock. "Yo, this chick is crazy, Brendan."

"Who you telling," he replied. He walked to the back of his condo and surprisingly it was intact. All the dresser drawers were open and it was apparent that Trina had taken all her belongings. Then as he took a seat on the bed to let everything digest, he notices a container of bleach on the floor near the closet. He jumped up and took a look inside. "You bitch," he yelled out.

"What?" Tanisha asked.

"This bitch ruined all my clothes. She put bleach on everything, even my shoes."

Tanisha covered her mouth in shock and took a look into his drawers. "Looks like she did your underwear and socks too."

Just then he heard a knock at the door and he ran to see who it was. When he answered he saw the same police officers who'd arrested him the previous night. "Oh great," he mumbled. "You're here to take the report on the car, right?"

"Yes, sir. The Corvette, right?"

"It looks like that's the only vandalized car in the parking lot from what I can tell," he spat out sarcastically.

"Brendan, don't get like that with them. They're here to help," Tanisha commented.

"It's okay, ma'am," one of the officers responded. "We understand that he might be upset."

"Upset? Nah, a nigga is past upset." Brendan pointed at his living room. "Look at this. I want that bitch arrested. Just like you dragged me up out of here and filed those bogus charges . . . resisting arrest, my ass. You need to go find her, and you better do it before I do."

"Sir, I don't think you want to make threats like that. We might have to take you in again."

"Man, fuck you."

"Brendan," Tanisha said before grabbing him. "Look, you go in the back, try to calm down, and I will handle this." She began explaining everything to the officers and headed out to the parking lot. After a glass of ice water and punching the walls a couple of times, Brendan walked out to join the officers.

"So are you guys going to issue a warrant for her arrest?"

"Well, sir, we don't have any witnesses, but we will question a couple of the neighbors to see if anyone saw anything that will help with the investigation."

"So the fact that she had a key and there was no forced entry isn't enough proof? The fact that she attacked me doesn't serve as motive?"

"Well, sir, according to her statement you attacked her once she told you that she was pregnant with your child. Does she have brothers or friends who may have taken issue with you over that? We can't just accuse her without any solid evidence."

Tanisha had a quizzical look. "Pregnant?"

There was silence. "Man, I don't believe this. Thanks for nothing." Brendan turned and headed back into his building.

"Sir, you're going to need this report for your insurance."

Once he reached the top of the steps he turned back. "Screw you and your reports, you probably lied on those too." Then he slammed the door.

Brendan exhaled the smoke and passed the joint back to Tuesday. She either felt sorry for him or was actually starting to dig him. He'd spent three nights in a row at her house.

Tanisha had been avoiding his phone calls since the officers had spilled the news to her that he was an abuser and, even worse, to a woman carrying his seed. He'd called Dee and immediately he insisted that Tuesday would come through for him and she did. His insurance company hadn't even cut the check, and Tuesday had already burned up two stolen credit cards and an assortment of bogus gift cards from Saks, Macy's, Best Buy, and Circuit City replacing all the items that Trina had destroyed.

All in all Trina actually did him a favor. His claim was for fifteen grand but Tuesday had gotten him twenty thousand worth of clothes and appliances. She was charging him half his insurance check and it seemed like an unlimited supply of head. He wasn't complaining. Tuesday was a superfreak in bed and the only thing that beats a superfreak is one with access to stolen credit cards. Brendan wasn't even mad at Trina anymore, except for the issue of calling the police on him. He had gone to her parents' house looking for her the day after she'd trashed his place only to get "She hasn't been around here." Her job claimed that she was on vacation. He gave up the search for the time being, though the pregnancy was on his mind nonstop.

"I really appreciate all that you've done for me Tuesday." He was high and feeling real sentimental. "I just want you to know . . ."

"Yeah, yeah nigga." She smiled. "Just put on your scuba gear and get back to diving." She hit the remote. Raheem De-Vaughn's CD came on as she spread her legs and leaned back on the couch. As soon as his tongue hit the spot, she shivered and purred like a cat. "Come on, let's take this to the bedroom."

Brendan got up and felt the effects from smoking. He was

already stripped down to his underwear. He watched as Tuesday moved past him and headed for the bedroom. He watched her ass as she swished her naked bottom. All the sexing between him and Tuesday was helping him forget his problems. As he approached the bed the only thing he remembered was to keep his shirt on.

13

No Ordinary Love

Sometimes the hardest thing to say is that which is already apparent. There's no formula to getting it out. No guarantee that your words will be received without contempt or understanding. It's more than a roll of the dice when lives and feelings hang in the balance.

"This isn't working for me," I said as I dried the last couple of plates.

"I cooked *and* washed the dishes. You're almost finished now so stop complaining," Shelly replied, flipping through the Sunday *Times*.

I dropped the dish towel and turned toward her. "That's not what I'm talking about. I'm talking about us. I'm talking about our marriage."

Shelly put the paper down on the table and a blank stare appeared on her face. Finally the corners of her mouth went up and then, "What?" The look she gave me asked the same question that I had asked of myself. *Was I crazy?*

"Shelly, I've tried but I can't go on with this. I love you, but we can't stay married." Her mouth dropped open.

"What's wrong? You're not happy?" She began to ramble. "Where is all this coming from? I thought that everything was going fine with us. I know you have been trying hard to adjust to being a father, but you and Amani are getting along, right?"

"Listen—"

She didn't let me finish. "How can you just come out of the blue like this?"

"Shelly, I haven't been unfaithful to you. I promise you that; however I haven't been completely honest with you."

"What does that mean? What haven't you been honest about?"

I walked over and sat down in the chair across from her to tell her what I didn't think I could. The pressure had been building up though, and I had to listen to what life was telling me. Life was telling me to be honest and to stop jeopardizing the future that I so desperately wanted. The only one that I knew I could live with. "I'm still in love with Nina."

The look on her face showed all the pain and confusion that it should have. She began to rant and curse me.

"What?" she shot out. "I know you didn't just say what I think you did."

I was silent for a moment, then I muttered, "Shelly, I'm sorry. I really am."

"Sorry? Sorry for being a no good piece of shit? Do you hear yourself?" She began to breath heavily and I feared she might hyperventilate.

I shook my head and said, "Shelly, please calm down."

At the top of her lungs she yelled out, "How long?"

"How long what?"

"How long have you been fucking her behind my back?"

"It's not like that, I swear. I would never—"

She cut me off. "Cory, there's nothing that I could put past you." She began to cry and moved toward me. I was still seated and as she stood over me she said, "This is it. You've made your bed now."

"Shelly, I'm sor—"

I didn't get my words out before she started to speak again. "You will regret this, I hate you, you will never see your daughter again," all came from her mouth in a combination of English and Spanish. Before I knew it I was on the receiving end of a few blows. I reasoned that I deserved worse so I took them for a few moments before escaping the house and heading to my office to spend the night.

"Hello," Nate answered the phone.

"Hello, Nathan." The voice was familiar. "I hope that I didn't ring you at an inopportune time. This is Anita. Anita Lawson," she added.

Nate was driving but was eager to give the conversation his full attention. He pulled into the parking lot of the 7-Eleven and turned his music down. "To what do I owe the pleasure of your call, Anita?"

She laughed, but he was serious. "Well, Nathan—"

"Nate, just call me Nate."

"Okay, uh, Nate. I was wondering if you had some time in your schedule, if you might be able to come past the house this afternoon. You see, Miss Bethany has been asking about you since you came by on Sunday. Each day she keeps insisting that she is sick and going to die if she doesn't see Doctor Baines."

"Say what?"

She continued. "From what I can gather, you do bear a resemblance to her former doctor. The last time this happened she went on for a few weeks nearly driving us all insane. She once mistook one of my girl friends for her former neighbor and began ranting about some unreturned items that she loaned out in 1965. Eventually to get her to let the whole thing go we had to get my friend to come back by and return an ice cream scoop and a sewing machine that we had to buy from Target."

"I understand," he responded.

"Do you really?"

"You want me to come by and *be* Doctor Baines for a couple of hours and tell her that she's fine."

"Yes, and also to tell her that you are returning down south to work or retire. We'll figure something out. That way you won't have to keep coming by."

"I honestly don't mind coming by," Nate shot back.

"That's good to know. So what time should we expect you?"

"It's a little after two now. How about six or so?"

"I'll see you then."

"No doubt."

Nate had mixed feelings about going back to Reverend Lawson's home. He honestly felt sorry for Miss Bethany and wanted to make her feel better. One of the things he wondered about was why God allowed old people to become afflicted or to suffer. His grandmother was aging and he hoped with all his heart that she would do so gracefully and without any pains and illnesses.

But truth be told he was going back over to that house for a reason that he didn't want to admit to himself. Anita had stirred up feelings inside of him that he hadn't felt in a long while. She was very attractive to him physically, but there was something else that he couldn't put his finger on. Something stronger than lust. Just the sight of Anita had turned him on so much that his desire for her almost caused him to break his abstinence. On the way to Charlotte he had prayed on it over and over. He realized that he was only going to use Janette because he was lusting after Anita. That Sunday Nate had made it all the way to Raleigh before pulling off of I-85 and turning around and heading back to D.C. As he'd headed back he had come to realize that he wouldn't be able to squelch whatever desires he had for Anita in the bed with Janette.

It was five o'clock and Nate was parked in Mrs. Winters's driveway. He had retrieved his Lexus convertible and turned in his rental. He was wiping it down when the Metrobus stopped at the corner. Nate looked up and saw Kim's mother step off the bus and start up the block. When she reached him her look showed surprise.

"Nate?"

"Hey how are you today, Mrs. Winters?"

"I'm fine. What brings you by?" She smiled.

"Well, I just needed you to sign some papers."

"What kind of papers?"

"The papers for your car."

"Well, like I told you, I was saving for a car. I don't have one yet."

Nate reached into the window of the Lex and pulled out the title and a bill of sale. "Well, you can use that money for the taxes and insurance." Then he pointed to the hood, "This is your car."

"What? You have to be kidding," she laughed out in disbelief. She insisted that she couldn't afford a car like this even if he was selling it for half its price.

"I'm not charging you a dime. The car is a 2003 and it's paid for. All you have to do is sign this paperwork and take it down to the DMV, get your tags, and you're good to go. The maintenance records are in the glove . . . hell, you can sell it and buy two cars if you want." He laughed.

"Nate, I thought we talked. You don't have to feel guilty or buy my forgiveness. I could never accept a car like this from you. It must have cost at least fifty thousand dollars."

"Closer to seventy."

"Oh my gawd," she said.

"Listen, Mrs. Winters, the only thing that I ask is that you drop me off at the car dealer. I've already purchased a new car. I don't want this one anymore. You need a car . . . summer's almost here . . . I know you tired of that bus. Besides, it would mean a lot to me if you would accept it."

Forty-five minutes later Nate was pulling out of the Porsche dealer in a brand-new Cayenne, next stop the Lawson's.

Jamison Hakito had been a little upset with my request. Mainly because my request sounded more like a demand. "Jamison, I'm sorry to break this to you in such an abrupt manner, but I need out of New York by Friday."

He stopped his golf club midair and slowly brought it to his side. "Cory, you know that that's not possible. We're preparing for the merger and I need you there."

"Jamison, I'm sorry but I need to leave. It's a personal matter that I'm unable to discuss. However, you have my every assurance that I can run the New York office from the D.C. office."

"Well, I will have to discuss this with the board because—"

"Jamison, with all due respect, I will have my office and files packed and ready to be shipped back to D.C. on Friday. I will report to my office there on Tuesday. If necessary, I will assume the rent on the apartment here for the next two months."

There was some more volleying on his part to get me to stay in New York for a couple more months. Getting annoyed at his persistence, I finally offered my resignation and he nearly choked. I had been the diamond in the crown of Hakito Electronics. Ever since I had come aboard, the company's expenses had dropped sharply while profits had risen drastically. I was gifted when it came to crunching numbers and configuring bottom lines that worked fiscally. On top of that, the Hakitos were superstitious and believed that I was good luck for them because as soon as I joined HE, their holdings in other businesses they owned had skyrocketed as well. There was no way that they would let me go. Once Jamison realized that I was deadly serious about resigning if there was a problem with my request, all resistance faded.

He was curious as to why I wanted to keep the apartment for the next couple of months. When I told him that my daughter wanted to finish the school year before moving back to D.C. and that my wife had agreed to stay behind, he insisted that they stay, no charge to me.

The tension was thick inside of our apartment. Shelly and I had attempted to stay out of each other's way and were both acting very subdued. It was almost as if we were both trying to keep an explosive situation from detonating.

"So when are you leaving?"

I was packing my belongings. "The moving service is coming this evening."

Shelly's arms were folded and she stood in the doorway watching me. I could feel her eyes piercing my back. "Hmmph," she said. "You know, Cory, I never figured you'd do something like this. You really didn't seem like you'd give up so easily."

"You know, it's odd." I stopped packing and turned to face

her. "I was thinking the same thing. I thought about all that life could possibly offer us if we stayed together. I tried to imagine something more than familiar faces doing familiar things, good sex, and memories of the past . . . but I couldn't. I want something new. I want something exciting. I want surprises." I walked up to her. "It's like we're stuck and we're trying to hold on to college dreams, afraid of the new."

"That's all you think that we could ever mean to one another?" Tears began to well up in her eyes.

"Shelly, I don't want to hurt you. I didn't mean to do that."

"Cory, it doesn't matter. Nothing matters." The tears began to fall. "This whole marriage has been a mistake." She began to laugh and cry at the same time. "I guess it's true what they say . . . you can't go home again." Then, as she walked away, she added, "Unless home is the little sister," and then threw the magazine she was holding at me.

I sat still on the bed for a moment and gathered my thoughts. I wanted to get out of the house as quickly as possible before round two started. I thought about everything that I would need right away and decided to make two separate piles of boxes. When the moving service arrived an hour and a half later they took everything except for two garment bags and my suitcase. Before I left I walked into the den where Shelly was seated. I handed her a check. "This is for her tuition and groceries." She motioned for me to drop it on the table. "So, do you think that we should explain this to Amani together?"

Shelly cut her eyes and gave me an ugly look. "Don't worry about her. Just like you came into her life out of thin air, you can disappear the same way. Trust . . . she'll be fine."

"Well, I won't debate that with you now, but you should know that I will plan to continue to be a part of her life."

"Oh yeah, with her aunt as her stepmother? Over my dead fucking body."

"Listen, I will have the legal-separation papers delivered here next week. Just let me know what it is you will want. I don't want to fight with you over money or visitation."

"Whatever." Then she began to mumble in Spanish. I knew that I didn't want to hear whatever she was saying so I grabbed my things and headed out the door. I went over to the office to go over a couple of reports before heading back to D.C. It was ten thirty by the time I finished and I thought about hitting the road. I wondered if Nina would be around when I got back to town.

Weeks ago, the night after I left the club, we had ended up spending the night together. We didn't have sex, though it wasn't because I didn't want to. She told me that she would never sleep with me while I was married to her sister. She also told me that she was seeing someone, nothing serious but serious enough for her to want to rush me out of her house when he called and said that he was on the way. We slept holding each other with my nose in her hair all night. When I left, I had no guarantees that we would ever get back together. I was encouraged, however, by a very passionate kiss and I knew that all promises aren't made with words. So with that I made my mind up. I was leaving Shelly.

After I packed up the files that I would need to look over during the weekend, I locked up my office and thanked my secretary for working so late. She didn't seem happy that on Monday she would be dealing with one of the company heads. It wasn't my concern at the moment. I was looking forward to getting back to working in my old office and with my hand-picked secretary.

I was headed down Fifth Avenue to Justin's. I was feeling

crazy stress and needed a drink so I decided to hit Justin's one last time before hitting the turnpike. I parked right out front and made a beeline for the bar. I started slowly drinking shots of Rémy V.S.O.P. and washing them down with ginger ale. "You all right tonight?" Terri asked as she removed the empty shot glasses.

"Yeah, I'm fine."

She could tell I was lying. "Stop your lying." She smiled. "What's on your mind, bruh?" I tapped the bar to signal that I wanted another drink. "This is your last one, understand?" she said and I nodded.

"Yo, T, I'm leaving New York, heading back down to D.C."

"You don't seem too happy about it." She laughed, "What, you gonna miss me?" Whenever I came through we always joked and flirted. She always told me that I might as well had considered myself a virgin until I'd had a Trinidadian woman.

"I'm leaving my wife. Well, we're gonna get divorced." I shook my head in shame. "We didn't even make it a year."

"Maybe you two will work it out."

"Nah, that definitely won't be happening."

"Hey, man, that happens ya' know. At least you didn't have to put too much time in it to find out that you weren't supposed to be together."

"You could look at it like that." I took the shot and threw it to my mouth. "One more."

"What you need is a princess from the islands like me," she said, smiling. Terri was a cutie, but *I* was the last thing she needed. "Here. Now this is definitely the last one." Between her taking care of the other patrons we talked for a full hour. I let her know of my plans to drive back in the middle of the night. I was in no shape to drive and she knew it. "Cory, why don't you wait for me to get off. You can drive me home and stay on my couch. When I get up for work in the morning you can hit the road then."

After agreeing I sat at the bar until she shut down and we left together. I was on her couch watching Conan O'Brien, trying to keep my head from spinning. Terri went into the kitchen and whipped up something in her blender. She placed a glass of something that looked like green juice with chunks of celery. "Drink this. It'll keep you from getting a hangover."

"What is it?"

"Just drink it down quick. Here," she said and pinched my nose as she guided my head back. I put the glass to my lips and still tasted the strong flavor of mint or ginger. "I'll run you a shower and make the couch up for you while you're in it."

Everything in her home had a natural feel. The candles burning in the holders on the walls gave off a relaxing scent that filled the entire apartment. The windows were open and a sudden breeze began to flow in along with the light from the flashes of lightning. Terri had gone back into her bedroom and I was wondering what to do about my clothes. I decided to take them off and make a neat pile right there next to the couch.

I had known her for about five months but only on a casual level. We'd hit it off but I always thought it was because I tipped well. I wanted to assume that she was merely concerned for my safety and that she might have felt some compassion for my situation. I was sure that from my drinking she had to figure I was depressed about my soon-to-be defunct marriage. In actuality, the fact that I had broken it off with Shelly hadn't really sank in. I was however filled with doubt about my future with Nina.

The water was just right and I moved up under it so that I

could let it run over my head. I stood there for about two minutes with my eyes closed. I finally turned to look for some soap and didn't see any. As if she was reading my thoughts, in she walked. "Cory, which do you prefer, Shea butter or Lever 2000?"

"I'll take the Lever."

She walked toward the shower. She pulled the curtain back slightly and I expected her to hand the soap to me. Instead she climbed in. I was stunned but still too drunk to show it. Instead I just looked at her. "Here you go."

I took the soap and began to lather up. As if we'd been bathing together for years, as soon as my back was turned she began to scrub it. Her scrub turned into a massage. Her massage turned into a caress and a few moments later we were in her bed.

"Cory, I've wanted you so long. Ever since I first saw you." I was a sucker for an accent and hers was thick and sexy. I was silent. My head was still swimming as she was kissing my neck and chest. Once I penetrated her, my breathing increased. She was tight and she asked me to slow down. "Take your time, baby, we got all night, even if it's just for tonight."

As I began to move in and out of her she got wetter and wetter. "Damn, Terri, it feels good." I was stroking her in a serious rhythm now and she was moaning loudly. Her legs were on my shoulders and slid off so that she could open up wide for me.

"That's right, enjoy me, baby. You're soooo sweet." As I humped, she humped back and I could feel my dick going deeper and deeper. "Ohhhh shit," she yelled out.

Her eyes were closed and I let out a smile as I looked down at her face. She showed the expressions of a woman in ecstasy. I was looking at her nipples and breasts as they bounced with each pounding. Her bed was shaking now as I found myself on the brink of an orgasm. In order to calm down I asked her to climb on top.

Terri lowered herself onto me slowly and let out a moan before she started grinding. I was beginning to think she was telling the truth about being a virgin until being with a Trinidadian woman. Her hips were moving as if she was doing a reggae dance. We had actually danced one night in the club while she was on break and I knew the sistah had rhythm but now she was blowing my mind. She put her weight on my shoulders and her breasts were on my chest. We began to kiss and as she lay on me I felt her legs lock onto mine and the grind continued. This time she was about to cum and started to cry out. "Ohhh shit," she yelled before jumping up off of me.

"What are you doing?"

She turned around and put her ass to me, "I want you to hit it from the back." Instantly I obliged. I gripped her cheeks roughly as I slid into her. Moving in and out trying to find a good pace, she interrupted me, "C'mon nigga, don't play with me. Hit it hard."

I did as told and took it a step further as I grabbed her braids and yanked her head back. I was hitting it so hard that the bed was sliding. As I felt my orgasm coming I noticed the whip that she had on the wall and figured that she liked it rough. I took it up a notch as I let the saliva run from my mouth onto the crack of her ass. Just as I was about to let loose I slipped my thumb into her butt.

"Ohmygawwd," she yelled out. We banged our bodies together for what seemed like an eternity until we both released. I didn't realize that I had sweat dripping all over my chest until I collapsed onto her back. We both panted until we drifted off to sleep.

I woke up with the condom still on my dick. She was ready

for another round and I figured what the hell. After another shower I ate her out and used the vibrator that I found sitting casually on her nightstand. I gave her a couple of intense orgasms and she returned the favor with some of the best head I had ever had.

This time I didn't wake up until nine in the morning. My cell phone was ringing. It was Brendan. When I answered he was ranting hysterically, "Cory, man, I am on my way to kill Trina's ass."

"What?"

"She's gone too far this time," he huffed.

I tried to calm him down so that I could make sense of what he was saying, but he was too angry after all that she had done to him. If she'd actually done half of what he was accusing her of, he definitely had a right to be furious. "Listen, B, I'm on the way back to D.C. As soon as I get there we'll hook up so you can explain what's going on. Right now, though, you need to calm down."

"Yeah, all right," Brendan said. "I'll get at you later." Then he hung up.

Terri cooked me breakfast and gave me a massage before I hit the road. If I had to leave the city and my wife under the circumstances I was facing, then she certainly made it bearable. As I got dressed, staring out of her bedroom mirror, two profound thoughts came to mind. The first was that I didn't feel any guilt about what had gone down with Terri. As a matter of fact I felt good about it. Sometimes, even when a man knows that he is at his worst, the approval he gets from another woman is enough to lift his spirits. And with that, there is no room for guilt, only selfishness.

The second thought was that I couldn't honestly say that I would miss being married to Shelly. Too much fussing and nagging, and not enough of a connection left after all we'd been through. It had dawned on me that, while we had been apart all those years, we had grown in different directions and it was unmistakable.

While tying my shoes I looked over at Terri's ass in her thong as she reached into her closet for a pair of shoes and thought that thanks to her I damn sure was gonna miss Justin's.

14

The Crossroads

Simply put, there are times when you gotta just let stuff go. In this case, though, Brendan tried hard but couldn't. After everything that Trina had done to his belongings in his condo and to his car, he'd decided to let the police handle it. Now that Tuesday had replaced everything that Trina had destroyed with newer and better, he had no real reason to complain. But the final straw had come Friday evening. As he prepared to leave work, he'd been invited upstairs into the floor manager's office.

She'd handed him a report from Nordstrom headquarters that contained information that Brendan had given away thousands of dollars' worth of shoes in the last few years, which he had. To validate the claims, the person, who Brendan had no doubts as to her identity, had given the shoe models and size numbers. They had run a check and had found enough discrepancies to warrant his dismissal. Just like that he was fired.

Apparently, Tuesday had gone into The True You to get a

manicure and pedicure and overheard Trina talking to Daphne about all the drama that she was causing for Brendan, including her Nordstrom exploit. Kim's death had caused Daphne and Trina to draw even closer, and it was the norm for her to spill her business to Daphne any time she stopped through. Tuesday listened to every word and quickly dialed Brendan.

"Brendan, this bitch is up in here talking mad shit about you," she whispered.

"You sure it's Trina?" he'd asked.

"I'm positive. I heard two different women call her by name. Plus she looks just like you described her."

By the time Tuesday had hung up with Brendan he'd gotten dressed and was headed to Georgia Avenue to confront Trina. He wasn't sure exactly what he was going to do once he caught her.

Hitting a woman wasn't his nature, especially a pregnant one, but he did want to do more than argue with her. He figured that since he was in a rental car, he would be able to follow her to where she was staying. Once he found out he would come and at the least destroy her car as payback. If it hadn't been broad daylight, he would have done it right there in front of the salon.

Brendan began driving as fast as possible when Tuesday told him that Trina was almost finished. He sped up on South Dakota Avenue and took Michigan Avenue past the Washington Hospital Center. Once he reached Georgia Avenue he was pushing the Ford Focus to the limit, trying to catch the green lights. When he reached the salon he slowed down because a Canada Dry truck was unloading in front of him. He pulled past it slowly and spotted Trina's car. He was looking for a parking space where he could remain inconspicuous.

While trying to parallel park, he almost didn't notice that Trina was already in her car and pulling out into traffic. She had walked out of the salon with newspaper covering her head to protect her do from the rain. His adrenaline began to pump and anger began to overwhelm him with the sight of her. He drove right up behind her and she didn't recognize him in the rental. He followed her closely for a few blocks before dropping back.

She headed down Florida Avenue and then down New York, toward downtown. He tried to stay a couple cars back but feared that he might lose her. Trina tried to get over into the left lane at the last moment to hit I-395 South, but Brendan gave himself away by swerving wildly just as she had done. He almost sideswiped a Jeep and when they'd smashed the horn at him Trina had looked through her rearview and noticed Brendan behind the wheel of the Focus on her tail.

Trina saw the look of rage on his face and in a state of panic she slammed on the gas and bucked an illegal U-turn. Like a man possessed, Brendan followed. As she tried to merge, he hit her bumper. Trina pushed the pedal to the metal once again and this time she began to pull away. His Focus was no match for her Avalon even though he gave a new meaning to the phrase "driving like a bat out of hell." Trina was catching the lights and it appeared that she was going to lose him. Brendan was stuck behind an Asian woman driving too slowly. It was beginning to rain. "Drive, you Chinese mutha . . ." Impatient and frustrated, Brendan pulled into the left lane to catch the light at the intersection of New York and Florida. He knew that if Trina hit 50 or the BW Parkway she was as good as gone.

As soon as he pulled out he saw the Escalade coming

straight toward him. There was a loud screech and he braced for contact. The Cadillac began to skid, swerve, and slide toward his door. Luckily the SUV stopped a half foot from knocking Brendan into the next lifetime. Everything slowed down and Brendan watched the look of horror on the face of the SUV driver turn to rage. By the time the driver could lean out the window to curse him out, Brendan had regained his composure and his focus. Trina had gone through the light and was on her way up the hill.

Brendan slammed his pedal and called upon all 150 horses in the tiny engine and took off after her. Almost being hit by the Escalade had thrown him off balance. Any other time he would have given an apologetic wave to the driver but today he was on a mission. Paying no attention to anything other than Trina's deranged ass getting away, he sped through the red light and saw a light flash. "Gotdammit. Oh I am gonna kill this bitch," he mumbled.

That was the last thing he clearly remembered before being crushed by the FedEx truck passing through the intersection. Brendan saw the front of the Focus disappear before his eyes, but by the time the car flipped he was already unconscious.

Paramedics had to use the jaws of life to free his body from the car.

It hurts. Everything hurts. Can you hear me? Brendan wanted to speak but couldn't. He was unconscious and his vital signs fading.

Is this how it ends? God, I got a baby on the way.

The EMS team fought to keep him alive the entire way as he was airlifted to Prince George's County Hospital.

I wasn't really gonna hurt her . . . just really angry.

It was a miracle that Brendan even made it to the operating room. He was suffering from massive brain swelling, internal bleeding, a severely fractured collarbone, and they feared a ruptured spleen.

During his surgery, Brendan could hear his grandmother's voice. *Hey, baby, it's been so long since I seen you. Grandma misses you so much, but you got a lot to live for your unborn child. Keep fightin', Brendan.*

Seven hours of surgery later and the waiting room was packed with his family and friends.

In the OR the doctors were frantic. "We're losing him," the doctor yelled.

I sat on my hands, eyes bloodshot. My best friend, my brother, was fighting for his life. I didn't know what to say to anyone. His mother and father were trying to be strong. Nate had beaten me to the hospital but left as soon as Trina had shown up with Daphne. He said that he was trying to remain steadfast and reasoned that the words he wanted to say to Trina were un-Christian-like. Dee was in Cancún and we couldn't reach him. I sat alone waiting and wondering if he was gonna make it. I hadn't been back in D.C. for twenty-four hours and I was feeling like I had come back too late. Maybe if I had come earlier or had time to listen to his rants, I could have calmed him down. The officers took a report that he was involved in a chase with an unidentified car, but of course I knew who he was chasing.

The doctors came out the doors and asked for his next of kin. As soon as they did that his mother nearly fainted. The doctors rushed to her and tried to make sure that she was okay. Mr. Shue was sweating bullets and didn't know what to do. His aunt began trembling and crying, "Oh Lord noooo."

I ran over and tried to help but I had the worst feeling in my stomach, and when I looked at the doctors and saw the blank expressions on their faces, I felt nauseous. It was a struggle to keep it together. As soon as we got his mother seated and stabilized, a small semblance of calm came over the room and I noticed Nate walk back into the waiting area. A beautiful woman was with him. She was holding a Bible and had Nate by the arm.

"Doc, we're all family here. Whatever you have to say . . . please just say it so that we don't have to repeat it over and over," Mr. Shue said with authority.

"Remarkably, your son pulled through the surgery. He has very severe injuries, he's lost a lot of blood, but he is young and very healthy. He is really fighting but he hasn't regained consciousness and even if he survives, there is no telling when or if he will," I heard him say.

"Oh gaaaawwwwd no," Trina yelled out.

"Please calm down, child," his aunt yelled out. "We don't need that right now."

"Noo, nooooo," she cried out again, stomping her feet this time. Then, she just blurted it out, "I'm carrying his baaaaaabbbbby."

"What?" his mother yelled out. "You're lying. Tell me you're lying."

The attention turned toward her, and Nate finally walked up to Daphne, whom he had feuded with for so long over his treatment of Kim. "It would be a good idea if you took her home." He was calm. Daphne never thought about cutting smart. She just stared into Nate's eyes as he continued, "She doesn't need to be so upset or upset his mother right now. I'll call you and give you an update in a couple of hours. Try to calm her down before she winds up in a hospital bed." Trina had snot running out of her nose and slob running out of the corners of her mouth. She was sucking air as if there would be no more of it to breathe tomorrow.

"You're probably right," Daphne said and Nate simply nodded as she took one of her business cards out of her purse. She handed Nate the card with her cell number on it and carried a reluctant Trina away crying and panting.

A thousand teardrops, prayers, and visitors later, Nate and I were finally able to convince Mr. Shue to take his wife home to get some rest. We were going to stay with him for the rest of the night. It was already four in the morning and we both were operating off the fear that we could lose our best friend.

Nate had brought his pastor's wife to come and pray with the family. He had been at the church feeding the homeless when he got the call. When he left the hospital the first time he told me that he had gone back to the church to pray and broken down in tears. Anita, the pastor's wife, had come upstairs and found him crying and helped him pull himself together. Afterward she insisted that she come to the hospital to pray with the family. She was nice. Not what one would expect physically from a pastor's wife. She had the body of a video queen.

"So what do you think?"

I was actually dozing off. "Huh?" I replied.

Nate was staring out the window on the opposite side of the waiting room. "Do you think he has a chance?" He asked.

I shrugged my shoulders like a kid with no good answers.

"I hope so." I didn't want to share my true thoughts. I wasn't very encouraged.

"Yeah." He walked back over and took a seat. "With Him, all things are possible."

"Amen to that."

The doctors were monitoring Brendan all night every fifteen minutes. He was shot up with the maximum amount of pain medication. He had more tubes running in and out of him than the Six Million Dollar Man did before they rebuilt him, bigger, faster, and stronger than he was before. All the attention was a good sign that the doctors were trying to bring him back.

As morning neared, the prognosis hadn't changed. Brendan was in critical condition but appeared to be headed into a coma. His body fought the sleep. He had so much to say to everyone, to Trina. *I just want to apologize, I could have been a man about things. I haven't been myself lately, all this running around lying and playing with people's feelings.* The voices that were with him spoke to him. *Don't worry about that right now. Save your strength.*

I'm really getting tired.

Don't quit.

It doesn't hurt anymore.

"How's his pressure?"

"Seems to be stabilized. He almost seems to be comfortable."

"Good," the doctor said. Though they could have been talking about anyone in the trauma unit, I knew they were talking about Brendan. I left the desk and went back out to the waiting area. His mother had told them that I was his brother. Being recognized as immediate family had given me the authority to make any emergency decisions in case they couldn't be reached. I was honored but sad as hell at the circumstances.

Nate and I both must have dozed off because at six thirty someone tapped me on the chest and I woke to see a familiar face standing in front of me. "Hey."

It was Renée.

I had no idea if Brendan could hear a word we were saying or sense what was happening around him. They say that it's possible for someone in a coma to hear and yet not process sounds and voices. Often, people who come out of them say that they could hear voices or feel the presence of loved ones. If that was the case, I had a theory on Brendan's state. He was up and down as far as his healing was going. But what I noticed over the course of the week was that every time Renée came to visit he seemed to smile. It was hard to make out since he had a tube running into his stomach feeding him and a mask over his mouth and nose helping him breath, but I saw it.

At the end of the week Renée was telling me that she was going to have to go back to Houston. She was preparing for a wedding. She was getting married to a New Orleans businessman named Tamarick Ledaye. We had a chance to talk about a lot of things, especially her and Brendan's friendship slash relationship gone bad.

We'd decided to ride over to Levi's, a soul food spot up in

Mitchellville. As we ate a late lunch she confided how devastated she'd been when she found Brendan in bed with Laney after what they'd been through. "You know, Cory, even though we had kind of called it quits or tried to go back to being just friends, it was still a shock for me to see him screwing her in my house."

"Yeah, but you weren't supposed to see that. You were supposed to be out of town, and you did tell him to make himself at home." I smiled, hoping that she could take me making light of it.

She laughed back. "I guess I did, didn't I?" Renée was a different type of woman. She was kind and had a bubbly spirit. She was the type who lived just to show love to those around her. She'd give the shirt off her back to you if you needed it, but at the same time she'd try to motivate you to go out and get your own. The Texas sun had roasted her skin and she was darker than I had ever remembered seeing her. With the cinnamon streaks in her hair she looked beautiful. I could also tell that she'd spent a lot of time in the gym, her stomach was flat as a board and she'd even bragged that she had gotten her belly button pierced.

"So you're really gonna get married?"

"Yeah, why wouldn't I? I have the man of my dreams," she shot back.

My eyebrows arched at her comment. "Okay," I muttered.

"What the hell is all that for?" she asked.

"I don't know what you're talking 'bout."

"Oh, yeah, you do," she pointed out "All that squirming and sarcasm."

"All I said was okay."

"It's the way you said it . . . like okay whatever." She seemed a little heated. "If you have something to say, brother, go ahead and say it."

I thought for a second about the picture that she had shown

me of her and Tamarick. "Well, I guess I just found it a little weird that your fiancé looks so much like Brendan." She was quiet. "I mean, don't get me wrong. I'm sure he's a wonderful guy, but don't tell me you never noticed how much they look alike."

Renée took a deep breath. I knew her well. Although she was Brendan's best female friend, she and I had basically grown up together as well and I knew that I'd just struck a nerve. "I find that funny, Cory. Funny that you of all people would have the gumption to speak on picking a fiancé look-alike. Aren't you the one engaged, married, or fucking the Sanchez twins?"

"Ouch. Hold on sistah. First, this isn't about me. Second, they aren't twins." I smiled to let her know that I wasn't trying to take it there. "I know I'm a little confused and can admit that I was dead wrong, but it's never too late to straighten things out."

"Whose life are we talking about right now, yours or mine?"

"Just speaking in general," I answered.

We finished lunch and I told her about what I felt her presence was doing for Brendan. "Why would you think that I am making such a big difference?" she asked.

"Probably because he still loves, wants, and needs you."

"Negro, isn't that a damn Patti LaBelle song?" She punched me in the arm.

"I'm serious, though."

"What makes you so sure?"

I looked her in the eyes and told her a lie. Not to hurt her or to lead her on, but because I believed in my heart that she was making a difference and because Brendan couldn't speak for himself right now. "He told me so not too long ago."

She bit her bottom lip and stared into my eyes. She didn't say a word and I could tell that she was moved. A minute later she said, "It's a little late for that now."

"It's never too late." I put in my Raheem DeVaughn CD and rolled the windows down and headed back to the hospital to spend the rest of the day with Brendan.

"Nate has been a Godsend at the church," Reverend Lawson stated to his wife and the board of deacons.

Every day he was there after his workout. He did everything from repair work to cooking for the homeless. Even more impressive was that he often used his own money. He had purchased fifteen new cribs for the nursery and asked that the church donate the remaining ones to teenage mothers. He had bought the materials and installed new floors in two of the bathrooms. He even paid some young members to make a hundred sandwiches a day to give out to the homeless.

What the reverend and his staff didn't know was that lately he was spending so much time there because he was looking for something. He was trying to find a deeper connection with the Master. He was a troubled soul and feeling weak. Nate was wondering if God was so good, why was his friend clinging to life in a coma. He was wondering why after all that he had done to change his life God had allowed him to still be tormented by occasional nightmares of Kim and why he had money but still felt empty. He'd given up the things he loved most in life, sex and women, but the loneliness he'd felt lately had begun to consume him. In fact the only moments of joy came for him during church and his visits to the Lawson house.

He had gone by to visit Miss Bethany several times since the first. She loved Nate and had even stopped calling him Dr. Baines. She'd heard Anita and Lloyd call him Nathan so much that she began to do the same. After leaving the hospital, he found himself headed unannounced to the Lawsons' home. He arrived to see Anita place a suitcase into her car.

She smiled when she saw him pull up. He climbed out and headed toward her. "Going somewhere?"

She brushed her hair from her face. "Yeah, actually I am. I'm headed to New Jersey to see my oldest sister and get away for a minute." Her body language and rushed speech gave the impression that she was running away from something. "Did you visit your friend today?" she asked nervously.

"Yeah, I just left."

"How's he doing?"

"Not much of a change, but thanks for asking."

She nodded. The front door opened and Lloyd appeared. He glanced out and turned and went back inside, slamming the door behind him.

"Whatever," Anita mumbled under her breath.

Nate was confused. "Is everything all right?" he asked.

She didn't answer but instead hit a button in her X5 and closed the garage door. Anita reached into her purse and grabbed a pen. She scribbled something on the paper. "Listen, Nate, I don't want to drag you into the middle of anything, but this is where I will be staying. My sister doesn't even know I'm coming. I may call her and I may not, but at least you will know where I am in case something happens."

Nate was concerned. "Nita, if there's something you need to talk about, why don't—" He was interrupted by tears welling up in her eyes. "Hey, c'mon now, what's wrong?"

Anita shook her head, "I just can't talk about it right now. How about I call you . . . I'll call you later maybe." The tears began to run down her cheeks and she turned and climbed into her car.

Nate was still trying to get his bearings together as she backed out of the driveway. Her tires kicked back gravel as she tore out of the court and up the street. After careful thought he decided to head into the house. He rang the bell and Lloyd answered it. He held what Nate considered to be his signature glass of Rémy in his hand. "Well, well, Nathan, come on in. You're here to see Nana, huh? I got to tell you, man, we all really appreciate this. You don't find many men of your caliber taking time out of their schedules to visit old folks and to volunteer their time and money to the church the way you do." Lloyd was rambling. Nate attributed it to the liquor or that he had walked in on a family argument.

"Reverend, if I came at a bad time I can leave and come back another time."

"Awww, don't be foolish. There's no bad time for you. You are doing the Lord's work. I don't know what she told you but she's just a little upset right now. She'll be fine."

"Okay, but it's none of my business, either way."

Lloyd nodded. He invited Nate into the family room and offered him a beverage. Nate declined the offer and when he asked for Miss Bethany, he was shocked when Lloyd yelled out, "Okay, cut the shit. What did she tell you?"

Nate was shocked and replied, "Huh?"

"Ya heard me, nigga. What did she tell you?"

When Nate looked at Lloyd his stare asked the question that he didn't come out with. "Negro, are you crazy?"

Lloyd went on, "Are you the police?"

Nate got up and headed toward the front door. He realized that this time Lloyd was actually drunk, not merely having a nightcap. "Man, I think you've had enough of that." He pointed to Lloyd's glass. "I'll see you around."

"What? How dare you say that bull to me? You know who I am. You would still be holed up in North Carolina hiding out if it weren't for me. I know the whole story about you man. I've had three or four members of the congregation tell me about you. They told me to watch you, nigga."

Nate was stunned at how Lloyd sounded like a street thug.

"Yeah, that's right. I know what you did . . . how you made that girl kill herself over you. I've heard that you'll fuck anything moving and don't think I don't see the way you've been looking at my wife, brother."

With that, Nate balled up his fist and headed toward Lloyd. "Reverend, if you know what's good for you, you'll control your mouth and put the liquor down."

"Oorrrrrr what," he said. "You gonna fight me? Shiiiit. C'mon, nigga, I was Golden Gloves back in the day. You don't want a piece of me."

Nate thought for a second about hitting him with a two piece, but decided that it wouldn't be worth it. He moved toward the door and reached for the knob when Lloyd grabbed him by the shoulder. "Man, I warned you," Nate yelled.

Lloyd jumped back for a second and then pointed his finger into Nate's face, "You stay out of my church and away from my wife. We're going to work this out," he said.

Without thinking, Nate grabbed Lloyd by the finger and bent it backward. Lloyd's finger broke with a loud *pop*. Nate's mouth twisted with disgust. He was angry with himself for having gotten physical with Lloyd. "I told you," Nate said, then repeated, "I warned you."

As soon as Lloyd realized his finger was broken he dropped to the floor as the pain rushed through his body. "Awwwwwww you crazy, nigga. You broke my finger. God is gonna punish you. Awwwwww." Lloyd was holding his finger and rocking back and forth. "I'm gonna call the police."

"Call 'em," Nate replied.

"I'm gonna sue you for every dime you got." Lloyd was groaning in pain; he paused and then continued, "What the hell do you do for a living anyway?"

Nate slammed the door shut behind him as he headed for his car.

*   *   *

After the incident with Lloyd, Nate decided to go for a drive to clear his mind. The roof was back and he was listening to *Marvin Gaye's Greatest Hits.* He pushed the Porsche to the limit while Marvin and Tammi sang "Your Precious Love." He enjoyed the ride and feel of the truck. The cool May air and the music kept his mind off all the drama. He still was dumbstruck at the behavior of the reverend and wondered what could have happened between him and his wife.

An hour, then two, and finally three before Nate had worked up the nerve to check on Anita. There was no denying his interest in her any longer. He thought long and hard about all the changes that he had made in his life. While he felt that most of them were for the better, he couldn't stop wondering if things weren't easier for him when he was the player of all players. He never had a chance to feel the loneliness that was strangling him at present. A big part of him was saying "Nate, you can't go back to living like that" but another part was winning out.

Two knocks and Anita came to the door. "Nate, what in the world are you doing here?"

"I think you know." She stood there for a second. Her eyes were puffy from sleep or from crying. They stared into one another's eyes for a moment and then she backed away from the hotel door allowing him to enter.

Renée was spending some time in the room with Brendan alone. She was heading back to Houston in the morning. I sat in the lobby with Shue, Brendan's cousin. I asked Shue why he had come to the hospital wearing makeup. "You know that is going to upset the family if they see you looking like that."

"All I have on is a little foundation and liner on my eyebrows. What's the big friggin' deal?"

I exhaled in disbelief. We all accepted Shue coming out of the closet a couple years back but he was taking it too far on occasion. I let him know that he could never hang out with me with any makeup on. To look at him now, it would be hard to imagine that a couple of years earlier he was dating women as well.

"You look ridiculous. I wouldn't be surprised if Brendan doesn't come out of that coma just to smack you upside your head when you go in to visit him." We both laughed.

"Okay, okay. You've made your point." He took out a baby wipe and rubbed his face off until there was no trace of makeup.

Seconds later Renée appeared from her visit. When she saw Shue she gave him a huge hug. Renée and I said our goodbyes and I promised to keep her updated on his progress daily. I left her out in the lobby with Shue so that they could catch up for a quick minute.

Ten minutes later I left so that the nurses could do their thing with Brendan. When I returned to the lobby Shue was sitting in the corner trying to look occupied with a magazine.

"What's up? You got only five minutes in there with him so get a move on." I noticed a stupid look on his face. "What?" I asked as he stood to head back.

"You know Renée is getting married?" he asked.

"Yeah, I know."

"Well, I didn't want to break it to her . . ."

"What?" I asked.

Shue twisted his lips, "While you were in there she told me all about her life in Houston . . . she's doing all right for herself . . ."

"Yeah, yeah, get to the point."

"Well, she showed me a couple pictures of her fiancé and her and I had the strangest feeling."

"What do you mean?"

"I mean, I think I know the guy she is marrying."

"From where?" I asked.

Shue twisted his lips and tilted his head, setting up the delivery for his own drama. "From the back."

"No."

"Yes."

"You sure?"

"If I'm lying I'm flying."

I couldn't and wouldn't believe that Shue would make a joke out of something so serious. "Please tell me you're playing. From what Renée tells me, he is such a great guy and really into her. On top of that, why would he want to marry her? Maybe you have him mixed up."

"If that nigga ain't on the down low, then Oprah's ass is broke and you know that ain't possible. I even remembered the Negro's name. You tend to remember a black man named Tamarick. I met him at the Bayou Classic one year. He was bragging about how much he had going on. He had it going on all right. All night."

"Damn," I yelled. "This is all I need. She has to know." I shook my head. "So, you're positive."

"A hundred and fifty percent."

"Just when I thought I'd seen and heard it all." I shook my head in both anger and disgust.

"When it rains . . ." Shue said.

"It pours." I finished.

"No offense, Shue, but why can't these switch-hitters pick a team. I mean I know that you went through a state where you were a little confused, but all the confusion in the world doesn't make it right. They're killing our sistahs with that sick, selfish behavior."

"I agree one hundred percent."

"Do me a favor."

"What's that?" Shue asked.

"Pass the word on to the gay community to out these down-low brothers at every opportunity."

He burst into laughter. "Yeah, that's a good idea."

"I'm serious."

"I didn't think you weren't serious, not for a second." He paused. "So are you going to tell Renée?"

I stood silent playing the scenario out in my mind. "I don't really see where I have a choice."

"No, you don't."

I had a sick feeling in my stomach as I prepared to leave. Not much was going right and I had a sense that some of it was actually the calm before the storm. I extended my hand to Shue and said, "Peace."

He returned, "If we're lucky my man. If we're lucky."

16

Love Electric

Anita and Nate sat on the floor drinking iced tea and vanilla crèmes that he had gotten from a rest stop on the drive north. He'd been trying to keep her mind off of what was bothering her and to cheer her up. He didn't so much as utter a word about what was going on between Anita and her husband. She had turned her cell phone off because she didn't want to be bugged. It was obvious that she was in shut-down mode.

At the door Nate only noticed her face but once inside there was no way to ignore how sexy she looked. She was braless under a faded Arden B tank top and her cheeks jiggled as she moved about in a pair of women's boxers from Vickie's.

"So, honestly, Nate, why would you drive all the way up here? And please don't tell me you were worried about me."

"It's funny because that's exactly what I was about to say." He stared into her eyes. "I don't know, Nita, there's something about you. Getting to know you the past few weeks has made me feel something. I'm coming to know God and trying to learn how to rely on him. Even still, there's nothing that can compare to the feeling that I have when I'm around you."

She was still and leaned her head back. "What kind of feelings?" she said almost in a whisper, feeling afraid of what would come next.

Nate leaned into her and placed his hands on her cheeks. "It's like I want to see you happier than you already are. Every time I think of you I can't bear the thought of you not being appreciated to the utmost. From the moment I saw you in the kitchen I felt a connection to you. I felt like you were put on this earth to be with me."

Anita softly said, "Noooo," while shaking her head. Her hands were trembling.

Nate moved closer toward her and kissed her gently on the lips. She only imagined resisting as his tongue parted her lips. While kissing her, he eased toward her until his weight caused her to lean back onto the floor. All Nate's instincts began to surface as he prepared to put down the loving of a lifetime. He was on top of her. Anita's hands were wrapped around his neck and she was beginning to breathe heavily as his hands began to explore her body.

She felt Nate lift her from the floor and place her on the bed. Her mind began to race with thoughts of what he would do to her. "Take them off," Nate commanded as he pointed to her clothes.

As if she were in a trance she grabbed the bottom of her shirt and lifted it off over her head. Nate hadn't had sex in over two months. It was the longest stretch he had ever gone with no pussy, and his dick was harder than a lead pipe. He had beaten her to taking off his shirt but when he dropped his underwear, Anita let out a sigh. She figured that there were at least nine or ten inches staring at her. But after dealing with the four and a half her husband had, almost anything would have looked humongous.

"Do you have protection?" she asked as Nate joined her on the bed. Then she said, "I can't believe I asked you that. We can't do this, Nate. Please don't—" Just then she felt his tongue press against her rock-hard nipples. "Ohhhhh," she cried out.

Nate danced his tongue all over her chest, taking time to squeeze and caress each breast. She'd forgotten what it was like to have her body freaked before making love. "Turn over," he commanded.

The way he spoke to her made her weak and inflamed her with passion. She did as told and in seconds she found herself being bathed in kisses from Nate. Anita shivered when he swirled his tongue into the small of her back. He could smell the scent of her perfume filling his head even on her lower back. With a cheek in each hand he spread her bottom and continued to kiss and lick. It was perfect and he tried unsuccessfully to calm himself down and hold back but he was too swept away. Seconds later, Anita jumped as his tongue brushed her hole on the way to her pussy. He gave her more of his sweet torture until he finally pulled away. He flipped her over and dived into her center, face first.

Smooth like a Maxwell cut, he licked her out. All of her passion raced to her middle and exploded as Nate used his tongue to take her mind and body to another place. Anita sang like a bird through her first orgasm. "Sssssooooooo goooooood, yes, Nate. It's beeen sssssoooo llllloooong since . . . since . . . oh damn . . . I'm about ta' . . . 'bout ta' . . ." Her body shook, shoulders lifted off the bed, she grabbed her own breasts and rode the wave down to her toes.

Nate moved up and with his face glistening from her juices, he kissed her full on the mouth.

Her head was in the clouds. It was like an out-of-body experience for Anita as she'd just realized that she had never had an orgasm before that moment. She wanted another. "Do it again. Please do it again," she mumbled as she stretched and cracked the bones in her feet and toes.

"We've got all night," Nate answered. Anita's eyes were closed and when she opened them slightly she noticed Nate's dick on her lips. She may not have been getting the best sex from her husband but she had become very adept at giving head. Some nights it saved her from being bothered with Lloyd trying to climb on top of her.

Anita caught Nate by surprise when she gripped him and took the head into her mouth. She teased him unmercifully and Nate was totally shocked when he felt his orgasm coming so quickly. Her hands were coated with saliva as she jacked him up and down while teasing the head. "You like that?" she asked.

Nate didn't answer; instead his face tightened and he locked into a grimace as he began shooting all over her. That part she normally hated but for Nate she allowed him to have his way. She continued sucking until he was spent only to notice that he was still hard.

Nate crisscrossed between the motions of making love to Anita and flat out banging her. It had been a while, and even though he was enamored with her, there was a lot pent up inside of him. He never realized how much of a release sex had been for him. Anita didn't know or care what was running through his mind. What he was doing to her was a dream come true. One minute she felt as if her body was being caressed and cared for as if she was a queen and a few minutes later her hair was being pulled as he slammed into her from the back.

Feeling sticky from the sex, she attempted to shower, only to be taken again by Nate on the bathroom countertop. When Anita finally finished in the shower and made it to the bed, she nearly collapsed. Her body felt as if she had been electrocuted, but in a good way. She barely had enough time to notice that Nate was already sleeping soundly before she curled up behind him and drifted off to sleep.

Trying to do something a little different, I took Nina to the Bar Nun. On Monday nights there was open-mike poetry. We arrived early and took a seat on the couches on the side of the stage. The decor in the basement where the performances took place reminded me of the spot in *love jones* where Darius Lovehall and company spit their prose in the movie. I loved poetry and had made attempts to get Nina involved before we broke up.

The atmosphere was relaxing and just what I needed. My mind was still heavy with all that was going on. I'd tried to check on Shelly, but my calls went unanswered. I assumed that she was still too angry with my leaving to deal with me and I had to respect her feelings. I was worn out from working all night and spending nearly every free moment at the hospital with Brendan. I hadn't confided in anyone but I honestly was beginning to fear the worst. He'd been unconscious for ten days and his condition was stabilizing but not improving. Though I tried not to think about it, I was trying to brace myself for life without Brendan.

The first few acts were okay but when the fourth went up to perform I was blown away. The sistah looked too young to be so damned deep. She went by the name Shaketa, and she performed her poetry over the soft rhythms of congas and a keyboard. I couldn't say if it was her words or the way that she delivered them with such obvious passion. It was obvious that her verse spoke of her own life and she seemed almost drained by the time she concluded.

When she finished she placed the microphone back on the stand and wiped tears from her cheeks. I looked over at Nina and saw that her eyes were watering. "You all right, baby?" I asked.

She nodded. We sat there and sipped our wine while the next poets went up. At the intermission Nina asked if we could leave, said she was feeling drained. As we made our way back to the car, a Hispanic man selling roses walked up on me. "Flowers for the lady, señor?"

Nina wave her hand to the man. "I'll take one." She handed him a five, took a rose, and handed it to me.

"*Gracias, senorita,*" he said.

"*De nada,*" she replied.

I smiled at her. "Thank you."

"You're very welcome."

We were in the car listening to Justine Love's *Love Talk and Slow Jams* on WPGC as we cruised toward Nina's house. She had recently purchased a town house in Wheaton. "So are you definitely getting a divorce?" she asked.

"Yes."

"When are you filing?" she asked as we exited the car and headed toward the house.

"Well, we have to be separated for a year before we can file, then it will take six months at the most after that."

She was quiet for a few seconds. "So what am I supposed to do until then, run around with my sister's husband?"

"I don't really know, Nina. I can't make that choice for you. All I can say is that I love you and I know that I made a terrible mistake. I'm trying to straighten it all out now."

"You know, I need to be honest with you. It bothers me. I

mean . . . you really messed things up. You come across as this together brother, and don't get me wrong, you do have it going on, but this is some crazy shit. You married my sister and now here you are, literally back at my doorstep," she said, turning the key and entering. She shut door and turned off the alarm. "Are you planning on spending the night?"

"If it's okay with you," I replied.

"Oh it's fine, but just know that you won't be getting any of *this* until you're divorced." She looked at the expression on my face. I really wanted to make love to her. Having sex with Terri a few days back had only made me hornier. If Nina wanted to play games, it wouldn't be anything for me to make a quick trip back up to Harlem.

True to her word we climbed into her bed and went to sleep without so much as a kiss good night.

At two o'clock in the morning we were both stirred awake by a banging at Nina's door. "What the fuck?" I said, being jarred from my sleep.

She jumped out of the bed and went to the window. Another series of bangs came at the door. "Oh no, this fool didn't," she grumbled. Instead of putting on a robe she slipped on a pair of jeans. "Be right back," she said.

I wandered to the window and looked out to see a police car double-parked in front of her home blocking her car in. I walked over to her door and went to the top of the steps. I heard her at the front door. "What the hell are you doing here? I'm sleeping."

Then I heard a male voice. "You've got company, don't you?"

"Listen, Felton. I don't have time for this. You ain't no jack-in-the-box so you shouldn't be popping up like you are one. Please don't make me call your superiors."

"What?"

"You heard me. I don't play this bullshit, comin' over here in the middle of the night harassing me, on duty at that. I'll call you tomorrow."

"Just tell me. Do you have company?"

"Leave now. I really don't appreciate you questioning me like this. Excuse me."

Then in a voice loud enough for me, or anyone who might be in the house to hear, he yelled out, "I better not catch anyone coming out of here." When he said that I walked down the steps in my underwear and without a shirt on.

When he saw me his eyes bugged out of his head. "Aha, I knew it."

"Aha, my ass. Felton, you are not my man." Then the Spanish kicked in and she began to curse him out.

"Not your man? Not your man?" He looked like he was about to throw a temper tantrum. "You didn't say that when I was buying all the furniture for this place."

"Go home, go tell it to your wife," Nina said.

I was shocked when she said that. I couldn't believe that she was dating a married man. He came back with, "You didn't say that when you were sucking my dick the other night."

I looked at Nina and saw rage in her eyes. "*Punta!*" she yelled. She said a few more words then grabbed a vase and hurled it at him. It hit the wall next to the door. Shards of glass went everywhere and he grabbed his face. "Geeeet the fuck out." He saw her looking for something else to throw and turned to take off.

Once he was out the door he yelled back, "Good luck, man, you can have the bitch."

"Your mama's a bitch," she shouted back.

I grabbed her and pulled her away from the door before she stepped on the glass. "Calm down, he's gone, and I don't think he's coming back."

She broke down in tears and ran up the steps. After I cleaned the glass up I joined her. She started trying to explain when I interrupted. "Hey, you don't owe me any explanations. None of that matters . . . all that matters is that I love you and I'm here. I'm going to make everything right and I don't care how long it takes. Your love is the energy that keeps my heart beating."

When I said that she stopped and stared at me. She stood up in front of me and undressed. "Please forgive me."

"I said you don't owe me any apologies."

"I wasn't talking to you," she whispered as she moved toward me. I wondered if it was hard for her, breaking her word and once again giving me her everything.

17

Masters of Disaster

I lifted my Corona in the air to chase down my third shot of Absolut. I was enjoying the flight that the alcohol had sent me on. I was looking around the bar, people-watching. It was my first trip to Chicago and at this point it could have been my last as far as I was concerned. My hotel accommodations sucked and my meetings weren't going well. In part because I hadn't been prepared for all the things that had gone wrong.

In the past few weeks Brendan's condition had twice taken severe turns for the worse, prompting around-the-clock hospital visits. My work had definitely suffered and I had contemplated a leave of absence, but it wasn't my style to quit because it was rough. Things between Shelly and me had gotten to the point where we barely communicated. The school year was fast coming to a conclusion and she would soon be back in town. I knew it was just a matter of time until the whole mess blew up in my face.

To top it off Nina and I weren't getting much right other than sex. Since the night at her house after the Bar Nun, we had resumed our affair and started making love again, she was constantly bringing up my leaving her to marry Shelly. She needed more reassurance than any man should have been forced to give. "Are you sure you don't still want her? How can I be sure you won't abandon me again?" were questions she asked me constantly.

It was hard to admit but I was beginning to think that I had made yet another mistake. Shelly was the rock and Nina was the hard place. I was beginning to wonder if I was cursed for falling in love with them. They both had traits that made them easy to fall for but damned near impossible to stay with. They were both beautiful and intelligent, yet they each had a nasty streak that caused them to lash out unmercifully when things weren't going well. To make it worse, they both nagged and held grudges way beyond what I felt was normal. There was no such thing as letting something go.

"You okay?" the waitress asked.

"Oh, I guess I'll have another shot and a fresh Corona, don't forget the lime." When she nodded, I said, "Thanks."

The spot was called Crocodile's and they had a nice little thing going on. The music was a mix of old-school R&B and new hip-hop. I didn't even realize that I was dancing in my seat as the deejay played "Enjoy Yourself" by Michael Jackson. Out of the corner of my eye I noticed a table of women sitting to my right, laughing. I immediately felt a little insecure at the prospect that I was the object of their amusement. I stopped dancing and heard one of them yell out, "Don't stop, brother."

"Yeah, don't stop till you get enough," then she burst out laughing.

I stood up and surprised them when I moved toward their table. "So this how you Chicagoans treat a brother from out of town? You just gonna straight clown a brother, huh?"

I looked at all three of them. Two of them were rather attractive, and one especially. The one who wasn't was, of course, the most vocal. When she opened her mouth I immediately thought of my orthodontist, Dr. David Harmon. He would have had a field day trying to straighten those choppers out. "No, my man, I was about to send you a drink over." She thought she was funny because she began to laugh and put her busted grill on display.

"I see."

"So where you from?"

"The Nation's Capital."

The prettiest one had the complexion of a Nestlé Crunch bar. She had the cutest button nose and eyes that looked as deep as the ocean. I had to catch myself to keep from staring. Her lips looked like she'd just left the Mac counter. They were a rusty red color and looked like they were drenched and sticky. To top it off, her cleavage was fighting for my attention and the only thing that kept my eyes from zooming in was her angelic face. She was cool, looking around the bar while I gazed at her. She just nodded her head to acknowledge my responses while the other two shot question after question about my business in the Windy City. What I noticed was that, unlike myself, the two asking all the questions were wearing wedding rings. I ended up joining them and when the waitress found me and brought my drinks over, I ended up buying a round for the ladies.

"What were you drinking, ladies?"

The funny face replied, "Bone crusher." It figured. I was thinking more like a tooth crusher.

"A Long Island iced tea for me," the second one chimed in.

Finally the unmarried sistah chimed in, "Another merlot, please."

After another round I realized that I was close to being fucked up and decided to start drinking water. My speech was a little slurred but I didn't think they noticed because all three of them had at least a nice buzz themselves. I was ecstatic when the two married sistahs got up to head for the bathroom leaving me alone with Miss Beautiful.

There was an uncomfortable silence for a minute while I thought. Why even bother. Why even try to connect with this woman. You have enough problems. I took a look at her and while she looked over at the dance floor I took in her beauty. She had something that I had never seen before. In addition to her good looks she had a radiance that personified class. Just staring at her I could tell that this woman had never been taken advantage of by a man like Nate or caught up in the type of confusion that I brought to relationships. She had probably never lowered herself or her standards to give a man a break in order to keep one. She was a real sistah in every sense of the word. I didn't have to hear it come out of her mouth. I could feel that she was powerful, energetic, and spiritual.

I didn't realize that while deep in thought, she noticed my drunken stare. "You all right, brother?" she asked.

I snapped out of it. "Oh, yeah, I'm fine . . ." I realized that I didn't know her name. "I didn't get your name."

"Faith."

"I'm Cory." She smiled. Before I knew it her friends were back and they were up preparing to leave. I tried to stand too quickly and the liquor made me move slowly. I was so captivated by Faith that I was unable to get the words out.

"Nice meeting you."

"Yeah, thanks for the drinks," they said.

"Hey, uhh, Faith, do you think . . ." the words escaped my mouth but went unheard. Too low, too drunk, and Faith was too powerful for my weak attempt. Before I knew it, they were headed out the front door.

Nate's calls went unreturned. He didn't know what to make of what had happened to his life. The weekend he'd spent with Anita had been the most beautiful one he could remember ever spending with a woman. Even more than the sex they'd shared, she had given him some serious soul satisfaction.

Lying in bed between their bouts of passion, Nate had confided things to Anita that he had never shared with anyone and he felt that she had done the same. Now he was torn between feeling foolish and feeling betrayed. What was different for him was that for once in his life he was able to take responsibility for his own actions and his feelings. He loved Anita and he knew that she didn't love Lloyd, at least not the way that a woman was supposed to love her husband.

He'd just finished unpacking the last of his things into his new condo. It was a two-bedroom spot located on U Street near the Lincoln Theater. As he sat down on his couch to catch a quick break he couldn't stop his mind from being overrun with thoughts of Anita and the time they spent. It was Saturday morning and he decided to go for a jog to try to clear his head. The one thing he hadn't stopped doing was working out. He hadn't been back to the church since his run-in with Lloyd and there hadn't been much else for him to do. He was through running women once and for all.

It was strange that when he thought of having sex now, he only thought of Anita. Janette had called him a couple of times, tempting him with erotic conversation, but gave up quicker each time, faced with his stern resistance. Nate wasn't interested in using her, or any other woman for that matter. An old dog had been taught new tricks.

Other than working out he had spent a lot of time at the

hospital with Brendan. He would take his Bible and visit him at least five times a week. He prayed and read scriptures while sitting in with him. He would talk to Brendan just like he always did, except now that Brendan couldn't hear him, he elected on occasion to pour out his heart to him about the heartache he was facing. He knew that if anyone could understand a broken heart it would be Brendan.

Each day he would leave with, "Sorry, B, I didn't mean to dump on you." Then he would come back, often the next day, and do the exact same thing again.

During his jog, Nate found himself on Seventh Street, and he noticed what appeared to be a procession of cars with their lights on. He recognized that it was a funeral, which was no big deal to him. He kept running, even picking up his pace. After a few blocks he noticed that the procession had begun pouring out from the parking lot of what had been, up until his run-in with Lloyd, his church, the Word Church. Nate slowed his pace down and took a closer look. He recognized a few of the cars in the procession and a couple of faces as people began to quickly climb into cars to catch the procession.

He was desperately looking for Anita to come walking out of the church as he crossed the street. Nate was mixed in with people leaving the church who were not headed for the interment. Still hoping for a glimpse of the object of his desire, he asked an older gentleman standing nearby, "Who passed away, sir?"

The older man looked Nate up and down. Unsure of why Nate would be asking he told him anyway. "Miss Bethany, the reverend's mother." Then the old man put a cigarette in his mouth and sparked a lighter.

Nate could still see the people around him, but everything seemed to go silent. The last time he'd seen Miss Bethany she was as healthy as a woman twenty years her junior should have been. Aside from the occasional dementia, which some-

times seemed feigned on her part, Miss Bethany s/
though she had many years left. Nate swallowed hard
held back the tears that were trying to form in his eyes. He
had really come to like the lady who'd first called him Doc.
Though she was originally just an excuse for him to go and
spend time at the Lawson home, over time she'd earned a special place in his heart.

She would spit one-liners to Nate out of the blue about
how tough it was growing up in the thirties and forties. "We
didn't have much, so we learned to feel rich inside . . . the only
way to keep from going crazy, killing a cracker, and getting
yourself lynched," she would laugh.

One day she'd told him that the world had turned upside
down and that there was no such thing as families anymore.
When he'd chalked up her sayings as nonsense and said, "You
have a wonderful family that loves you right here," she had responded by warning him about trusting appearances.

"I'ma tell you, Doc, like my momma told me," she had said,
"everybody that lends you a hand ain't trying to help you up,
sometimes they just want to get a firm grip on you so they can
make sure you go down as hard as possible."

As he stood there watching the church parking lot empty
out, he felt alone again. He thought about his own grandmother and how much she meant to him over the years. She
was truly all he had left, with the exception of Cory and Brendan. As he walked away he heard someone talking about the
repast in the cafeteria that was to take place in two hours. He
took off jogging, contemplating returning with a card. *It
would be a bad idea,* he thought to himself, but the thought of
seeing Anita was tempting.

"Listen, baby, I do miss you . . ." Nina was hitting me with
one question after another. "It's just that I've been busy up

here . . ." She was trying to catch me in a lie. "Yeah, I did step out for a minute last night . . ." Wasn't gonna happen. "Okay, so I left my phone in my room . . . I wasn't out long . . . just needed a . . ." She hung up.

I was on my back staring at the ceiling. I began to reflect, as I often did when things weren't going well. One half of my best friend duo was still in poor condition. Although I never admitted to anyone, my hope of him making it out of the coma was beginning to fade like the sunlight before a fast-approaching storm. Nothing was working for me. Nate was going through some things and it seemed like he had changed so much that I hardly knew him. I wanted to take his new-found spirituality serious, but he had been so treacherous all his life that sometimes it was hard to believe that he had given up all the womanizing. I wasn't happy in my marriage and I was finding out that all the flip-flopping back and forth wasn't working either. I realized then that I had to come to some type of decision to get control of my life. I wasn't going back to D.C. into the same type of confusion and despair that I left. I decided to do something that I hadn't really done in a long time. I got down on my knees and prayed.

I had two hours before I was due to check out at one p.m. I must have prayed for an hour. I asked for direction. I asked for a sign that would lead me to where I needed to go. Mostly though I prayed for Brendan, his family, and Nate. On the back end I sent one up for Renée because I was worried about her. Going into a marriage when I knew she still loved Brendan.

The airport was packed, but I moved through quickly. The flight was nice and smooth. Up above the clouds I peered out the window and collected my thoughts. I thought about my life and wondered if I had the opportunity to change anything about it and the decisions that I'd made, good and bad, would I have?

I thought about when I was happiest or truly happy, period. I scanned over my life, chapter by chapter. As I pictured scene after scene I came to the conclusion that I was like a leaf blowing in the wind that somehow never seemed to hit the ground. I thought of each accomplishment, each woman I had conquered, the milestones reached, and the places I had seen. Finally it dawned on me that while I was thankful for each experience, I had never really made anything happen for myself. I had always drifted from one thing to the next, letting life take me on a journey and never carving out my own path. Even with my work. I hadn't pursued the change in companies. The position with HE had fallen in my lap.

Women, jobs, and good times had been my life. Since my father passed, I couldn't recall making a tough decision when it came to choosing a path to follow. I'd always taken the obvious choice or the path of least resistance. I had never committed to anything that threatened to be rough. When I thought about that, an epiphany came crashing down on me like a ton of bricks.

I hadn't been happy since my father died. I hadn't suffered from depression or anything like that, but I hadn't been happy. Without his guidance, I had drifted into manhood without a plan or a map. As I was growing up, my father had always been my confidant and without the words of encouragement and discipline coming from him, I had never matured into the man I knew he planned for me to be. With that realization, I breathed in and closed my eyes tight and held back the tears of shame that began to pour from the inside out.

18

I Wish You Well

I got the phone call from Brendan's mother at one thirty in the morning. I'd just gotten into bed after cleaning up and unpacking from my trip to Chicago and wasn't sound asleep yet. I spent almost an entire hour lying still in the bed listening to Frankie Beverly and Maze's *Greatest Slow Jams*, trying to come to terms with myself. I was uncomfortable with my life and had finally admitted that fact. After our earlier argument I still hadn't heard from Nina, which I felt was a good thing. I definitely needed more time to clear my head after the realizations that I had on my flight.

For the third time in a month I jumped out of bed and headed straight for the hospital. I called Nate and woke him with the news and immediately tried to get Shue on the line but he didn't answer. I sped down the Beltway and hit the BW Parkway headed to P.G. Hospital. Nate was closer and beat me to the hospital. When I got upstairs Brendan was back in surgery. He had started bleeding again internally and his pressure had dropped drastically. There was a serious threat of cardiac arrest. His mother was in pieces when I saw her. Mr. Shue showed the wear and tear of all his family had been through on his face.

In that instant a weird thought came to my mind. I felt bad for thinking it but looking at his mother I couldn't shake it, so I took a seat next to Nate and closed my eyes. I began to pray. "Dear God, please forgive me if what I'm asking is wrong. It's just that this has been the hardest three weeks of my life, even harder than when my own father died. What I ask is not for me or even Nate. I ask on behalf of Brendan, because I know that he would want this"—I took a second before going on— "God, I ask you . . . if You won't allow Brendan to recover from his injuries . . . could you please . . ."

"Yo, Cory." Nate nudged me, interrupting. "You all right? You sweating like a dog over there and it ain't warm in here."

He startled me and when I snapped out of my state I realized that I was sweating. I took my palms and wiped my forehead. "Yeah, I'm cool."

"Did you talk to Shue?" he asked.

"No, I tried him but no answer."

"Same here. I hit him on the way to the hospital."

I nodded as I noticed the doctors approaching us. I thought about my prayer that was interrupted and how I was about to ask God to end Brendan's life and pain. When the doctors spoke I couldn't believe what they said.

His mother almost fainted *again*, and his father burst into tears. I looked at Nate and then my watch. At six thirty-three on this June morning, after two and a half hours of surgery and three hours in the recovery room, Brendan had come out with flying colors and was out of the coma.

"Groggy doesn't quite describe his condition," one doctor

said. "He did manage to ask for two things before drifting off to sleep."

"What's that?" his father asked.

"He said he wanted some Kool-Aid and does he know someone named Renée?"

19

Where Do We Go from Here?

He thought long and hard about his decision before going through with it. Nate had followed Anita from her home like a bona fide stalker. Once she pulled up to Starbucks he carefully took a spot a few cars down so that he wouldn't be seen just yet. Instead he waited until she came out with her latte and muffin in hand before walking up to the side of her car. When she saw him, her mouth dropped open, revealing her shock.

"Nate, what are you . . ." she muttered.

He grabbed the handle on the passenger side of her BMW. "Listen, I'm not going to make a scene out here, but you need to speak to me. I have called you repeatedly and you have yet to return my calls."

Her face showed shame. "I'm sorry, Nate, it's just that I felt so bad about what I did with you that night."

"I understand, but you still could have been woman enough to give me a call back." Nate sounded calm and it was hard for her to get a reading on him. "I mean, I felt like we shared more than just sex." Anita tried to turn away because he was so right. They had connected on a deeper level. She had confided things to him that she had never told her husband. Anita had revealed parts of her past that still haunted and shamed her. As she stared into his eyes across the hood of her car she regretted telling him about the child she'd put up for adoption, and about her four-month stint in a mental ward after being raped by her first husband's best friend.

Her husband hadn't believed her when he'd walked in on the rape. Anita had blanked out during the attack and hadn't fought to get away, nor had she let out a cry for help. She had been living the fast life then and drugs were a part of the scenario, though she was by no means an addict. She had merely dabbled around with cocaine, since it was readily available in her home. This night, though, her decision to get high at a party had cost her dearly. Her first husband Daniel's friend, Shane, had sensed her vulnerability the entire evening and the second he had her alone in the basement he had pounced. Shane had sworn that Anita had come on to him. Daniel left her pregnant a month later and unsure of the paternity. She was only twenty when it all happened and most of her ordeal she had gladly forgotten.

The day Nate had pulled up and saw Anita leaving, she had just a couple hours earlier walked in on Lloyd—the man who had been her savior and protector since the time they'd first met at an AACLU rally, and the founder of The Word Church—with the twenty-one-year-old daughter of the Guatemalan cleaning lady. Although Lloyd hadn't raped the girl, it later became clear that he had taken advantage of her. The next week when he spoke to Anita, he admitted to paying the girl for sex. The only thing that mattered was that as soon as Anita had seen Lloyd with the girl, thoughts of being raped and feeling defenseless had all come back to her. She had run out of the house and only returned long enough to pack her things.

It had left her so confused that she couldn't tell whether she slept with Nate out of anger or if she was truly attracted to him.

"Nate, I'm sorry . . . I care about you. Honest, I do, but I just don't know . . ." She tried not to look into his eyes, because when she did, she did know the truth. She wanted Nate. It was more than sex. He was the type of man she had always dreamed of having. Just the sound of his voice sent chills down her spine. Before she'd slept with him, Anita had observed him. She often dreamed about what it would be like if she were a single sistah in the church and had laid eyes on him. One thing that she was sure about was that she somehow would have found a way to make him hers. "I can't leave my husband, Nate."

"Why?"

She paused before coming up with, "It would destroy the congregation."

Nate stared at her coldly. His whole life began flashing through his eyes. Only once before had he ever fallen in love. First with Sahleen, and now with Anita. Now for the second time, he likened the feelings that washed over him to being kicked in the teeth. Though he tried to restrain his emotion, he couldn't. He had exposed himself to Anita that night as well, poured out his soul to her. Shared his regrets, hopes, and even told her how he'd come to make his fortune. Now he shook his head in disgust. Anita was a coward. She was afraid to love him because it was going to cost her and her precious congregation too much pain. Without a second thought he yelled out, "Fuck the congregation and fuck you too. You'll be sorry."

Nate had been pushed over the brink. He had gone

through too many ups and downs since Kim's death. He walked back to his Porsche and climbed in. Anita began to cry and she dropped her coffee to the ground. Nate slammed into reverse, gave her one last look, and pulled off.

"So what do you mean you can't see me right now?"

I repeated myself. "I need some time to get things into perspective."

"Nigga, you've lost your mind." Nina was dumbfounded. "So what is it? You just wanted to come back and hit it a few more times, huh. And why the fuck did you have me meet you here? We could have done this bullshit over the phone." She was referring to Haines Point.

I had chosen the park hoping that the sunshine and scenery would have an affect on Nina's response to what I had to say. At the very least I had hoped that we would be able to come to terms without a major scene or hurtful remarks thrown back and forth. "Nina, I just wanted you to understand that this isn't about you or me not caring about you—"

She cut me off as she stood up and headed toward her car. I caught her and she stopped short of hitting the alarm. "You know, Cory, I'm not even going to go off out here. I swear I should have expected this from you. You are the most pitiful brother I have ever met. I feel sorry for my sister because she is stuck with you and a baby. Luckily for me, I'm not." She was poised and pointing her finger at me while she talked. "But guess what, Brotherman, I am so over you and this foolishness. I'm done losing sleep over you. I need a real man. I don't care how much money he has, 'cause I'm gonna make my own. The only thing I care about is that he won't be a selfish, immature, lying bastard like you."

The insults were starting. "Nina—"

"No . . . fuck this, Cory. You think you can jerk people around like this. You are sick. The worst thing about this is that I must be just as bad as you if not worse for allowing this, but no more. I have destroyed a relationship over you and I know that I will always regret it. I am going to apologize to my sister and assure her that I will never so much as acknowledge that you breathe air. I just hope that one day she will forgive me because, looking back at all this, it is so clear to me"—she brushed her hair from her eyes and went on—"being with you was never worth it."

That comment cut deep. I didn't expect it or the way she was attacking my manhood as she was delivering her points. "I'm really sorry."

"You're damned right you're sorry. The sorriest of the sorry." She showed anger in her face and a few drops of spit flew from her lips as she proceeded. "I won't front and say that I don't love you, that the sex was whack or that you're not a fine-ass nigga . . . but the sad thing about that, Cory, is this . . . even with all you do have going on . . . you're still an asshole . . . a got-damned cancer, destroying everything you touch. If you don't do anything else with your money, do this—get some professional help and find out why you're such a loser." She opened the door to her car and shouted, "Never, ever, call me again. You understand me?"

I nodded yes. Though I was only hoping for a small break in our romance, some time to think things over, it was clear that she was done with me for good. She was, after all, right. With that she climbed into her car. I heard the radio come on loudly and in the next instant she pulled off and left me there. I sat down on a bench to collect my thoughts. Nina had said so many things about me that were right on point. By the time I climbed into my car I was crumbling inside.

* * *

Two days after Brendan had come out of his coma I still hadn't been able to contact Renée. On the evening of the third day I found out why. Shue had called me with some news; he had set up Renée's fiancé, Tamarick. It was almost one o'clock in the morning and Shue had been tucked inside the closet, sitting on the luggage holder. He had the camcorder rolling as he was gathering all the evidence he would need to break Renée's heart and save her life at the same time.

It had taken Shue less than a week in Houston to find out where Tamarick's real estate company was. Shue also took the time to find out which gym he worked out in. Shue had enlisted the help of a friend, Charles, who was a male exotic dancer in Galveston to come to Houston for a few days and pose as a potential client looking for some commercial real estate to open up a day spa. When the dancer walked into Tamarick's office with a woman he introduced as his partner, he was sure that he'd gotten a certain telling vibe from him.

Two days later Tamarick didn't question the coincidence of running into Charles at the gym. Instead he seemed excited. After working out together, Tamarick had taken the bite and agreed to a complimentary massage.

Shue had spent nearly two thousand dollars putting his scheme together but it had proved to be worth it. He had slid out of the closet with the camera and now had a view of Tamarick enjoying more than a massage. Charles had oiled him up and was having his way with him, all on tape. Once Shue had given the silent thumbs-up to Charles, he took Tamarick into the shower as Shue dipped out of the hotel room with the home video of a lifetime.

He immediately made a copy of the tape and had Charles deliver it to Renée the first thing the next morning. Charles pretended to be a jilted lover doing the innocent girlfriend a favor and letting her know that her man was a dog and a phony. Shue parked outside Renée's home all day in his rental with a switchblade. He flinched as he saw her throw what was obviously some nice merchandise into the trash cans outside her place, including sheets and a few suits, which obviously belonged to her soon-to-be ex. He stood just below her window when Tamarick finally came over to talk. Wanting to make sure there was no violence, he stayed there until he saw Tamarick leave an hour later.

When Tamarick pulled off, Shue did the same, only he headed straight for the airport and home.

Now Renée walked through the door of Brendan's hospital room like an angel coming to usher him back to safety. He was improving bit by bit but there was still cause for caution. Somehow, though, when I saw Renée standing there I knew everything would be just fine.

"Is it time for my shift, doctor?" she asked playfully.

Checking my watch, I smiled, "You might be late, young lady, but you're just in time." I laughed and stood as she approached me for a hug. Her squeeze was so tight that I felt something in it. When we broke free I asked her, "So how is everything?"

"It's a long story, but I'm home now. Home for good."

"Seriously . . . but I thought your fiancé . . ." I played dumb, like I didn't know the whole sordid story.

She cut me off and said, "It's over between him and me and there's a zero percent chance of us getting back together."

"You okay? If there's anything I can do, please just let me know."

"I'm fine, but I really don't want to talk or think about it for that matter, if it's all the same to you," she said.

"Of course," I responded as I looked into her eyes.

Her demeanor showed the obvious. No one ends a relationship, and engagement no doubt, and is fine in the days immediately following. I know that I wasn't. Not that I was losing any sleep over love, it was more of a haunting feeling. I couldn't stop thinking about the way I botched both relationships and the hurt I'd caused Shelly and Nina. Nina's words echoed inside my head on the hour like a news update.

Though Renée was trying her best to seem like she was cool with her breakup, I decided to keep a close eye on her. Since Shue had been right about him being a down-low brother, then she was better off. And to be honest I had been planning to call her and break the news to her. It had worked out for the best. I decided not to quiz her about it. Instead we talked about Brendan's condition and the doctors' prognosis.

We sat for thirty minutes until he opened his eyes. Renée stood over him and stroked his hair. "Brendan, can you hear me? It's Renée."

His eyes showed that he recognized her. He tried to get words out but she stopped him. "Don't try to speak. I know, sweetie . . . I know."

I sat back and prepared to leave. It was a beautiful reunion seeing them together, even as friends, and it made my heart feel good. Renée held Brendan's hand for a few more minutes and he drifted back off to sleep. For the first time in a long time, it seemed like things were getting headed in the right direction. It made me feel even more determined to right my own course. I was thankful and was ready to send up another prayer, this time strictly for thanks, when Trina walked through the door.

Renée turned to look at her and the two locked eyes for a moment. Then Renée looked down at Trina's slightly protruding stomach. I saw a momentary look of pain slide over her face before she coolly came up with, "Hello, Trina."

"Hey, Renée."

It wasn't that I expected a catfight but they were extremely cordial with one another and I was a little surprised. In the next few moments, I observed and listened as they made small talk. Finally Renée excused herself and I stood to leave with her.

We said our good-byes and left Brendan with his family.

20

Just What I Needed?

I needed to cleanse my soul and ease the guilt that was crashing down on me. Renée needed to find a way to get comfortable enough to share her pain. She desperately needed a shoulder to cry on, to finally let it all out. Nate for his part had been so off balance in the past couple of weeks that he seemed like an out-of-control aircraft. One moment he'd be distant and out of contact, and the next he'd be zooming in for some camaraderie. I was beginning to think he needed a runway. I wasn't sure if it was a crash landing or an emergency takeoff that the brother seemed to be seeking, but I had a feeling the night would reveal all.

All three of us had different motivations, but the end result was that we were all looking to get drunk and forget what was on our minds. It just so happened that one of Nate's old flames, Tracye, was throwing a party on the *Spirit of Baltimore*. Her company, IKON Entertainment, was throwing a star-studded event to kick off the summer. Plenty of celebrities were in town for Big Tigger's annual charity basketball game and she was sure to have quite a few of them on board.

"You guys have everything you need?" Tracye asked.

"We're good for now, thanks, but I may need some of your attention later on," Nate replied with a smile and a smooth tone that made him sound like the player he once was. I glanced at him quickly, wondering if the old Nate was finally going to show up. We were seated in the VIP section and we had several bottles of champagne on the table. Two of the bottles were popped and we'd made quick work of them.

"I'll be sure to come back and check on you *all.*" Tracye shot back before she walked away.

Hiding whatever feelings we were harboring about what was going in our personal lives, we all made one toast after another until the Moët had us acting a little silly. "Here's to love," Nate said, raising his glass. "The most overrated thing that a man and a woman can attempt to share."

"I'll drink to that," I said.

"Shiiiit, my brother. You ain't never lie," Renée answered and threw her glass to her lips. She had just downed her fifth glass.

I raised mine again. "Here's to Brendan. I love that dude. I can't believe he's gonna be okay . . ." I paused, feeling a little choked up. "For a while there, it didn't look good, so here's to miracles."

"God is good," Nate chimed in and we clanked our flutes together.

There was more sipping and laughing. Before I knew it Renée made a toast of her own. Her speech was slurred but her point was loud and clear. "Here's to you sorry-ass Negroes, especially my fuggin' faggot of a fiancé."

When she said that, Nate's mouth dropped open and I almost spit my champagne out. "What the . . ." Nate said.

I kept a straight face except for the exaggerated expressions that hid my knowledge of what had happened. She told the entire story of getting the videotape of Tamarick being ridden like a pony and of him giving better head than she could. Shue'd told me about how he'd gone all-out to set the brother up upon his return from Houston. I was shocked, but I didn't pretend to be upset. Actually I thought it was a nice gesture on his part. We were all family and if you messed with one of us, then you had to be prepared to take the retribution.

When she finished, Nate and I sat silent, not knowing what to say in response. Finally Nate came out with, "How about another bottle?"

"No doubt," Renée answered. A few moments later our next bottle arrived and when Nate pulled out a wad of cash the waitress said that the bottle was paid for already.

I was puzzled and Nate said, "By who?"

"By me," came a voice from behind me. Emerging from her posse was Shawn Simmons.

"Omigod," Renée shouted. She was tipsy and she began rocking back and forth in excitement. Renée was wearing a pink spaghetti-strapped dress and when she leaned forward I noticed that it looked like one her breasts was going to fall out the top of it. I grabbed her leg to calm her and noticed that Shawn Simmons was staring and looked as though she was lying in wait.

"Long time no hear from," Shawn said as she smirked at Nate.

"Yeah, it has been . . . a long time, that is." Nate looked over at me and Renée. "Let me introduce you to my friends. This is Cory and Renée." We extended our hands and shook as he said, "Cory and Renée, this, of course, is Shawn Simmons."

"We know who the hell it is," Renée blasted him as she stood up. "It is so nice to meet you. I love your music. I have both of your CDs and the ones from when you were with Plain Jane."

"Thanks." She flashed a genuine smile. "So you guys look like you're having a good time." She pointed to the empty bottles. "Mind if I join you for a bit?"

"Of course not," I said.

Renée joined in with, "Please do."

Nate coolly slid over on the love seat and made room for her. She was looking every bit the star she was. She was wearing a white silk dress that stopped mid-thigh with a slit on the side of it that rose completely to her hip. When she crossed her legs, revealing the side of her tanned thighs, I felt a rush wash through me. Nate seemed almost too cool to be sitting next to one of the hottest female singers in the industry. His demeanor hardly changed, I figured because he'd had her already.

When the deejay played Shawn's latest hit, a duet featuring the once-retired Ma$e, everyone hopped to the floor. Renée grabbed her glass with one hand and my hand with the other. "C'mon, Cory, let's dance."

I followed her to the floor and we moved around to the beat like the two drunk fools we were. Twenty minutes later and we were still dancing. It felt good to move around as the boat cruised along. I was sweating a little and Renée wiped the beads from my head with a hand and a smile. She surprised me by being a better dancer than I remembered, but she shocked me when she turned her back to me, grinding it against my crotch as they played Lil' Jon's "Get Low."

Nate never made it to the dance floor. He stayed behind with Shawn and that was the last I saw of him. When the boat docked we came to a stop and the lights came on. As the crowd moved toward the exit, I tried to locate him in the crowd. I tried his cell six times before Renée and I left the parking lot in my car.

"Don't worry about him," she smiled. "He's a big boy."

I laughed as we cruised out of the harbor. "Yeah, I know

that. But he was doing so well. He had really turned over a new leaf. Stopped all the womanizing and everything. I just hate to see him backslide."

Unconvinced, she looked at me. "Uh-huh."

"Uh-huh what?"

"I think someone might be a little jealous."

"What. Jealous of what?"

"Of you know what. Don't hate the player, hate the game." Renée laughed. She was still feeling the alcohol. I was still buzzing too and laughed right back.

"A'ight. A nigga might be a little jealous." I laughed again and we cruised on down the Parkway. The laughter felt good, and effortless. There was nothing heavy on our minds, signaling the evening had been a success.

I woke up and looked at the clock; it was seven thirty. My full bladder had been my alarm clock and I climbed out of bed. The air conditioner had been blowing all night and the cold air was a shock to my naked body. I looked at my face as I passed the mirror on the way to the toilet. I took a long leak and thought about the night's events. The party had been nice and a real celebration to Brendan's recovery, even though he couldn't attend. I began to wonder how long it would take for him to completely recover and for us all to be able to hang out like old times.

I flushed and washed my hands and ran them over my face. Eyes still a little puffy from too much drinking and not enough sleep. I took a quick swish of mouthwash to combat the morning breath and moved back into my bedroom. I slid back into the warmth of the bed and when I did, Renée turned over and looked at me.

"Sorry, didn't mean to wake you."

She yawned and replied, "It's all right. I need to get up anyway. I have an appointment today at Abada Hair Studio."

"Your hair looks like you just got it done." I smiled.

"Boy, please. This do is two weeks old. I will be in the chair at ten getting right. That's one thing I missed while in Houston. There's something about the way the sistahs do hair here in D.C., especially Amani, my stylist." I nodded my head. She went on. "What about you? What are you going to do today?"

Her stylist shared the same name as my daughter and it got me thinking that I needed to see her. I hadn't pressed the issue since asking Shelly for a divorce. But simply hearing the name sparked my desire and the decision was made instantly.

"Well, actually, I have to go New York and get the last of my things from my office and apartment and close out a couple of other things there. I was going to wait until Monday, but I have a meeting back here so I figured I'd just go ahead and get it over with. Plus I would have the whole day to spend with my daughter tomorrow."

"So how is that going? It has to be hard adjusting."

"That's an understatement. But honestly, I think that Amani and I have connected, or at least we *had*."

Renée's sentiments were hard to read. I waited for her to bring up what had happened between us. When she didn't after some more small talk I leaned in and kissed her on the mouth. "Thanks," she said.

"For what?"

"For last night. I had a good time hanging out with you and Nate. And somehow you knew I didn't want to be alone last night."

I did sense it. On the way home I picked up her subtle flirting. It had been muggy outside and with the air blowing from the car vents straight onto her chest, I had noticed her nipples hardening. She kept leaning over toward me to change CDs and before I knew it I was aroused. It felt sort of taboo. We'd known each other forever it seemed. We'd even slept in the same bed before one night after a party during Howard U's homecoming, but hadn't had sex. Of course, that had been our little secret.

The tension was there but after everything that had happened over the past couple of years, neither of us could have expected that anything would happen like this. "You know what?"

"What?" she responded.

"I didn't want to be alone either." With that I climbed on top of her and with a free hand I reached into the nightstand.

I began softly kissing her neck. "Boy, we are wrong for this you know," she whispered and followed with a chuckle. "Plus you're married."

"Separated."

"Whatever," she moaned. "Oh, man, that feels nice."

My hands were all over her. She grabbed them and wrestled me over onto my back. "Here," I handed her the condom.

She tore it open and while she stroked my dick, she playfully said, "You're just using me."

"True." She reached down and pinched my nipple when I said that. "Ouch."

"That's what you get." She straddled me. "But it's all good because I'm just using you too." With that she eased her bottom down onto my thighs. I slipped into her and she humped me like she was on a mission. There was something supremely erotic about the way Renée made love. She made me feel as if she was going to explode with every stroke. Her nipples jutted off her chest and she whimpered like a baby.

While we screwed I thought about her being with Brendan and wondered how he would feel if he knew what she and I were doing. I wondered if she cared. She had her hand on her clit rubbing it while she rode me. Renée was a nice girl, the kind you could take home to your mother, but here she was on top of me after being with my best friend just a year earlier.

"Oh, Cory, I feel it. It's in my stomach." She began to buck while her hands were doing more work than I was. "Oh sheeeeiiiiit."

My whole pelvic region was wet. She began rubbing my chest and my mind drifted from all the thoughts and clarity that the morning after brings. Now I was beginning to focus on my own orgasm, and my dick grew harder inside of her. Within moments we had both zoned out and we were in a place where no thoughts or emotions existed. No guilt or second guesses. We were just using one another's bodies to get some stress off.

She slammed down on me and it felt as though I hit her G-spot. She screamed out and began to pant in short spurts. Right then and there I began to involuntarily lift my hips from the bed as I filled the condom up and collapsed with an, "Ohhhhhhhhhhh dammmmmn."

For a couple moments we lay still taking in the gravity of what we'd just done. After the silent stares we broke into smiles that gave way to laughter. We were grown. Then she spoke.

"Nigga, you know you took advantage of me."

I laughed again. "Shit. You know you used a brother for his body."

She nodded in agreement. "Maybe so," and then she covered her eyes and ran them through her hair before continuing, "but thanks, I needed that."

After her shower she walked out of the bathroom and grabbed her clothes. She was dressed in ten minutes. I walked her to the door and we parted with a hug and words from her that I know she meant. "Take this to your grave, your hear me?"

"Of course," I said.

She pointed a finger in my face. "No telling Nate, Dee, or anyone else. I'm serious."

"I feel you."

She kissed me on the cheek. "Cory, you're a sweetheart. It was beautiful."

"Thanks."

"I'm not finished," she said. "I enjoyed it. I really did, but this can never happen again. Never. You understand? I still love Brendan, though, even if he and I never work it out. I would never want to hurt him . . . at least not the way he hurt me. You got me?"

"No doubt," I shot back because I understood.

With that she walked out the door as if we'd done nothing more than chitchat. I was glad that she appeared to be okay with it. I got up and packed for my trip up to New York, hoping that everything would go smoothly. Though we had hardly spoken, I knew I would have to face Shelly's rants when I saw her. I started to call Nate to see if he'd ride with me and run interference. Recalling Shelly's temper, I knew if she had something to say, it wouldn't have mattered if the pope showed up with me, she would have her piece.

21

Now . . . for the Moment You've Been Waiting For

Nate had yet to entertain anyone in his brand-new U Street condo. Shawn Simmons would be the first. Though when he'd had Jewel Green, one of D.C.'s top interior decorators, put her skills to work on it, he had hoped it would be Anita Lawson whom he would christen his four-hundred-thousand-dollar, two-bedroom condo with. Shawn would have to do instead.

Shawn had ditched her security and rode back from the party with Nate. She'd been impressed with his Porsche Cayenne. She'd owned one the previous year. Once she had seen his place, though, she was taken aback. The living room was furnished with furniture that was imported from Fiji. Her mouth dropped open when she noticed the stainless steel Viking appliances. His kitchen was immaculate and the dining room looked like something out of a model home. Nate hit a button and the electric blinds slid down, a second button and Amel Larrieux's CD came on.

She had taken her sandals off at the door and the feel of the plush white carpet between her toes made her coochie wet.

"Your place is phat, man. Can I look around?"

"Knock yourself out."

Shawn looked into the guest bedroom, which was furnished with a cherry-oak sleigh bed, a customized aquarium, and a red mural painted on the wall. There was a fifty-five-inch plasma screen in there that paled only slightly in size to the one in the living room. She wondered who did his decorating because it was incredible. Each room was color-coordinated to a tee. When she reached his master bedroom she screamed "Wow."

She noticed the one wall that was completely glass, overlooking the street below. The moonlight was shining into the room and she could make out the furnishings. She moved toward the bed and Nate was standing behind her. She plopped down onto it and let out an "Ahhhhhh. This bed feels so good."

"It's a Vi-Spring, there isn't a better one in the world. Be careful, you may not want to ever get out." Nate laughed.

"And maybe I won't." She motioned her finger for Nate to come to her. It was just like old times. Most men dreamed of the opportunity to even catch a glimpse of a star like Shawn. Nate had never pursued her and it made him all the more mysterious and desirable to her. She was used to rappers, actors, and moguls going all-out to spend time with her. Nate had never even cared enough to lock her number into his phone.

Ten minutes later and they were in the mix. Shawn was completely naked, trying her best to sound sexy as she moaned and gyrated. Nate, on the other hand, was going through the motions trying to bring the player inside of him back to life, but he was having a problem. He couldn't stop thinking of Anita.

"What's wrong, baby?" Shawn was asking while pulling on his manhood.

"Not sure," he answered. He wasn't. He had never had a problem like this before.

"I'm not turning you on?" she asked seductively before taking him into her mouth. He closed his eyes, trying to get into her but he couldn't. He felt nothing for her and as far as the sensations went, there was nothing at all. All he could see was Anita.

He pulled away and said, "Listen, sweetie, I'm sorry about this." Then he said the unthinkable. "I'm in love with someone."

There was silence as Shawn took in what he'd said. She drew a blank look and replied, "So what. Does that mean we can't fuck?"

Nate shook his head in disgust. "Let me just take you back to your room. Where are you staying?"

"What," she yelled out. Shawn couldn't believe her ears. Was she being rejected? "What the hell are you talking about?"

She stood up and it was apparent that she was about to throw a temper tantrum. "Where are you staying?" Nate repeated.

"At the Capital Hilton, but why does it matter? I'm not leaving here without getting what I want."

Nate was stunned by her behavior. "Shawn, come on now, you can call up anyone you want and get laid, don't make a big deal over this."

"Don't make a big deal? You got to be kidding me. *You* sound like the bitch. Now you got me naked up here in your crib, pussy dripping wet, and you want to send me home?" She shook her head. "Oh hellllll nooo."

Nate began to wonder if she was serious. "So what are you gonna do, Shawn, rape me?" He laughed at her.

Disgusted and humiliated, she screamed, "Fuck this. Nobody tells me no. I got something for your ass, Negro. You just be ready to turn yourself in tomorrow."

"That's cool," Nate said. "So you would do some foul shit like cry rape on a brother?"

She folded her arms. "You got-damned right. If I don't get what I want, there's gonna be hell to pay. Plus, who you think the cops are gonna believe? I got a nigga in Miami sitting in jail right now just for pissing me off, doing three on an eight-year bid. All that nigga did was eat my pussy all night long. But he got cute and wanted to start fucking with that bitch, Nia Harvey." Nia, who had a similar-sounding voice to hers, was being called a younger version of Shawn Simmons. Subsequently, she'd become Shawn's top rival in the industry. "Now you fuck with me and see what happens."

Nate laughed hard for a couple seconds and then stopped suddenly. He walked over toward Shawn and shouted, "You better get the hell outta my house, you crazy bitch. I'm calling you a cab and you'll be all right."

"You obviously didn't hear me."

"Oh, I heard you. Loud and clear. It's just that I don't play like that."

"What's that supposed to mean?"

"It means that I have a state-of-the-art surveillance system that will show that I didn't rape you; as a matter of fact, it will show that you suck a mean dick or at least you try."

"You didn't."

"I did."

Five minutes later and Shawn was in tears, riding in a cab headed back to her hotel, all thoughts of false accusations gone from her mind. Her only concern was that she didn't wind up with her name linked to a sex scandal like Paris Hilton. However, on the way out of the building, she began to welcome the thought of some free publicity.

Nate, although still a little tense from the exchange, began thinking about Anita again. He was relieved that he been able to convince Shawn that he had her on tape. He decided then and there that he was going to actually have a security camera installed.

He waited until the last of the congregation had filed out of the church after the early morning service. Nate knew the schedule by rote from all the work he'd put in. By nine thirty the church and the altar would be empty, and by ten thirty the people piling in for the next service would begin to arrive. Just when he knew she'd be there, Nate walked up behind Anita. Just as she did every Sunday, she was organizing her husband's note cards, putting them back in order.

She thought she was alone in the pulpit but then she felt someone's presence. When she turned around and saw Nate standing there her heart dropped and she gasped. "Nate, what are you doing here?"

"I've come for you," he said. "I love you and I know you don't love your husband."

Anita batted her eyes. She took Nate in. He was dressed in a tan suit that hung on his body like it was sculpted on. He had on a pink tie from Hermès and a matching handkerchief. Her mind began to spin and her flesh was weak for him. She had told herself that she was fine as long as he stayed away. Day by day she had built her wall up with the notion that he'd probably found someone else.

Damn, she thought. He had just told her that he loved her. She had long since conceded to herself that she felt the same way about him. "I don't know what to say, Nate."

"Tell me you miss me too. Tell me that you'll leave him and be with me. We're soul mates."

Anita took a deep breath. "Nate, you shouldn't be here. If I promise to call you later, would you leave?"

He sensed desperation in her voice, not fear. She didn't fear

being caught with him. It was just that she couldn't stand being so close to him. While he stood there, she began thinking
of all that had transpired between them. They had shared so
much, and for the first time she had fallen for a man both
physically and emotionally. Nate was her *it*. But she needed
him to leave before she begged him to take her away.

"I won't leave without you. If I do, I'll never hear from you.
Baby, listen, you don't need this. You don't need him. There's
nothing for you to worry about. I'll treat you right . . . love
you a lifetime. Plus, I have enough money to take real good
care of you. Just leave with me now. We can go get your things
and never look back."

Anita stood there in silence. Nate's eyes pored over her
body. Her face, in spite of the tortured look she sported, was
angelic. Even in a somewhat conservative dress, she was stunning. He could make out the traces of lace in her bra under
her dress. He also marveled at her small waist and the way her
hips gave a hint of the beautifully shaped bottom that she
possessed. "An ass so phat you could see it from the front" was
how his boy Dee had described it after seeing Nate with Anita
one day at the hospital.

Finally a tear formed in her eye. "I want you too, Nate. I
love you too. I do want to be with you—"

He interrupted. "Then what will it take? We can go tell him
now. Where is he?"

"He's not here. He stepped out for an hour." She shook her
head. "Honestly, I think he went to have a drink."

"We'll wait, but this has to end. I can't stand not being with
you another day." With that he forgot where he was and move
closer to her.

"What are you doing?" Anita said, attempting to slide back.
She moved too slow and Nate caught her by her wrist. She
dropped the note cards and let out a sigh as Nate grabbed her

by the back of her head and pulled her face to his. "Nooo, not here, Nate."

Nate didn't stop. Their kiss was love personified. His tongue danced with hers and she couldn't keep her passion under control. The kiss was long and full. His hands began to wander all over her body. First to her hips, then her ass. Next he found her breasts and palmed them. "Ohhh, Anita, I missed you so much."

Nothing but a moan from her. Her lips were on his earlobes and his neck. They lost all track of space and time. Nate pulled her dress up enough to grip her panties. One firm tug and they were ripped from her body. "Ohmygawwd no," she whispered when she felt his fingers reaching her center. He backed her against the wooden barrier in front of the choir benches. One finger, two, then three inside of her as he kissed her neck.

Anita was high on passion. Higher than she'd ever dreamed of going. She wanted Nate. She was in love with him. She'd been unable to sleep without dreaming of him, but right now she was in a different place. Her desire for Nate, coupled with the contempt she held for her husband, had her wanting to do the unthinkable. "Nate," she murmured.

"Yeah, baby," he answered.

"I want you to fuck me," she moaned as his fingers danced on her clit like a guitarist on the strings. "I want you to make love to me right here, where that hypocrite stands and delivers messages that he doesn't live by."

With that Nate spun her around and lifted her dress. Within seconds he began pushing inside her. Each inch brought a deeper moan and remarkably a cry of passion that could have been heard up the block.

He moved slowly at first until she asked, "Did you miss this?"

"Yeah, I did, baby."

"Then act like it. You want me to leave with you?"

"Yeah, baby, please leave."

"Then, ma . . . maaa . . . maaake me wanna . . . ohhh shiiiiit."

Nate began banging her like a man who was just released from prison on a weekend pass. His strokes began coming like thunder. His thighs clapping against her perfect ass. Her wetness was drenching him and he was beginning to lose control. She was now screaming at the top of her lungs as she began to feel her orgasm approach. Nate was magic. No man had ever made her cum before, and here Nate did it every time. "Ayyyyyeeeeeee," she screamed out. "Don't stop, doooonn't stop. I feel . . . I feeeel iiiittttt."

With that she began to grunt and her legs trembled underneath her. Nate began to shoot inside of her. "Yess, oh damn yesssss," he mumbled as he finished.

"What the fuck!" They both heard a voice yell out.

They turned to see Lloyd and Thomas, head of the board of deacons, standing next to Sister Toya Sanders, the treasurer. Her mouth was hanging wide open. Part of her display of shock may have been due to her witnessing the size of Nate's huge, glistening penis. He had just pulled it out of Anita upon their arrival.

Lloyd swooped in on Nate for his rematch. He did successfully get a couple of licks in while screaming, "He raped my wife." But by the time Nate was able to pull his pants back up, he had regained control of the situation. He'd punched Lloyd in the ear a few times and caused him to recoil.

The women were screaming while Thomas tried to break it up. Anita was professing loudly, "He didn't rape me. I love him."

A crowd gathered and by the time the situation had some semblance of control, people were beginning to arrive. It was a mess, to put it mildly.

Old women were treated to a barrage featuring Lloyd's true colors. "Bitch, get out of my church. Call the police."

Nate had gotten his wish as he and Anita scurried from the church like two teenagers eloping. They went straight to the house in Mitchellville and packed Anita's things. An hour later and Anita sat in a daze in Nate's marble superbath whirlpool tub, sipping a glass of wine. The two hardly talked while Anita's mind drifted back from the absurd display of the morning's events that kept playing over in her mind. Nate knew she needed some peace and quiet time. He didn't mind giving it to her; after all, he'd gotten just what he'd prayed for and he wasn't about to blow it.

I didn't want to sleep with Shelly. I merely wanted to use the couch to take a nap since it was late when I arrived. A summer shower had slowed traffic down on the turnpike and it was murder making it through the Holland Tunnel. When I parked my car I had only one thing on my mind, some peace, quiet, and rest. I even tried checking into a nearby hotel but they were all booked. Saturday night in Manhattan gets that way.

I reached my floor and headed toward my door. Inside all was quiet and there were boxes everywhere as Shelly was preparing to vacate the apartment. I looked down the hall and could see the television on in Amani's room and headed that way. I didn't want to wake her. She hadn't seen me in almost two months. I walked up to her door and saw that she was sleeping soundly. What I also noticed was that she had company. There was another little girl sleeping at the foot of her bed. They looked like two little angels that had overdosed on pizza and soft drinks. The empty box was on the floor next to the controller of the GameCube. There were a couple of DVDs on the floor next to the television as evidence that there had been a little party going on.

I watched her sleep for a moment and then I turned and headed for the living room. On the way back I walked to the master bedroom. I looked in and saw my wife sleeping soundly. I have to admit that I felt a strange mix of feelings take over me. She was still beautiful and still my wife, but she was in a negligee, one I'd purchased no less, lying in bed with another man. He was sleeping so soundly you would have thought that it was his house.

Not knowing exactly what to do, I did nothing. I took a closer look and recognized him. The guy with the daughter at Amani's school, it made sense. I had been replaced with the other half of a ready-made family. Ricky Reyes. I hadn't forgotten his name. He was a Lenny Kravitz–looking mofo, with his shirt off in an apartment I was paying for. I thought about walking over to him and cracking his head open just for general principle, but then a thought came over me. It was the same type of clarity that I felt when I'd been on that flight from Chicago. My mind raced with thoughts of all that I'd done and taken Shelly and Nina through.

Right there in that moment, she had peace and comfort. My daughter was in her room in child's heaven. She had a friend and a sister perhaps. Me, I'd been a user, irresponsible, and the opposite of a real man. I'd crossed forbidden boundaries and had hurt the union of a sisterhood. Worse than that I hadn't yet been worth it. By ending things with Nina, I had started to right the ship. By walking out of that apartment and swallowing my pride I would take another step.

I turned around to walk out and as I gathered my things I heard a voice, "Daddy."

I looked over and saw Amani. A smile formed on her sleepy face and I felt my heart melt. She'd called me "Daddy." In that moment I had all the answers I would need. My daughter would love me, no matter what. "I missed you, honey, so much," I said in a whisper.

"I missed you too." We were locked in a hug.

"Listen, sweetie, I want you to go back to bed and I'll come and see you tomorrow. We can go anywhere you want."

"Can Kali come?" she asked.

"If her daddy says it's okay."

"It's fine with me," I heard a male voice say behind me.

I looked at him and he looked back. I turned back to Amani. "Baby, go on back to sleep. Daddy just stopped in for a second to see you, but I'll be back in the morning."

"What time?" she shot back.

"What time would you like?"

"Eight o'clock."

"That's a little early. How about noon?"

She nodded her head. "Okay." I gave her a kiss and she headed back to bed.

I made my way to the door, bag in hand. "Tell Shelly I'll see her around noon if you don't mind."

"No problem. Nice to see you again."

"I bet," I said as I exited. Trying to keep from getting an attitude, I thought of all the things I had done to bring this on myself. My pride was crushed for the moment but I had it coming. It was life. My life.

"**Look what the** cat done dragged in," Terri said as I made my way to the bar. I had driven straight to Justin's. I had an hour till closing and I knew that Terri would set me straight. "The usual?" she asked.

"And then some," I replied. "You know I'm really beat."

"You look it," she said. I'd begun to forget how sexy she sounded with that accent. "Where you staying, sexy?"

"With you if you've got the space in your bed."

She laughed. "You know your ass is a funky trip. You come through, hit it on your way out of town. I don't hear from you for what . . . two months . . . now you want to come back unannounced and come lay up?"

I smiled. "Hey," I said.

"You fine and all but I don't know who you think you are?"

I grabbed the shot she'd given me and slammed it. "I'm Rick James, bitch," I said imitating Dave Chapelle.

She burst out laughing and poured me another. "You tired," she said, reaching into her purse. "Here." She threw me the keys. "You remember my apartment right, it's 209."

"124th?"

"Yeah, I'll see you in a couple hours."

"Thanks."

She smiled, letting me know that she was glad to be of some help to a brother in need.

There was no sex with Terri, she'd let me sleep. Told me I was snoring when she came in. I woke up and she was getting ready for church. We made some small talk while she fixed me a quick breakfast of bagels, eggs, and turkey sausage on her George Foreman grill.

We kicked it like buddies and I explained to her my reason for coming to the city this weekend. She gave me some advice that I heeded. "Cory, no matter what, keep the bond strong between you and your daughter. If you move on or if she does, don't be a fucking hater. As long as that man is good to your seed, then don't worry your head 'bout it a bit."

After breakfast I left Terri, promising to do better with keeping in touch. I headed downtown to spend some time with my daughter and to set up a time in which Shelly and I could file our papers for a legal separation.

SIX MONTHS LATER

Brendan was recovering quickly. He was still in therapy but was now working out vigorously. He ached at night but he didn't complain, he was lucky to be alive. He was self-conscious about the slight limp he walked with. The doctors told him that the next surgery would eliminate that and he'd be back to normal. Aside from the two-inch scar on the side of his head, which was now covered by the curly fro he'd grown out, he had no visible marks from the accident.

Each morning he would get up and go to therapy. After that he would go to the gym with Nate and Dee. Nate was on a mission, working out like he had never before. His regimen inspired Brendan to push himself to the brink and had been part of the reason for his speedy recovery. Dee, in the mean-time, had gone back to college and was trying to regain his youthful physique for the college girls. He'd decided he wanted to be an elementary school teacher, of all things. It was a noble profession, but hard to imagine a guy with the history that he had molding young minds.

In addition to his partners working out, Brendan was getting even more inspiration from his newborn son, Khalil Brighton Shue. Trina had reluctantly given their son his last name. She had been trying to convince him to give their relationship another chance for the sake of their son.

Brendan, for his part, told her that he merely wanted to take it slow. There was so much damage to repair. Before he even wanted to tackle the idea of trying to become a family, he needed to get well physically first. In addition, he was seeing someone who had been there for him through it all. He wasn't willing to turn his back on his blossoming relationship and blow what could possibly be the type of love that he'd always wanted by giving yet another chance to Trina's psychotic, lying ass.

I arrived last to Nate's crib. When I got there I could smell the food when I hit the door. I walked in and took my shoes off as was required. "Hey, Cory," everyone spoke.

"What's good?"

Brendan walked in off of the balcony. "What's up, dog?"

"I can't call it," I answered. "Where's the baby?"

"Renée is in the back changing him for me."

"So, playing Mr. Mom is rough, huh?" Just then Renée walked out of the room with a freshly changed baby. "I see you brought in some reinforcements."

Renée handed Brendan the baby and gave me a kiss on the cheek. "Hey, love," she said.

Nate had on an old-school mix CD playing, and currently "Joy and Pain" was bouncing through the system. I looked around the room as I found a seat and thought about how fitting the title of the song was to everyday life. We each had been through our own personal turmoil in the past couple of years. Then I wondered why it was that the *joy* that was so elusive and the *pain* so easy to find.

On a positive note I looked at Nate over there with his fiancée. Anita's divorce wouldn't be final for two more months but she was already wearing a five-carat diamond ring straight from Harry Winston, and had said yes to Nate's proposal. He had flown her down to North Island in the Seychelles where he'd rented one of only eleven secluded villas. They had spent four nights in the 4,500-square-foot villa. Nate had told her that the trip was only for her to clear her mind and relax, but on the second night there, he presented the ring to her as they watched the sunset. He'd told me that the vacation was the best fifteen grand he'd ever spent. I wasn't sure if it was because of the wedding he was now planning or all of the incredible lovemaking he'd claimed they'd done.

My life was settling into a steady pattern of woman sampling. I wasn't ready for another relationship. At least I kept telling myself that to keep from getting bent out of shape about the poor luck I was having finding a suitable mate. I looked over at Brendan holding his son and found it hard to believe that he too seemed to be on the verge of settling down. Even if he was going to have a baby's mama situation on his hand, he seemed content. I figured having a new lease on life will make a man put things into perspective. He had been repeating that "life was too short to be involved in a bunch of drama."

He definitely had a point, but I was having some trouble finding out what was the point without the drama. My crew was getting boring.

"Listen up, everyone," Nate yelled out. "I have an announcement."

"Turn the music down," I said. "This is gonna be good."

His grandmother was smiling, waiting to hear her loud-mouthed grandson profess his love for Anita or shower her with some other outlandish romantic gesture. Everyone else in attendance tuned in as he clanked his fork against the side of a wine bottle.

Nate made his way out to the middle of the floor and for some reason he pulled his T-shirt off. "Man, it's hot in here," he said.

"Come on, man, what is it? A brother is ready to sample some of that grub," Brendan said. "What's up, you posing for *Playgirl* again?" The room erupted into laughter.

"Not quite," Nate said. "But I will be making a return to the public eye."

He had us all at attention.

He reached into his pocket and pulled out his necklace with the diamond-encrusted boxing glove charm and put it around his neck. "I'm coming out of retirement. I'm going to fight again." He was grinning from ear to ear; meanwhile everyone in attendance, except for Anita, sat there with a blank look of surprise.

"What?" I said.

"What did you say?" Brendan chimed in.

"You heard me," Nate barked. "I'm fighting again. Don't try to talk me out of it, I listened to your concerns before and I retired in my prime. I have my wife-to-be's blessings and that's all I care about."

"C'mon, man, you haven't fought in seven years," Brendan said. "Who's you gonna fight, Sugar Ray?"

"I already have a deal lined up. Two tune-ups and then Henry Scott for the light heavyweight title."

"You got to be kidding," I said. "Henry 'the Horse' Scott.

Why would you want to fight him of all people? This is ridiculous, man. I mean, why would you want to fight, period, it ain't like you need the money."

Nate was quiet. Then he looked over at Anita. "The stock market has been a bitch. What can I say?"

I shook my head. I couldn't believe what I was hearing. Nate Montgomery had been the youngest welterweight champion in boxing history at seventeen. He had skipped the Olympics and started fighting professionally in order to get an early shot at the belt. He had surprised the champ at the time, Marco Revera, with a patented overhand right. The odds in the fight had been thirty to one. Revera was 29–0 at the time. Nate was in only his tenth fight. He had gambled every bit of drug money that he'd ever made at that time and even gotten his uncle to loan him the money that he'd be earning on the fight. In all, Nate had bet close to two hundred thousand dollars on himself. He'd walked away with nearly six million dollars.

Nearly every fight the odds were against him and every fight he bet on himself. By the time he reached twenty wins, he was worth nearly twenty million dollars. He had planned to make a hundred million in the ring like his idol and fellow D.C. boxing legend, Sugar Ray Leonard, but in his twenty-first fight he had suffered a head butt that knocked him out cold. He had landed on the back of his head, bursting a vessel in his brain, nearly dying.

He recovered and saw four of the best doctors in the world; to his dismay, they all agreed. His career was over. Not one punch, but the accumulation of head trauma caused by sparring, could and most likely would prove fatal. Even with headgear it wasn't safe for him to absorb punishment. No sparring, no boxing, it was simple as that. Or at least I guess until the money ran out.

"Man, this is crazy," I yelled. "If it's money you need, I got you. We can start some kind of business and we'll be all right."

He shook his head no. "Sorry, brother, I don't do handouts. Besides, I can whoop this nigga. You saw his last couple of fights."

It was true. Scott was showing signs of aging and he no longer had the same speed or power he'd shown early in his career. But against someone who hadn't thrown a punch in the ring in seven and a half years, he didn't seem old at all. "Yo, how much could you make off a fight with him?" Dee asked.

"Five million, maybe as much as six."

"Yeah, but you'd have to win two fights to get to him, right?" Renée asked.

"He'll win." Anita said, trying to sound supportive. "He has been training like mad. Look at him." Nate flexed and indeed he did look rock solid.

"Seriously, though, folks," Nate stated, "I'm gonna need all of your support and no negative energy allowed. Understand, Nana and Cory?" He was looking at us.

We all debated with him for the next hour before we began reminiscing about his career. By the time we'd eaten we'd all given in and were either going to support him or keep quiet. I had resigned myself to the fact that I was going to be carrying his casket. Nate might as well have been fighting a gorilla as far as I was concerned. There was no way he would beat Scott, but you couldn't convince him of that, so I gave up trying.

I had to go and pick up Amani from my mother's house. School had started and I was taking her all week. Her mother and I had worked out arrangements that suited us both. One week a month Amani would stay with me the entire week and I got another weekend. In addition, she had started taking her past my mother's home on a regular basis. My mother was thrilled that she was given an opportunity to play catch-up and spoil her youngest grandchild. So much so that she redecorated my bedroom in the latest cartoon for girls. Every Saturday she would pick Amani up and take her to dance class.

The advantage to Shelly was that she had more free time to run back and forth to New York to see Ricky Reyes. Things seemed to be serious between them. It was no shock that she was in a hurry to get the divorce papers through and didn't ask for a dime in child support, said she trusted that I would do the right thing.

It was a good-money bet that she and Ricky would be getting hitched or at least shacking up as soon as those papers came through. We had a court date for the week before New Year's. For her, it would be out with the old and in with the new in more ways than one. But I wasn't mad at her for moving on so quickly. As a matter of fact, I had to admit that the brother had some long cheddar and he was obviously feeling Shelly. He spoiled her in an almost sickening fashion. They say that diamonds are a girl's best friend. If that's so, then a man who owns a diamond store obviously runs a close second. Followed third by a man who will buy them.

Though I had nothing lined up as far as a relationship, I was ready to move on with my life. I was enjoying my time with my daughter and our bond was growing tighter each day. I was finding that my life did have meaning beyond a relationship or sex with a woman. Eating dinner, braiding hair, and doing homework were becoming my favorite dates and the only ones that I came to look forward to.

It was becoming obvious that life has its own way of developing you. As I drove toward my mother's home, I thought about all that I had to go through to obtain the type of growth that I had. I'd once heard that no matter what you go through you always wind up in the same place, which was learning. I'd learned that even if I loved women, I needed to respect boundaries. A pretty face and a piece of ass are never worth causing a bunch of confusion over. I realized that, in my past, all I'd ever done was chase women based on those criteria. Married or not, sisters or not, and even with Renée, I realized that yet another line had been crossed. I shouldn't have done it. She and Brendan were special to one another and I had violated that bond.

I was more like the old Nate than I had ever realized. The only difference was that he was who he had been by design. He always embraced being a conqueror of women. I did it without intention. And without thinking. I didn't know which was worse.

Truth Hurts

A packed crowd filed into the D.C. Convention Center to witness Nate's return to boxing after a layoff of seven years. Everyone and their momma had come down to the brand-new facility to be a part of one of the top social events of the year in Chocolate City. Many of the spectators hardly remembered Nate's previous efforts when he was at the top of his game. What they did know was that even though tonight's battle was supposed to be the first of two tune-up bouts, he was coming back to eventually fight the Horse.

His fight was billed as the co–main event, but everyone knew that *his* definitely was the fight that everyone had come for. It was evident by the cheers of the crowd when the music came on, signaling that he was prepared to make his way to the ring. I wondered how he was feeling as he came out of the locker room and heard the roars from the crowd. The cameras were rolling, the fight was being broadcast on ESPN2, and a host of other media outlets had their people on hand to cover the event.

Nate came through the tunnel as LL blared "Mama Said Knock You Out," wearing a pair of silver-and-red customized boxing shorts by Sean John. Brendan and Dee were in his corner working with his trainer, manager, and cut man. Nate had asked me to sit with Anita and keep her calm, which I was having trouble doing myself. I was nervous as hell for him. He had a lot to lose. The street credibility that he valued so highly, his dignity, and even his life.

Like most events held in D.C., the fight had become a fashion show. There was an ocean of Christian Dior–, Gucci-, Prada-, and Cavalli-clad women walking around the hall. The crowd was filled with the finest women in the city, most of them half-naked, trying to see and be seen. Of course, every baller and wannabe baller in town was posted up trying to see who was wearing the most expensive gear. There was a lot of standing around until the hour had come for Nate's bout. I noticed a few local celebrities, including the mayor, who was seated five chairs to my left, next to a bunch of other local VIPs. A couple of players from the Redskins and Wizards sat ringside. Of course, some D.C. fighters had come to support Nate. Sharmaba Mitchell, Darrell Coley, Chop Chop, and "Too Sharp" Johnson were in the stands.

Suddenly the crowd came to its feet as Nate climbed into the ring.

He looked over toward me and Anita and I saw him shout, "I love you," as loud as he could.

Anita knew what he was saying and mouthed the words back.

It took no time for the announcer to bring the other fighter to the ring. He was from Saint Louis and surprisingly garnered a loud applause from the crowd. I expected Nate's trainer slash manager, Wally Booker, to get a fighter who didn't look as imposing as this opponent. He was an inch taller than Nate and his muscles made him look like the Hulk or at least Hulk Hogan.

When the bell rang, my fear gave way to excitement for my friend. I didn't care whether he won or lost the fight, I just wanted him to stay alive. After watching the first round it was evident that either Nate had truly prepared himself for the ring, or that the Hulk he was fighting was too slow to hit air.

To open the fight Nate had hit his opponent at least thirty times while getting struck no more than twice. The second round was the same as the first, only this time Nate caused the Hulk to cover himself up after being stung by a barrage of punches.

Forty seconds into the third round and the Hulk made a desperate attempt to throw a wild, lunging punch. Nate easily ducked back and was able to put his full force into a counter-punch. The right hook that Nate connected with landed flush on his opponent's jaw. The mouthpiece flew from the Hulk's mouth, followed by a grunt as his neck absorbed the horrible impact of Nate's punch. Two seconds later, after the sound of the thud echoed through a silenced crowd, the referee was standing over him and counting him out.

Ozio's Cigar Bar on K Street had been shut down to the general public. Invitation only, or you had to know somebody, namely our crew to get into the after-party. It was a surprise for Nate to celebrate his successful return to the ring. Dee and Brendan had prepared the party. I had paid for it. Dee made sure that the place was filled with women. Brendan made sure that all of our family and close friends were there.

Nate arrived in a stretch limo. He stepped out in a white T, a pair of Evisu denims, and all-white Air Force 1s. The diamonds on his bracelet, Rolex, and chain had him looking like a rapper headed for an award show. When he entered the party all eyes were on him as he moved in search of Anita. There was an embrace between them before he began hugging and shaking hands with all of his well-wishers.

"What's good, my niggas?" he asked as a smile slid across his face.

"Your right hook, I guess," I laughed back.

We were a little too close to the speakers. Biz Markie was on the turntables spinning a mix of old-school hits. Nate pulled me to the side.

"So, Cory, tell me, bro. How did I look?"

I tried to keep from blowing his head up any bigger than it probably was by now. "Man, you looked sharp in there. I have to admit that you surprised me. That was a big boy that you knocked out in the ring."

He nodded then commented, "Yeah. But that kid wasn't all that experienced. My next fight will be more of a test. I'm gonna go against Anton Moncrief. He's that German guy who was locked up for attempted murder. He just got out after four years. He's 7–0 since being released. If I whoop him I get the Horse."

"Yeah, I know about him. He stabbed an animal-control worker who tried to pick up his dog. They say that he's a little off in the head."

Nate shrugged his shoulders, letting me know that he wasn't a bit worried or at least wanted me to believe that he wasn't. Dee and Brendan walked up on us, each holding a bottle of Cristal and glasses. "Come on, take a glass," Dee yelled.

Brendan began pouring glass after glass. Just then I noticed Renée and Anita walk up. Anita seemed to be glowing. She didn't realize that she had done the incredible by capturing

Nathan Montgomery's heart. I was waiting to see if she could do the impossible in keeping him a one-woman man. I looked around the room as we all put our glasses in the air. I saw nothing but hungry women. Who wouldn't want a piece of what he had to offer? Brendan summed it up with his toast, "To our friend, our brother, the once and future champ, Nathan Montgomery."

"Here here."

"Thanks," Nate said. "Thanks all of you."

The look on his face said it all. When I reached the lobby and made my way past the doorman, Brendan was standing on the curb eyeing me. I stepped out into the light of day to face him. He'd been outside my apartment when Renée had come down twenty minutes earlier. He hadn't said anything to her, instead he watched her stroll to her car with the look of a well-rested and satisfied sister.

"So it's like that, huh, Cory."

I didn't really have a response, so I responded with a futile, "Listen, B."

"I don't understand you, man. How could you do that shit to me?"

My response was silence.

He went on, "We supposed to be family. How could fucking her be so important that you would throw twenty years of friendship away?"

"Man, I wasn't trying to do that."

"What the fuck were you trying to do? I mean come on—" He was so disgusted that he was having trouble speaking. "How long has this been going on?"

I didn't know if he really wanted to know but I had to be man enough to give him any answers that he asked for. "Not long. It's only happened a few times." The truth was that Renée and I had become booty-call partners. We would hook up usually once a week, sometimes twice, if one of us went out and had drinks. On the way home, the effects of the alcohol would usually take over and the other would get a call to hook up. Understandably, I was in a holding pattern after the Shelly-Nina situation came to an end. I wasn't ready to get into anything serious. And the truth of the matter was that Renée and I thoroughly enjoyed fucking one another.

"How long, man?"

"It didn't happen until after you came out of the coma."

"Man, why didn't you tell me?"

I told him the truth. "She begged me not to. She said she didn't want to hurt you even though you had broken her heart with the whole Laney mess."

Brendan stood there for a moment. He had his hands in his pockets and he slowly pulled them out. He handed me the keys to my apartment. "Well, it looks like I got hurt anyway, huh?"

"C'mon, Brendan, can we go talk about it?"

"There ain't shit to talk about. Things will never be the same between us. I love you like a brother and I always will, but I could never see us having a friendship on any level less than what I have had with you over the years. It's no sense trying and, to be truthful, I'd rather not even have to deal with someone like you. You go your way and I'll go mine. . . . Hell, at least you got a decent piece of ass out of the deal." With that, Brendan turned and walked away.

I walked behind him and once he climbed into his car, I said, "Brendan, I'm sorry, man. Like you said, we've been friends too long to let something like this come between us. Besides, man, you and Tuesday are supposed to be so close. I didn't think you would care what Renée was doing."

He gave a slight laugh. "Bro, you are a piece of work. Yeah, I dig Tuesday . . . no, let me check that. I love Tuesday. She's been there with me through all of this drama with Trina, the accident, and now the baby. She is a ride or die chick and it's hard for me to imagine a life without her. She has earned a place in my heart for sure. But I have my doubts and lately I have been thinking about Renée, if she and I should have given it a serious try."

"B, I had no idea—"

He cut me off. "Let me finish. Last weekend I invited her over to talk about it. I was honest with her about my feelings for Tuesday and for her. I told her I wanted to make sure that there was no unfinished business between she and I before I let go, ya' know. She and I ended up making love and afterward she cried for an hour and kept apologizing for not being stronger." He put his shades on. "I didn't know exactly what she was talking about then, but now I do."

I nodded because I felt his pain. Then I thought of Renée and how good she was at keeping secrets. I knew I was wrong but I couldn't believe Renée had slept with him and didn't tell me. There was truly no honor among thieves.

He went on. "It was strange that I noticed how you looked at her last night at the party, like you wanted to eat her up. But, hell, I chalked it up to her looking good and didn't think twice about it. Then I called her all night and got no answer. I tossed and turned thinking that I might have to let Tuesday down easy after all. I came over here this morning to talk it over with you . . . maybe get some advice. What a fucking joke."

"Man, I swear if I knew . . . I would have never—"

"The point is, you should have *never* any damned way. You got a problem, man, and this time it's gonna cost you. Peace."

Brendan pulled off. I was in shock. First of all, I couldn't believe that I had gotten caught. Second, I had just lost one of my best friends. I had the worst feeling of shame as I moved toward my building. One by one I was destroying the people close to me. I thought back to Nina's words "you're toxic."

I shook my head in disgust and at that moment I wished I was never born.

Nate had tried his best on more than one occasion to get his boys back together. I was hoping that he would be able to help smooth things over with my boy but Brendan wasn't feeling it. Nate had gone on and on about how much time I had spent at his side in the hospital but nothing softened his heart. "I will always love him like a brother, but I'm not fucking with him after this. It's one thing to treat women in the streets like this, but to do *me* dirty . . . I can't get past it," Brendan had told Nate.

After the last attempt, he had told Nate flatly that he could make one of two choices. Either respect the fact that he and I would never be cool again and be both our friends, albeit not at the same time and place, or he could pick a side and roll with one of us and not the other, period. Knowing that Nate would never choose one over the other, Brendan was able to get his way, and Nate decided to stay out of it.

It made getting together awkward, especially with Nate's demands that everyone be by his side. I found myself being the one to concede to hanging out in order to avoid the tension. Renée had shied away from showing her face anywhere she thought Brendan might be. They'd had only one discussion since the incident. She'd called him a couple of days later to apologize to him and he'd hung the phone up on her after a few choice words.

Ten minutes after Brendan left my home after busting me with Renée, I'd called her on the phone and rifled her with verbal assaults. From that day forth she and I had been on some seriously ill terms. There had been a bunch of finger pointing on both of our parts and ultimately we disagreed on just about everything, especially on who was most at fault. She had ultimately gone too far, calling me a backstabbing mufucka, and I had done the same in calling her behavior whorish.

The sad part about it was that deep down inside we each had to admit that there was some truth in the things that we'd said about one another. Even still, one night after yet another argument, we'd wound up back in my crib doing the nasty. For most brothers it was hard, if not down right impossible, denying the one steady piece of ass that you had.

On the Saturday morning of Nate's second fight, sitting ass-naked once again in my hotel room at the Sands, she tried to explain. "Cory, sex with you is great. You always make me feel completely satisfied, but the real reason why I keep coming back to *this* is because I know you can't hurt me. I could never fall for you."

She took the puzzled look on my face as a request to continue.

"To most women you seem like a great catch on the surface, handsome, intelligent, and having a slamming job doesn't hurt. But the *real* Cory, he ain't to be messed with."

Finally I interjected, "What makes you say some shit like that?"

"For one, you're too selfish to ever love another person as much as you love yourself. The tricky part of it with you is that I believe you actually do want to love . . . maybe you're scared or maybe you just don't know how." She stood up and headed to the bathroom. On the way in she shouted back, "Plus, loyalty is definitely not your strong point."

Her words were strong and it was hard to face up to her negative perception of me. I sat there on the bed and digested each word, bit by bit. She was right for the most part and I had to fight to keep from slipping into a funk behind realizing that. She showered and threw on the same outfit that she had worn to my hotel room the night before and headed back to her room. When the door closed behind her I decided that this would absolutely be the last time we'd be together.

During the bout, I noticed someone I hadn't seen in a long time sitting a couple of seats down from me. When she saw me she had the look of someone who was trying to recall where she'd made my acquaintance. She must have figured it out because all of a sudden a smile appeared on her face. I smiled back and waved. The fight had our attention.

This time Nate had a much tougher opponent. By the end of the fourth round he was bleeding from his left eye and it was beginning to swell. Nate's speed was being neutralized by Anton Moncrief's power. The German was walking through Nate's punches and landing shots to his body and head. Even though Nate was ahead on points, the few punches that he was being hit with were taking a toll on his body.

In the fifth round the doctor took a look at the cut on his eye to determine if the bleeding was impairing his vision to the point where it wasn't safe for him to continue. They went on.

I looked over at Anita and noticed the look of concern on her face. Then I said to her, "Anita, after tonight you have got to find a way to get him to hang up the gloves. It's not worth it."

She was looking at the ring intently but paused to answer me. "Cory, I never wanted him to fight. I just want him to be happy. He's the first man that I've ever known who truly knows who he is and what he wants. It's his decision and his alone. He told me that it wasn't easy for him to decide to fight again. He told me that he was scared to death to get into the ring again." She paused when the crowd erupted with a loud "*awwwwww*." Then she asked what happened.

Renée was seated on her other side and said, "Nate got a warning for hitting Moncrief with a low blow."

We watched while the referee gave Nate's opponent a minute to gather himself. Foolishly Moncrief only took twenty seconds. He stepped back in to motion toward Nate. Nate had made him angry and he knew it. A good boxer never fights out of anger; he uses his head to make controlled decisions in the ring. Moncrief was not a good boxer. He immediately tried to take Nate's head off with a series of wild punches. He next tried to land a low blow of his own and missed. In all, he threw more punches in the minute following Nate's warning than he'd thrown the entire fight. With forty seconds left in the round, he was completely punched out and had no energy left.

If I didn't know better, I would have sworn Nate had a smile on his face as he began decorating Moncrief's face with punches. Nate must have thrown and landed forty punches in the last forty seconds of that round. The round ended with a stunned Anton covering up in the corner.

At the start of the sixth round, Nate continued to pound on the head of a winded opponent. Halfway through the round Nate faked a left. Moncrief attempted to duck and Nate hit him with an uppercut. The fight was over.

The after-party was held at the Atlantic City Sheration Hotel. The line was halfway out of the parking lot. I wasn't going to miss this for anything. I even climbed in the limo with Nate, Brendan, and Dee. Brendan and I pretty much avoided eye contact and I knew that he was wishing that I hadn't come, but I decided that it was going to be his problem. Dee kept cracking jokes about the fight and the low blow, which did cut the tension a bit. He also hyped up the party and all the women that would be there. Anita had been tired so she had decided to stay at the hotel and get some rest.

We pulled up and climbed out of the limo. "Follow us, please," a gentleman in a wine-colored suit said.

We were led through the lobby to an elevator. A moment later we were in VIP. "Daaaamnn," I said aloud. It was involuntary but I couldn't help it. There were so many beautiful women in there that it was hard to believe.

"It's like that," Dee laughed out.

We had a table reserved. It was more like a section with three leather couches. There were buckets of champagne. "What the fuck is this?" Nate asked the waiter assigned to our section. He was holding up a bottle of Moët White Star.

"Sorry, but we don't have any Cristal, señor."

"Well, somebody better find a bottle of Nectar Imperial at least or run they ass to the liquor store."

"Yes, sir," he responded.

"Take all of this with you. We don't drink this bullshit."

The waiter gathered all of the bottles and headed off to the kitchen. I stared at Nate and wondered where all of the humility and Christian attitude had disappeared to. I didn't say a word. He was in a celebratory mood I was sure. I eased back into the chair and noticed Brendan staring dead in my face until I stared back into his. When I did he began speaking to Nate.

"Yo, I can't believe you actually listened to Dee and threw a low blow," Brendan said.

Dee was laughing. I was stunned to find out that the punch had been intentional. Nate responded, "For real, that nigga was killing me with those body shots. Like Iron Mike said about some dude he fought," then in a Mike Tyson–like squeak he went on, "Dat nigga hits so hard, he punches like a mule kicks."

We all fell out laughing. Dee said, "Yeah, I remember he said that about Razor Ruddick."

I interrupted the laughter. "So, man, you all right with winning like that? I mean an intentional low blow. C'mon, dog."

At the same moment the waiter came back with three bottles of Moët Nectar Imperial. Nate leaned in toward me. "Listen, that's why they call it the fight game. Get it . . . it's a fight. He's trying to take me out and I'm trying to do the same to him."

"By any means necessary, huh?"

Nate shrugged his shoulders and showed his palms as he said, "It's whatever. It's a war out there."

I wasn't feeling him. He never had to resort to any of that before and I wondered if he was truly all right with it himself. Before we could get into it any further, I saw Nate's demeanor change instantly. He was looking over my head and he stood up. I turned around and saw her for the second time.

"Oh man," I said. "I forgot to mention that I saw Sahleen earlier at the fight." Nate glared at me and turned his attention back to Sahleen's glowing face. She was more stunning than when he'd seen her last. I watched as a host of emotions welled up inside of Nate. Standing before him had been the only woman to ever break his heart.

He had finally admitted that finding Sahleen in bed with Shawn Simmons had been just as much the cause of his temporary downward spiral as Kim's death. By the time he realized that he was falling for her, she had given him a dose of his own medicine. The morning that she told him that she wasn't in love with him had been one of the most humiliating experiences of his life. It was an understatement to say that he now had mixed emotions to see her standing before him, especially on a night where he had solidified his chance to fight for a championship belt.

"I hope I'm not intruding, but I just wanted to come over to congratulate you on your victory. I had no idea you were such a talented fighter," Sahleen said as she moved toward Nate. "It's good to see you," she said. "Hello, boys."

A chorus of hellos came in response.

"Yeah, it's good to see you again. Been a while, huh?"

Sahleen wasted no time. "Still no wedding rings or children?"

Nate laughed. "Why would you ask?"

"Well, I have a couple of my friends with me. If you let us join you, I could explain it to you."

Nate nodded his head and called for the waiter to bring a couple more chairs. Two of Sahleen's friends came over. They were both tall model types and were snooty as hell. A few minutes after they announced that Allen Iverson was in the party, he came by to congratulate Nate before going to his table. When Denzel showed up and stayed for a glass of champagne it was over. The model chicks started acting really giddy and talkative.

Nate was still sitting there but he was so wrapped up in the conversation that he was having with Sahleen that he may as well have been on another planet.

Twenty minutes later I left. It wasn't my scene. I was there for Nate anyway. He was enjoying himself and that was all that mattered to me. Before I left I headed for the bar to get a drink. In no time at all I had drank a couple of shots of vodka. My mind was heavy and I wanted to be alone so I walked through the cold December air in Atlantic City.

Stopping to warm up and get some hot chocolate at the gas station, I contemplated taking my phone out to call Shelly. In the cold night air I was missing my wife. The harsh reality was that she no longer belonged to me. We were a thing of the past. She had moved on. The next few seconds had me thinking of calling Nina, but the idea of a cursing out didn't seem to do much for me. I put the phone back in my pocket and moved quickly toward the hotel. Ten minutes later I was in the lobby all set to go upstairs and spend a night alone.

I pulled the phoned out and dialed the number. On the first ring she answered. "Hello."

"It's me."

"What's up?"

"I'm on the way up to my room . . ."

"So . . . what's up?"

"You coming over?"

"Give me a half an hour."

"All right, see you then."

Renée was on the way. I was content yet disgusted with myself at the same time. Then I said to myself, "Get over it, man. Her shit is the bomb."

This was the absolute last time.

One More Round

Brendan was filled with anger when Trina called from Children's Hospital to tell him that eight-month-old Khalil had grabbed a box cutter off the table and opened a nasty gash on his hand. "I was putting together a new desk earlier and forgot to put the cutter away," she screamed frantically.

If Tuesday hadn't been there to keep him calm he might have passed out as Trina described how the blood was pouring out of his son's hand. "Wrap his hand and get him to the hospital. I'll meet you there," he'd commanded.

By the time they reached the emergency room, Khalil had calmed down, partly because he was a little weak from blood loss, in addition to his treatment. It was Brendan's first time dealing with a health issue and his son. He was overly nervous about Khalil feeling any pain and had a thousand questions. Tuesday greeted Trina when she and Brendan walked into the room where Khalil was being treated. By the time Brendan had gotten there the doctor had Khalil stitched up and was preparing to give instructions on how to care for him until his hand healed completely. His hand was all bandaged up and it looked like he was wearing a white catcher's mit.

"This is his father," Trina said, forcing a half-smile.

"Dr. Bennett," he said, extending a handshake to Brendan. He was a young doctor and seemed really energetic in his treatment. "As your wife will tell you, luckily he didn't sever any tendons or nerves and that's great news."

Brendan thought about correcting the doctor but kept his mouth shut. He was surprised when Trina belted out, "Oh, he's not my husband." Then she rolled her eyes at Tuesday.

"Sorry," Dr. Bennett said. Then he went on with his directions as he stared at the chart with Khalil's information on it and was about to write a prescription. "Is Khalil allergic to any medicines?"

Brendan didn't know so he looked at Trina. She replied, "No."

Then, simply trying to make conversation, Dr. Bennett made a comment. "I see it says here that he has sickle cell. Is that the trait or the anemia that he suffers from?"

"He actually has the milder form of sickle cell, it's not quite the anemic state." Brendan looked surprised. He had no idea.

"So have you had many problems with it growing up?"

Trina answered and, without knowing it, changed the fate of three people. "Oh, I actually don't have it at all."

Dr. Bennett then turned to Brendan, "Okay, well, as a male you'll be able to help him deal with any problems, and that's only if any arise. He may never have any serious crises from it."

Brendan was merely listening and nodding his head. Until Dr. Bennett's "Did it affect you much growing up?"

Brendan did a double take as he processed the question. "No . . . doctor, I didn't have it either."

His eyebrows rose. "Are you sure?"

"I'm positive. My next-door neighbor had it and that's the only reason I know anything about it."

"Maybe you should both get checked. One of you has to have it in order to pass it on to your son."

Instantly, Brendan's mind began to race as he processed the words. He stared at Trina and for a split second he saw the fear in her eyes.

Trying to play the drama unfolding off, Trina answered, "Okay, that sounds fine."

A few minutes passed as the releases were signed and then everyone headed for the exit. Brendan's mind continued to run wild with thoughts, only now his blood began to boil with thoughts that he might have to seriously break Trina's neck. As soon as they reached the outside, he paused.

"We need to talk," Brendan said.

Trina looked back as she had walked ahead. "Listen, Brendan, I need to get him home. The doctor said that he will be in some pain when the local anesthetic wears off."

"Yeah, whose fault is that?" he barked back.

Trina smacked her lips. "I don't have time to argue with you. I feel bad enough."

"Not as bad as you're going to feel if I find out that Khalil is not my son."

Tuesday's mouth dropped open. Trina breathed deeply, and with Khalil still in her arms half-asleep she returned, "Nigga, what?"

"You heard me. You tried to play that shit off. I don't have sickle cell and neither do you."

"True, I don't have sickle cell, but I may have the trait, for all you fucking know."

"Bitch, please. For once in your life, tell the truth."

"Me tell the truth . . . isn't the reason we're not together because you were fucking around on me this time?"

"No, the reason we're not together is because you fucking destroyed my condo. Don't try to flip this around on me." Trina turned and headed toward her car. Brendan was walking behind her fussing all the way. He accused her of everything under the sun and brought up everything that she had done to him from the day they first met. When she had put Khalil into his car seat, she turned around to face him as he said, "This isn't over. We're going to get to the bottom of this."

"What's that supposed to mean?"

"I think you know. I want a paternity test."

Trina grew a smirk on her face. "Knock yourself out, Negro. It's your money."

"Yeah, it is and I won't be spending it on a kid that's not mine. I don't hear you denying the possibility of him not being mine."

Trina flipped him the finger and climbed into her car. "You make the appointment and I'll have him there." Then she slammed her door.

Brendan stood there as she backed out. Tuesday watched the exchange from a distance. After witnessing the confidence with which Trina had carried herself, Brendan thought, *Damn, maybe I do have the trait.*

After the last series of crunches Nate's body was glistening with sweat. His abs were in washboard form and his back looked like he hauled bricks for a living. The lights were low, the gym stayed cooler that way. He climbed off the mat and headed for the ring for one last workout. He ended each training session with three minutes of vigorous shadow boxing. His logic was that if after two hours of training he still had enough in the tank to go one more round at a furious pace then he would be fine in an actual fight if it came down to fighting through exhaustion.

It was supposed to be his day of rest, but he had elected to come to the gym without his trainer. He was focused almost completely on the fight. As the timer wound down she shouted, "Thirty seconds," just as Nate had instructed. Nate began to throw a serious flurry of punches. "Ten, nine, eight, seven . . ." Nate was throwing at blinding speed.

When he finished, Sahleen made her way through the ropes with a towel and a bottle of water. "Impressive," was all she said.

"Thanks." He took a drink from the bottle. The second squirt he spat right onto the mat.

She began to towel him off. "Are you going to shower?"

"Got to cool down a bit first," he said, eyeballing her.

The only word to describe the way that Sahleen had made her way back into Nate's life was to say slithered. Nate had told her all about the changes he'd been through and how he came to find Anita.

Sahleen had been intrigued by the Nate she now encountered. He was back on top. She saw no vulnerability in him and found it extremely appealing. What appealed to her, she usually found it necessary to possess. This time was no different.

In their first dealings Nate had given in too easily, but now he seemed happy in his life without her and she needed to do something to change that. Immediately following their hooking up in Atlantic City, Sahleen's interest peaked to the point where she had to act on it.

Once she made it back to her place in D.C., she played it cool over the first couple of weeks, calling Nate just to say hello. While he was training, she would ask, "Is it okay if I stop and drop something off at the gym? How about a quick bite to eat?"

There were a couple of casual lunches at the organic foods

café. After offering to treat him to an evening out several times, a walk in Old Town Alexandria and dinner at the Chart House finally had been the opening she had waited for. From that date on, it became obvious that Sahleen had been on Nate's mind, just as much as, if not more than, the fiancée he had fought so hard to get. After that, every day was an opportunity for her to recapture Nate's mind and heart bit by bit. Text messages that read,

I have really missed you,
I missed your friendship,
No man ever moved me like you,
I would never want to come in between you and her,
I wish things would have worked out differently,
I was a fool to let you slip away,
I'm happy that you have someone who makes you happy,
I just want to be your friend.

It had all come down to this. The buildup to a moment in a darkened gym. She stood before him. A cut-off Baby Phat T-shirt and a jean miniskirt that she worn on purpose. She kicked her sandals off as she moved toward him. "I want you" rolled off her lips.

Staring into her eyes Nate thought about everything that he had been through with her. Falling for her the first time had been a mistake. Her beauty was too intoxicating, too much of a struggle to resist. He leaned into her. He had toweled off but was still sweating. She didn't flinch when she felt his wet body touch hers.

Their mouths met and Nate realized that he felt something, but it wasn't love. It was contempt. He continued on as he realized that he didn't like what he was doing. He hated doing something that he knew would hurt Anita. It bothered him that he was giving Sahleen the pleasure of being with him. He was disgusted with himself for being weak enough to deal with her. He thought about how he had dissed Shawn Simmons. Now was the perfect opportunity to do the same to Sahleen.

Within seconds Nate had shoved the one-time supermodel into the corner of the ring. He had placed his hands on the top of her head and was gripping her hair. She smelled the odor and tried to pull away. "You need to shower first."

"Fuck that," Nate said. His dick was hard and he swiftly guided it toward her mouth. "Suck it," he groaned.

"I don't want to."

"Do it." She tried to resist but he tightened his grip on her hair and repeated himself. "Do it."

Reluctantly she opened her mouth. She was turned on by his forcefulness. She worked him for a few moments until she began to gag when he pushed in too deeply. He was punishing her and she began to sense it. Once she accepted the punishment she began to enjoy it. Once she saw that her submitting to his forcefulness was turning him on she began doing her best impersonation of a porn star and was deep-throating. Before he lost control Nate stood her up and pulled her skirt up. She was naked underneath. Nate eased her up to the corner and put her legs through the ropes. "Hold on," he said. She wrapped her arms around the pole in the corner and resembled a cat climbing up a tree. Her skirt was hiked up and Nate eased up behind her.

Sahleen let out a moan that turned into a scream as Nate penetrated her from behind. "Ohh shit, Nate. I forgot how big it was," she mouthed.

"You can handle it."

She was giving it her best, bouncing up and down, trying to take what he was dishing out. His hands were on her waist pulling her down onto his dick. Nate's mind began to drift and his subconscious was being overrun with thoughts of how he felt the night he'd walked in on Sahleen with another woman.

He started banging her harder. "Oh please," she screamed.

He remembered how he felt when she told him that she wasn't in love with him after he'd broken all of his own rules and fallen in love with her. He now had a fist full of her hair as he was working her over. She was panting like a wounded animal and her arms let loose of the post. She nearly collapsed but Nate caught her and made sure she kept her feet. In one motion he slung her body a foot to the left and now her head was hanging through the ropes like a fighter knocked silly. Nate was thrusting so hard that she had her hands clinging to the ropes trying to keep from falling through them to the floor.

Sahleen had never been taken so violently. Nate kept it up for five minutes until she almost passed out from the alternate waves of pleasure and pain. Finally Nate went over the edge and came inside of her. In that instant he realized that he no longer held any feelings other than contempt for her. Sexing her had been all about his ego and revenge.

He wiped off with the towel and stared down at Sahleen. She was lying on her side on the mat like a beaten fighter. It wasn't until she heard him speak that she realized that she had been unsuccessful in recapturing Nate's heart.

"Baby," she said, finally making it to her feet, "can we go get something to eat.

In the coldest tone imaginable Nate responded, "I have to get home to my fiancée."

Sahleen digesting his disdain replied, "So you don't have any time for me."

"No, I don't, actually." Nate headed over to his gym bag and quickly hurled a few items into it.

Getting herself presentable to walk outside, Sahleen smoothed out the wrinkles in her skirt, climbed out of the ring, and walked toward him. "So, Nate, what's up?" Her voice gave away the fear that she'd been used. "I thought we were trying to work on something here."

"Sweetheart, you thought wrong," he delivered. "I was up-front with you. I told you that I had someone from the start. You had to know that I wasn't looking for anything . . ." Nate had to hold in the feelings of joy that he had welling up inside of him. Sahleen's bottom lip was quivering and her eyes looked as if they were about to erupt with tears. He had done it. Ripped her heart out the same as she'd done to him. The fact that this was probably more an ego thing for Sahleen than a love thing didn't matter to him. All that mattered was that he wanted to win. He repeated himself. "I wasn't looking for anything. At least nothing serious."

Her arms were folded. She didn't know what to say so she stood there motionless. When he turned and reached for the bag and motioned for her to exit with him, it was all she could do to move her legs. Her pride was wounded, feelings crushed, and her pussy felt like she'd been screwed by a donkey. Not wanting to let him know how she felt, she did her best model strut out of the door.

When she reached her car Nate asked, "You're all right?"

"But of course," she responded, but it was obvious that she was about to shatter into a thousand pieces.

He watched her pull off, and burst into laughter. He was back on cloud nine. It had been a long time since he felt so good. Thinking back he couldn't recall wanting to put a bitch in her place more than he had Sahleen. Now that he had done it, there was nothing left to do other than win the fight.

He pulled off and thinking about his rise back to the top, he never even noticed the Reverend Lloyd Lawson parked across the street waiting and watching him.

27

Don't Forget Your Way Home

It had always been hard for me to use the term *best friend* because I'd always had two of them. Since my fallout with Brendan, it felt like a big part of my past had been erased. All that we had been through, the good times that we'd enjoyed and the way we'd bonded, helping one another through the tough times was now all for naught. Brendan had made it apparent that I needn't call him if I caught a flat on the highway in the rain, he was no longer going to be there for me.

I would find out to my surprise that Brendan had stopped by my mother's home on her birthday and taken her flowers and Godiva chocolates, same as every year. When she brought up the subject of our friendship, assuming that she knew the details of our rift, he spoke openly about what had happened between us.

My phone rang five minutes after he left with the demand that I come right over. "There is nothing wrong but I want to see you right away," she'd said.

"Ma, I'll meet Brenda there at four to pick you up for dinner."

"No, I want you over here right now."

"Ma, what is so important that you can't say over the phone?"

"Cory, we need to talk in person."

"I have stuff to do before . . ." I heard her sigh into the line, signaling she was about to go off. I didn't want to upset her on her birthday so I said, "All right."

As soon as I agreed to come she hung up in my ear.

I cruised around the Beltway, wondering what was so urgent, as I took bites of my breakfast from Taco Bell. When I arrived at my mom's, Mr. Fields, her boyfriend who was also her neighbor from across the street, was in the front yard trimming hedges. He didn't stop to talk when I got out of my car. Instead he gave me a salute as a general would before sending troops into battle.

"Hey hey," I yelled, walking through the door. I yelled because Moms was blasting Patti LaBelle's latest CD. She was indeed Patti's greatest fan. She made it a point of going to see her perform at least once a year.

"I'll be right there," she said.

That meant five to ten minutes, so out of habit I walked into the kitchen and looked through the fridge. I found a bowl of grapes, ran some water on them, and went to work. I was in the family room when my mother came down.

"Happy birthday," I said.

"Thank you, sweetheart." She took a seat across from me and wasted no time. "So do you know why I needed you here right away?"

Looking at her, it appeared everything was fine and I was a little puzzled by the urgency of it all. "Actually, I don't."

My mother took a deep breath. Then a second that was even deeper. I knew then that she was trying to calm her nerves. "Cory, I don't know what's become of you."

"What do you mean?"

"I mean that you are not the man that your father and I set out to raise. Don't get me wrong. I'm proud of your accomplishments in the business world. You're very generous to me, your sister, and her children. That's not what I'm talking about."

I sat there, a blank look on my face. The one that only a parent or respected elder can put on the face of a grown man.

She went on. "Brendan came over here a couple of hours ago. He told me about what happened. I was so shocked. What were you thinking, son? How could you do something like that? You two are like brothers. Hell, you are brothers as far as I'm concerned. Now that damned Renée, she really surprised me. I had no idea she was that loose."

"Ma, it's not like that. She was really vulnerable. She had just caught her fiancé with . . ." I started to say another man but decided against it for a variety of reasons. "She caught him with someone else. She was hurting."

"She was hurting. You were hurting. Brendan had just come out of a coma. Your answer to all of that is to fall into bed with her? That's just what I mean. Where is your head? I expected you to be a much better thinker than that. But you should know by now that you can't think with the little head, Cory."

She paused for a second and turned the volume down on the music. "Listen, son, we all make mistakes. Some mistakes are necessary. But I want you to take a look at yours. Remember what your thought process was before you made those mistakes. I'll bet you were always thinking the same thing."

She had my attention. It was just like being a kid all over again. "Like what?" I asked.

"Oh, I'm not a mind reader. You would have to tell *me*. But

I'm betting that you were thinking that you were going to feel something. Feel better, feel good, feel happy . . . I don't know. But it's obvious that from all of the silly crap I seen from you in the past couple of years that you're obviously lost." I sat and listened to her, wanting her to tell me what I needed to know, but never thought to ask.

"You're trying to find yourself, Cory. You're trying to discover who you are as a man. You don't seem to realize that it's a combination of what you do and how you do it that will define you. It's not about what you achieve or what you can get away with that will make you a man or *the man*. It's not about which woman winds up on your arm or who you fall into bed with. It's about what people take away from you when they come in contact with you. Is a person's life better and richer for having you in it? Have you taught, loved, or blessed your friends?"

I was thinking about all of the people in my circle. The reality was hard. True, I had my good points, but what had I truly added to the lives of those around me?

Almost like she was reading my mind, she said, "Son, you've done a lot of wonderful things and most of the time you've meant well, but your lack of definition has caused a lot of heartache."

"Lack of definition?"

"Yes. You don't have definition. You don't know who you are. Are you a player hater, or a decent man?"

"You mean player?" I laughed at her attempt to be hip.

"You know what the hell I meant. Are you a dog? If you want to run women, then run 'em. But be up front about it. That's what a real man does. He tells a woman up front if he's not looking for anything serious instead of playing games."

"What if I don't know what I want?"

"Then tell them that too. That's what women want. We want honesty, a choice. If we decide that we want to chase you or to change you after you're up front, then it falls on us. But give a lady a choice. If you really and truly don't know what you're looking for, then there ain't nothing wrong with spending some time by yourself. There are worse things in the world than being alone."

I nodded my head in agreement.

"As for the way you deal with your friends. You know better. Honesty and integrity are the only way. You don't screw your friends over."

I started looking down at the carpet.

"You know what Brendan said to me this morning?"

"No, what did he say?"

"After he and I spoke in detail he said to me that it wasn't so much what you did. It was how you did it. He considered you two, along with Nate, his best friends. He couldn't believe that you would keep anything like that from him."

"But, Ma, it wasn't like we planned it, or even thought about it. Sometimes things do just sort of happen."

"Did he catch you the first time?"

"No."

"Well then. The first time it might have just happened. But what about the third, fourth, and fifth times? At some point you have to think about what you're doing."

My mother went on for another half hour and when she was finished I felt about as small as Tom Thumb. She hadn't said one wrong thing. The last thing she said was, "Son, I need you to do two things. The first is for you to capture yourself."

My look showed my lack of understanding.

"Capture yourself. Gain control of your life and you decide who you will be as a man. Shape your life instead of always allowing life to shape you."

I smiled. It was more timely advice. "What else?"

"I'm not saying you're crazy or depressed, but maybe you should see someone. Like a counselor."

"You mean a shrink?"

"A professional," she shot back. The doorbell rang. "At least think about it." She hurried to the door and walked back into the family room.

When she returned, she smiled. Brendan was standing behind her. "Well, I'll leave you two to talk." She hugged and kissed Brendan on the cheek and said to him, "Thanks, love, now this is the best present you could have given me. Don't get me wrong, I love the chocolates, baby boy." She laughed and headed out.

"Your mother told me you wanted to apologize. Just like you to get her to fight your battles for you," he laughed out.

I stood up and walked over to him. I didn't say a word until I embraced him. "I love you, dawg. I'm sorry. I'm so sorry."

Just like a friend. He forgave me and I didn't have to beg. Although, after the talk my mother gave me, I would have.

Lying in bed, Nate was watching Anita sleep. He looked at the lump in the sheet her ass created. He then stared at her, inspecting every inch. She was flawless. What more could he want in a woman? She was sweet, smart, sexy, and she adored him.

Like all men do at some point, Nate was wondering if he was doing the right thing by trying to settle down. He was three weeks away from re-creating the Legend of the Phoenix. His once-promising career had been completely destroyed with no hope of resurrection. Unlike anyone before him he'd risen from the ashes and now he was the hottest story in sports. There was much ado about the dangers that he faced fighting again. It didn't bother him when ESPN had him on *Sunday Conversation* and drilled him about the possibility of his death coming in the ring against the Horse. It didn't even bother him that the Horse had said that he would use his head for a punching bag and let the chips fall where they may.

Nate wasn't afraid of any of it. The only thing that scared him was the thought of actually committing to a marriage. Although Anita satisfied him sexually, he still found himself thinking about conquering other women. Women he couldn't put a name or a face to. He'd already been with Halle, Madonna, and a few other stars, but he thought about the stars of tomorrow that he might want to screw, not to mention his penchant for round-the-way girls. He thought of the Afro-centric chick who worked at the juice store across from Howard's campus. The sexy security guard down at the FedEx building. The hairdresser at the salon where he got his nails manicured.

He thought that he had moved beyond all of that. It was shallow and he knew it, but he still couldn't shake the desire to fuck them all. It dawned on him that the deeper he got into his training, the more his old mentality was coming back. And with that, the more he thought about leaving Anita. He had to make a decision before it was too late. He did love Anita, but he was, in fact, an old dog.

Nate was jogging to clear his mind. This would be the last week that he would train in D.C. Next Saturday he would be leaving for Lake Tahoe for his last couple of weeks before the big fight at the MGM Grand in Las Vegas. He had on his MP3 player, listening to all his favorite hits. "Jesus Walks" was pumping into his head and he found himself bouncing to the beat of the music. He loved running and thought that if he hadn't boxed he could have been a track star.

The sun was out as he made his way down U Street. He turned right on 14th and headed up the hill. He ate the hill up and had barely broken a sweat. He was in the best shape of his life. He was so focused that he didn't notice that once again he was being followed by Lloyd. Nate reached Park Road and turned onto it. He was picking up his pace now. He was listening to the R and was singing along in his mind.

Nate noticed the Hispanic men outside in Adams Morgan. They were in front of their homes, wiping down cars, playing checkers, and just kicking it. Nate turned up an alley to hit a side street in order to circle back toward 14th Street. He was going to run down to the MCI Center before heading home. When he did, Lloyd decided to seize the opportunity. He turned into the alley behind Nate. Nate couldn't hear Lloyd as his engine revved as he slammed on the gas. There would be no witnesses. The front tag was removed just for this purpose, and when he hit the corner he planned to be moving too fast for anyone to read his back plate.

Nate never even heard the impact or the sudden squeal of the dog or the screech from the breaks. Nate continued on his path, never once realizing that his life had been spared. For all practical purposes, life should have ended for Nate right then and there. Instead Lloyd ended the life of someone's Labrador retriever. What was strange is that Lloyd was prepared to run over or through Nate, but yet he swerved when the dog ran out from behind the Dumpster. Meanwhile, Lloyd looked at the outcome of the incident as divine intervention. The bottle of Rémy had flown from his passenger seat on impact, as had his Bible. He looked over onto the floor and saw that the alcohol had spilled out and saturated the pages of his Bible. The Bible had been a gift from Miss Bethany on the day he had preached his first sermon. Now it was ruined, like his spirit. He held so much anger toward Nate that he had been willing to throw his entire life away to take Nate's.

Lloyd got out of his car and looked at the lifeless dog and he began to cry. He fell to his knees and began to pray. He begged for forgiveness. He thanked God because he realized that his life too had been spared. He then did something that surprised even himself. He prayed for Nate and Anita.

He got up and climbed into his car. As he moved slowly past the dead canine, he let out a sigh of relief that it was lying there instead of Nate.

28

Thicker than Water

It was a cool summer night. The breeze more than likely signaled rain was on the way but I didn't care. I was feeling good. I'd just completed my second session of counseling. It was odd but I wanted to shout to the world that I was in therapy. Leaving the doctor's office, I tried to decide whether I would head home or out for a drink. I opted for the drink and called Brendan to see if he was going to be able to hang.

He was leaving in a few days to help Nate in his last week of training before the fight. Dee was going with them to work in Nate's camp and said that he wanted to hang out before he rolled. We all decided to meet at the Red Tavern Grill at the Boulevard at the Cap out in Largo. Once we got there we realized that everyone must have been thinking the same thing because the spot was packed.

We positioned ourselves until we managed to get seats at the bar. "Yo, here's to our boy. The future light heavyweight champion of the world," Dee said as we sipped our drinks.

"No doubt," I responded as we clanked glasses.

"So you think he's ready?" Dee laughed out.

"We'll soon find out," Brendan shot back.

"On the real, I'm starting to think that he has a chance to beat this nigga," I said. "I just wish he wasn't doing it for money."

"Money seems like a good-ass reason to me," Dee commented. "I'd fight the Horse for a million. Shit, I'd have platinum chains and fronts, the whole nine."

"You'd need more than a million just for your medical bills if you fought that nigga, Dee," I said, laughing at the thought. "On top of that you wouldn't have any teeth left to put platinum fronts on."

"Speak for yourself, he's have to catch me to hit me. And if he got off a good shot on me, it would probably be to the back of my head 'cause I'd be running the whole fight," Dee laughed out.

Brendan was quiet and it made me curious. "What, B, you nervous or something?"

"Nah, I was just thinking 'bout something."

"What?"

After a second he commented, "You both should know that Nate is far from broke. He ain't fighting because he needs the money."

I was dumbstruck. I was convinced that there could be no other reason why he would risk his life other than to protect his lifestyle. "You kidding, right?"

"Nah, I'm serious as a heart attack. I overheard him talking to his broker a few weeks back. He was talking about moving a couple million from one fund to another. When I confronted him . . . he admitted it. He said he told us that just so we wouldn't question his motives for fighting. So then I asked him why he was risking everything to fight."

"What did he say?"

"He said the reason was simple. He wanted to be champ again before it was too late. Said he didn't want to be sitting around wishing he had done something more in the ring. He actually told me that one day while he was sitting in Charlotte he saw a special on ESPN that showed the top fifty greatest fighters in history and there were two fighters in the top fifty that he had knocked out."

"And?"

"It pissed him off. He knew in his heart that if he hadn't stopped fighting, he would have been listed in the top fifty. He said the next day he got up and went to the gym."

"So he doesn't need the money?" I said, thinking aloud.

"Nope."

"Ain't that some shit," Dee said. We were all silent for a second and then Dee raised his glass. "Here's to some Rocky Balboa–type shit. May Nate whoop his ass like Rocky did Mr. T."

We all laughed and argued about which was the best Rocky movie, which stars were sexiest, and who we wanted to see in Vegas at the fight. It was after midnight when we paid the tab and headed out.

I paused at the door and said, "Let me hit the bathroom right quick."

"All right, we'll be at the door," Dee said.

I made my way to the restroom and handled my business. I was digesting the idea that Nate had lied about his motives. I wasn't mad at him. He was right in assuming that I would have never let up if I knew he was fighting just to take one last shot at glory. As much as I didn't think that it was smart, I recognized that my fears were not his fears and I needed to respect how he wanted to live his life. My therapy was helping me put a lot of things in perspective. I had come to realize that while my life was affected by the actions of those around me, it was most affected by my own actions and decisions.

On the way out I was stopped in my tracks when I saw her standing a few yards in front of me, going through her purse. It was Nina. She hadn't noticed me and I couldn't decide if I should speak. I figured that she was more than likely waiting for her date.

Before I could say a word, the door to the ladies' room swung open. I looked over and saw Shelly walk out and say, "Let me see your cell, baby, I have no signal in here."

Nina instantly handed her the phone and they walked off toward a table in the back. I was stunned to see them together, but happy at the same time. There had been a tremendous amount of guilt that I had never realized was still bothering me about coming between the two of them. Suddenly it was lifted. The last thing I wanted at this point was for them to see me, but I followed them anyway. I watched them walk back to their table. Two other girls were seated with them. I was in a daze as a quick couple of minutes slid by. They were laughing and I could tell that they were engaged in heavy girl talk. They were sisters again. I turned and walked away.

"Man, I thought you fell in back there," Dee said. "What'd you do, take a shit?"

"Hell no," I laughed. "I saw someone I knew."

Brendan and Dee had spots up close so I said my good-byes and headed off across the lot to my car. "You need a lift to your car?" Brendan offered.

"Nah, I'm just over there. I'm good."

"All right then. Peace."

There was a reason for everything that was happening. Nate would be fine. I knew it. It would be a stressful time for all of his friends, but I decided to enjoy the ride and give him one hundred percent of my support. There was a lesson to be learned and I was more than willing to accept it, whatever it was.

*   *   *

I woke up late and decided to take the day off. I wanted to do some shopping for the trip, so I showered and headed for Mazza Gallery to Saks Men and Neiman's. I got there when they opened and headed for the elevator in the garage to get up to the main shopping area. When I got on the elevator I was shocked to see Trina with Khalil in his stroller. Trina was hugged up real tight with a brother looking really comfortable.

When she saw me her eyes got big but she spoke. "Oh, hey Cory. How you doin'?"

"I'm good," I responded. "Look at him. He's getting really big."

The guy gave me a goofy grin. I was sure I shot him a weird look in response. There was no issue with her being with another man. She and Brendan were no longer together. What was odd was the way she was trying to rush and control the conversation.

"You all ready for the fight?" she asked.

"I'm getting ready for it now. Picking up a few things," I said as the elevator hit our floor.

The door opened and she tried to escape the elevator as if I had passed gas on it. As she began to exit she said, "Good seeing you. Take care."

"You too," I responded and then took one last look at the baby, then at her friend. Instinctively, I said, "Oh, my bad, brother. My name is Cory, by the way. I've know Trina for years."

He turned and extended his hand for a shake. "Nice to meet you. I'm Khalil."

A Story to Tell

The Ghostbar was pumping. Everyone was in Vegas for the fight. Half of the crowd in the club tonight was VIP. The Horse always brought out the stars to his fights. He was from Compton and his West Coast following was unreal. There were at least a hundred A-List actors and models in the party and at least twenty groupies or wannabes for each of them. I shouldn't have had a hard time staying upbeat with all the excitement but I found myself struggling to stay in a partying mood.

My mind had been heavy for a full week. Ever since I had uncovered Trina's dirty little secret, I had been trying to find the right time to break the news to Brendan. My answer had come to me when she had stopped at my mother's home and left me a message to call her. When I called her she wasted no time admitting everything to me. She told me that she loved Brendan. She always had and she always would. The boldness and honesty of her words after that both shocked and repulsed me at the same time. After she finished and I had a chance to digest them, I realized that what they really did was scare me.

The discussion had been heated. "Trina, how can you say you love him? All you've ever done is lie and cheat on him."

"Cory, but I do. I can't even imagine my life without him."

"Well, you better get used to the idea. 'Cause this time there definitely won't be any forgiveness. As a matter of fact, you might want to get the fuck out of town. 'Cause if it was me you pulled this on, I would be ready to kill you."

She paused. "It's not how you think. The only reason why I was with him that day was because . . ."

I cut her off. "Trina, please. I'm not Brendan, so there's no sense in you trying to feed me any of your insane bullshit. You actually named the kid after this other guy. How foul is that?"

"I only did that because I was so upset with Brendan for cheating on me. Yeah, I did fuck around on him with Khalil. But it wasn't like I was in love with Khalil."

"But you decided to name the kid after him? You must have been feeling him," I snapped loudly. I was hating her at that moment.

"Khalil was out of the picture, Cory. He didn't even find out that the baby was his until a couple of weeks ago. Did Brendan mention the incident where the baby had to get stitches?"

"Yeah, I remember him saying something about it."

"Well, until that day it had never dawned on me that one of the parents had to have the sickle cell trait in order for Khalil to have it. Two days later I called Khalil and had the test done."

"You ain't shit."

She ignored my statement and asked, "So you're going to tell him? Or have you already?"

I sighed. "Don't you think if I had you'd be dead by now?"

In a sarcastic tone, she spit, "You didn't kill Shelly for keeping your baby from you and having another man raise her for five years. Neither did he for that matter. Stuff like this happens. I'm not saying it's right."

"Trina, for real. What's your point? What did you want?"

"I want you to give me some time. Some time to tell him in my own way."

I paused for a second. "Listen, let me ask you something."

"Go ahead."

"Why do you do this shit? Why do you fuck around on him time after time?"

She snickered a bit into the line. Not in the way that would indicate the she thought there was any humor in the situation, more like she laughed to keep from crying. Then she answered. "Cory, to be honest with you, I don't know why. I have always been promiscuous. I love sex."

I listened and thought about some of the things that Brendan had told me over the years about their sexual antics. She went on into a short explanation of how she came to be the slut that she was. "Cory, when I was twelve, my next-door neighbor's son, Ralphy, was in the army. One time he came home for a month. The nigga was like twenty-one and fine as hell. All of us little girls would sit out front and dream of the day we'd kiss a boy who looked like him. One day when he was out front cutting the grass, I walked up to him and told him I wanted him to be my first. He laughed, thinking that it was a joke. When I didn't budge, he realized that I was serious. He told me to come over the next morning after his folks left for work. I remember getting up at seven as soon as my parents left for work. I waited patiently on the steps for his parents to leave. His mother's car was barely down the street before I was at his door. As soon as

I made it inside his house he was all over me. I was scared at first, too excited to stop him. By the time he finished, my body felt strangely satisfied." I noticed that her voice trailed off a bit but she continued, "I went back almost every day until he left to go back on duty. The truth is he turned my twelve-year-old ass out. After that it was on. I was never satisfied. I became known as the fast ass of the hood. Once my body filled out, the attention I received was overwhelming. I got used to going from one boy to the next. Most people would say that basically I became a freak or whatever, but to them I say *at least* I became one on my own terms."

It was a tough pill to swallow, realizing that women like Trina existed. I was quiet and wondered if she was finished spilling her guts. "You have until we get back from the fight to tell him," I said sternly.

"Cory—" she said.

I hung up.

"Yo, Cory, this joint is off the hook," Dee said. "I can't believe we are doing it like this. The promoters are treating us as if *we're* the one's fighting. Nate is at the hotel chilling. He said he needed complete seclusion. Anita wasn't even allowed to his room."

We were sitting off in a so-called private lounge with everyone from Team Nate. Tuesday was up underneath Brendan, looking very much in love. It was hard to get a handle on Brendan's feelings for her, or anyone other than Trina for that matter. He'd always worn his feelings on his sleeve when it came to her. He loved her in all her slutty glory.

Dee, meanwhile, was having the time of his life. He was Nate's authorized, yet unauthorized, spokesperson. He had done interviews on Nate's behalf that aired on sports shows all over the country. More than anyone, he was enjoying the limelight and the women crowding him trying to get a line on Nate.

People were popping bottles everywhere, dancing wherever they could find room. The women had on the slinkiest, albeit most expensive dresses you could imagine. It was almost like sensory overload. Because of where we were seated, people were stealing glances, trying to see if Nate was going to appear.

I saw plenty of nice-looking women but hadn't made a move on any. I had been in a real holding pattern since starting therapy. I was embracing my solitude, getting my life quieted down. It was strange that as soon as I began doing that, all the problems that I had making decisions about my personal life were no longer an issue. The women who were chasing me became less than appealing and the quiet that entered my life in their absence was welcomed. I was just as turned off by their desperation as I was by the fact that I finally began to realize what I wanted in a woman. There was a long list of qualities that I was looking to find in one woman. I was still working on myself but I knew that ultimately I wanted a wife. It wasn't hard for me to realize that none of them were it.

It had happened gradually, a missed or ignored call here, an unreturned e-mail there, and suddenly I wasn't dating anyone or sleeping with anyone for the first time in years. I had a clean slate.

At three in the morning I left the party and headed for the hotel. Waiting on the corner of Flamingo Avenue for a cab, I noticed a sister heading in my direction. She was holding a pair of shoes in her hand and was walking barefoot. As she moved closer I could make out the fact that she had a dynamite shape and, even moving without shoes, she was as graceful as a runway model.

A cab pulled up and I got a glimpse of her face. She reminded me of Melinda Williams, the girl who played Bird on the Showtime series *Soul Food*. But once she was within clear sight I recognized her, though for a second her name escaped my memory.

Somehow, right on time, it came to me. "Faith," I said.

She looked at me, puzzled. I realized then that I obviously hadn't made the same impression on her in Chicago as she had on me. "How do you know my name?"

"I met you and your friends one night. You're from Chicago right? I was at a bar and bought you all a drink."

"Oh, yeah, I remember you. You were doing the robot off of the Michael Jackson music," she laughed out.

"You want to share a cab? My treat."

"Sure, but that really wouldn't be sharing now, would it?" she said and then climbed in.

Once we were both in we said the same thing to the cabbie, "MGM Grand."

We both smiled when that came out.

"So you're a big fight fan," she asked.

I began explaining my ties to Nate. She explained that she was a fan of the Horse but that she would be praying for my boy. She said it in a joking manner but I was hoping she was serious.

When we reached the front door of the MGM I gave the driver a twenty and hopped out. I had done well at the crap table earlier, plus I was in a great mood. "Thanks for the ride," Faith said.

"Yeah, don't mention it," I said. "Hey, are you hungry?"

She looked like she was trying to figure it out. Then she looked at her watch, "It's a little late to eat, don't you think."

"Let's just call it early for breakfast," I said. I thought about it for a second. I remembered how she had slipped away in

Chicago and how it had been for the best. Now that I was well on my way to self-discovery, here she and I were, crossing paths more than half a country away from where either of us lived. "Listen, tomorrow is going to be a really busy day for me. To be totally honest with you, if I had the chance to spend some time with you, nine out of ten times I would blow off whatever for the chance. But this case is different. I'll be ringside with my boy. My flight leaves Sunday at four, so it's almost now or never. Please don't make it never."

She stared at me, peering deep into my eyes. "Brother, you are so intense."

"Only when I'm sure about something. And believe me, it's been a long time since I've been sure about anything."

"Well, what makes you so sure about this. And what exactly are you sure about?" She adjusted the strap on her dress. It had slid down her shoulder.

"I'm sure that I want to get to know you better. I was sure when I saw you that night in Chicago that you weren't the average girl. You had class and sex appeal. You were so confident, it blew my mind."

She nodded her head and held her bottom lip with her teeth before she responded. "Wow" was all she said.

I reached for her hand and she gave it to me. I led her through the lobby.

I woke at ten a.m. to a knock at the door. "Housekeeping."

"Got-dammit," I grumbled.

"It's too early," Faith said. Then she yelled loud enough for them to hear, "Come back later, please."

We were both still in our clothes from the night before. We had fallen asleep, talking after eating steak and eggs from room service when we'd come in.

Her dress was wrinkled and her hair a little mussed but still she was still gorgeous. I scooted up against her and wrapped my arm around her. We drifted back off to sleep for another hour before my cell rang. Nate needed me, or more so wanted me. He told me that he wanted to talk to me about a few things, alone.

I didn't want Faith to leave, so I asked her if she would come back at four to have dinner with me before the fight. I was feeling her tremendously. We had talked until almost six, and it seemed like it was only twenty minutes instead of two hours. By the time she left my room we had all but planned a trip for her to come to D.C.

My divorce had become final and I was free to pursue Faith with a clear conscience. I was honest with her about my situation, although I saw no need to go into all the details. I had learned to let some sleeping dogs lie. Although she had never been married, she had been engaged for two years. She had broken off the engagement when she realized that she was settling. Her fiancé had been a corporate lawyer and had done some modeling. He was long on money and looks, she'd said, but short on all the intangibles that she was looking for in a husband.

"Believe it or not, you asked me more of the right questions in a few hours than he did in three years," Faith said as she embraced me before she left my room. "I really enjoyed you, Cory."

"So, I'll see you later?"

"For sure."

I entered Nate's suite; it was as dark as a tomb. He had candles burning and the curtains closed. Dee answered the door and he was preparing to walk out past me.

"Where you headed?" I asked.

"I'm headed down to do a preliminary press spot for pay-per-view, then coming back to pick up his food. He has a personal chef across the street preparing some type of organic shit . . . don't ask."

Nate called out, "Cory, come on back."

He was in the rear room of the suite soaking his feet. "What's up?" I asked.

"Have you seen Brendan?"

"Not since last night. Why?"

"Dee said he talked to Tuesday this morning. She said Brendan got a call from Trina last night and went off. He started throwing shit around the room. Then he told Tuesday he needed some time alone. She slept in the room with Anita and this morning he hasn't answered his door or his cell."

I was worried, so I tried calling him. No answer. "I'm going down to his room," I said.

"No," Nate said emphatically. "Listen, I don't know what he's tripping off of because of that crazy bitch, but I can't let that negative energy invade my circle, you feel me?"

I nodded and he went on, "I am going to need you in my corner tonight. Brendan's head isn't right but I can't let that be my problem. So it's me and you. Pops will tell you what to do. Mostly just be there for me . . . just like always." He sounded nervous.

"You got it," I said. We sat and talked about nothing in particular. I told him about Faith and how strange it was to run into her.

"Sounds like love at first sight." He laughed. "Or is it lust?"

"Nah, it's deeper than that with her. I think she's beautiful and sexy, but I want so much more from her right now other than sex. It's like I can't wait to soak up knowledge about her like a sponge." He pursed his lips up like he was going for the line I was giving him. Then I added, "Don't get me wrong . . . eventually a brother will want to tap that ass."

Then I continued on about how much fun it appeared that Dee was having. After a while Nate seemed to relax a lot more, then we talked about him and Anita. He told me that he was going to settle down and do right by her. He was going to win this fight, marry her, and relocate. In that order too. He said he liked Charlotte, Atlanta, and Miami. It was funny but Faith told me that one day she wanted to relocate from Chicago to a warmer climate. I was shocked when he told me that he wanted to raise a family with Anita, hopefully no girls. He said he would be too overprotective and rightfully so. That's how men feel when they think that their daughters could one day meet a man like them.

I didn't tell him what I had learned about Trina. I didn't want his mind to be on anything other than his fight. His dreams and, most important, his life depended on it, so I kept it light.

30

Don't Ever Wonder

"I had to know if I could do it," Nate repeated over and over. "Cory, how am I doing?"

It was a lot different being up close and personal to the action. I was in his corner and right there at the side of the ring. The lights and the crowd noise were so distracting that I had trouble focusing on the action at hand. From what I could tell, Nate was doing fine. He had lasted three rounds with the Horse.

Pops yelled out, "You're doing fine." He reminded me of Mickey in *Rocky*. The whole scene had my head spinning. *Hand me this, hand me that, give me the sponge, more water.* It was demanding work in the corner.

At the start of the fourth round, Pops said to me, "Son, for some reason he's looking to you for encouragement. You gotta pump him up. Pay attention, and if he ask you something, tell him," then he smacked me on the side of my head as if I was stepping into the ring.

As Nate move away from the corner, I yelled, "Whoop his ass."

Pops smiled at me and turned his attention back to the fight. The fighters gave the crowd reason to cheer as they had a violent exchange of punches in the middle of the ring. It was the first clean punch of the night for the Horse. Unfortunately for Nate it gave him confidence. After the exchange the Horse began asserting himself. It became obvious that it was his time on top as he began hitting Nate with a barrage of punches. Although he was never in danger of going down, the punishment was evident on Nate's face. His left eye showed some swelling when he came back to the corner after the round.

I didn't hesitate when he asked how he was doing this time. "Nate, he's bigger and stronger, but you're quicker than he is. Don't stand there and trade punches with him." In my mind I was thinking that it could prove fatal if he did, but I said, "Use your speed. Come on. This is what you wanted, right? I know you don't need the money. So, if you're fighting for pride or ego, then show it, man."

With that he turned and looked at me and nodded his head. Pops shouted a few curse words about his performance but I knew that he was hanging on my words.

The next two rounds Nate was barely hit while throwing twice as many punches as his opponent. The seventh round both fighters seemed to tire and looked as if they were resting up for the finale. The crowd didn't like it and everyone from the cheap seats down to the celebrities began to boo. I looked over at Faith, whom I had given my seat to, to make sure that she wasn't joining in. When I looked over at her, she was already staring in my direction. Our eyes met and she smiled.

Nate surprised everyone by not just surviving the next few rounds. It was possible that he was ahead on a couple of the judge's scorecards. In the corner we were all yelling at him, trying to keep him pumped up. "You're doing it," I yelled.

"Pops, I told you I could do this, didn't I?"

"Yeah, you did."

"Damn right I did."

"Okay, stay loose and be careful. You only have two rounds left to go. It's yours. Listen to the crowd." They were chanting for Nate. The whole place had turned, not so much against the Horse, because he was a great champion. It was more of a swelling up for the underdog.

Nate stood, anxious for the bell. Across from him the Horse was a confused and frustrated fighter. He couldn't understand how he had underestimated Nate so badly. He had cursed his cornermen so much by this point that they were silent in between rounds. The bell rang and the two met in the middle of the ring.

As they danced around, Nate's mind began to drift. He began to think about the ESPN special. He began to think about the history he was on the verge of making. No boxer had ever come out of retirement to defeat such a formidable opponent. This was bigger than Leonard versus Hagler.

Nate was no longer focused on the punches. He was focused on the end result. The crowd was chanting his name as they had for the past two rounds, but suddenly he could hear them. He began to wonder how it would feel to wake up as the champ again.

The first punch came and Nate ducked it, the second he backed out of the way. Nate had lost track of where he was in the ring. His back was against the ropes and there was no escape. The third was not to be denied. Nate felt the impact and his knees buckled. A fourth and fifth punch to the head sent him reeling to the canvas two feet in front of me.

I could see his eyes rolling up in his head and, for a minute, I wasn't sure if he was okay. When I saw him trying to shake the cobwebs out of his head at the count of five I was encouraged. At seven he had his hands on the ropes. At nine he was standing straight up. The referee asked him if he could continue. "Hell, yeah," he replied.

I was quiet. I was hoping he would quit. I wondered if Brendan was watching somewhere. I looked over at Dee. His face showed concern. As I looked in his eyes, I tried to see if he could make it. For the first time he was slow to rise. "Be ready to stop it, Pops," I yelled.

He ignored me. I repeated myself, "Son, shut your mouth. You don't know boxing. He's okay."

"You're worried about a paycheck. I'm worried about his life. If he looks shaky, I *will* stop it." Pops gave me a mean look but I didn't give a damn.

The crowd was on its feet. Nate pulled himself together enough to make it through the next minute. After the knockdown it was obvious that the Horse was trying to fight safe. He wasn't throwing many punches and allowed Nate to regain his energy. As the clocked ticked down to the final minute the Horse did something extremely stupid. He responded to the chants of the crowd. *"Knock him out"* they screamed, and he tried.

He threw four hard punches that all landed to Nate's body and head, but they had obviously lost steam. The Horse had backed Nate into the corner but the Horse seemed too winded to do anything. The champ threw a lazy punch that Nate easily moved out of the way of.

The next thing the crowd saw sent them into a frenzy. A right hand to the champion's temple stunned him and caused him to stumble backward. From that point Nate threw no less than fifteen punches. The Horse reached out in an effort to grab Nate but only took more blows to the face. Cameras were flashing, hundreds by the second as Nate threw punches like a man possessed. The last punch from Nate landed flush on the Horse's chin and sent him stumbling to the canvas.

The crowd went off as Nate threw his hands up in victory. We watched from the corner on pins and needles as the referee counted to ten. The Horse couldn't make it to his feet and just like that it was over.

Nate was the champ once again.

Anita came down to the ring. When I saw the way Nate's eyes lit up when he saw her I knew that they would be all right. I was next to him keeping the crowd back. I heard him say to her "I love you" over and over.

She was in tears. "I love you too. I told you you'd do it."

"You did. You told me." He was crying.

"I love you," was all I heard. Then I saw the Horse come over to congratulate Nate.

"Great fight, man," the Horse said.

"Thank you, man. Thank you for the opportunity."

"Rematch?" the Horse asked with a smile on his face.

"We'll talk, baby," Nate said and winked.

A few moments later and Larry came over with the microphone. After Larry's opening statements and questions, Nate started, "Larry, I know we all say this, but honest out there people, listen up. To God Be the Glory. Anything else I can say is pointless. I didn't do a damned thing in this ring but show up. God kept me alive."

"He sure did, Nate," Larry said and went on, "So what will you do now? Is there anyone you'd like to fight or are you willing to give him a rematch?"

"At this point, I honestly don't know yet. I have to go and talk it over with my fiancée. We're getting married as soon as this swelling goes down." Nate laughed.

"Congratulations. So with all the speculation about health concerns, were you at all scared for your health?"

"Never," he lied.

"Did you ever imagine that you would be here back on top of the sports world and did that fuel your return?"

"I wondered almost every day for the past six or seven years what this would be like. But I listened to everyone else's reasons why I had to give it up. But I got one word of advice for everyone out there. Dreams don't come easy, ya' know. Life is short, you have to live your dreams. If you sit around wondering when the time will come that life will make it easy for you to live them, you may wait a lifetime. Don't ever wonder, baby. Don't ever wonder."

The End . . . almost

31

Don't Wanna Be a Player No More

ONE YEAR LATER

We were sitting courtside at the Miami Heat play-off game. Shaq had made ten of eleven free throws, the Heat were winning, and the crowd was going crazy. Life was good. Nate had sprung for the tickets since we were guests in his town. Brendan, Dee, and I had all flown in with our ladies for the weekend for a special occasion.

Nate was hosting a baby shower for Anita. Of course, he had gotten a lot of help with the whole thing from Tuesday. During the past year, she and Anita had become the best of friends. Even with the distance, they talked on their cell phones every day, all day. When Nate gave Tuesday the green light to plan a baby shower to end them all, she'd jumped at the chance and had spent two weeks in Miami putting it all together.

Nate had purchased a home on Miami's exclusive Star Island. The nine-million-dollar price tag was cheap compared to what some of his neighbors had spent. His crib was a five-thousand-square-foot, five-bedroom, MTV crib-worthy dig. The house had a dock in the back with a boat and four Jet Skis hooked up to it. It was equipped with a pool and Jacuzzi.

Nothing was too good for his family, now that he had truly decided to give it his all. As promised, he'd married Anita on New Year's Day in St. Margaret's on the beach, no tux or gown, they both wore white linen and were barefoot. By that time the baby was already on the way and due to arrive in July. Nate's grandmother was moving down to become the nanny. They were expecting a girl. Nate was doing well in his efforts to be a do-right man. He truly appeared to be a changed man, a reformed player.

After the game we hit the club without the ladies. Each of us admitted that it had been a while since we had been out individually or as a group. I had been spending all my free time with Faith. She had moved down to D.C. from Chicago and we were giving our relationship a real try. Faith, believe it or not, was a psychiatrist. She hooked up with one of her professors from Brown University who had a practice on Connecticut Avenue. The greatest thing about her, other than her sex, which was incredible, was that she was the fairest woman I had ever known. She realized that no one was perfect, including herself. She would say that if people wanted patience, acceptance, and forgiveness, then they had to be willing to offer it. On top of that she made a nice piece of change.

We cruised down Washington Avenue toward the club Bed. We jumped out of the limo and walked straight past se-curity. Nate was greeted with, "Hey, Champ," and "Good luck on the fight," by the people waiting in line.

Nate had given the Horse a rematch four months after the first fight. This time the doctors had stopped the fight after six rounds. Nate had opened a cut over Scott's eye in the second round that was pouring blood, impairing his vision. After Nate had hit him with ten straight hooks to the head, it became too dangerous to let the fight go on.

Afterward Nate signed a three-fight, thirty-million-dollar deal with HBO. His camp handpicked the opponents. He was definitely going to retire after the fights. "No need pressing my luck, nothing left to prove, and plus I'm rich, beyaatch," he had said.

The bottles came and so did the ladies. They came two, three, and four at a time. Each time Nate said, "Sorry, ladies, we're having private celebration over here. Just the fellas. But please allow me to buy you a drink." He signaled to the waitress to take care of anyone he turned away.

"We've got a lot to celebrate," Nate said and raised his glass. We all raised ours to meet his. "Here's to my baby girl," he said, all teeth.

"To my godchild," I said.

"Our godchild," Brendan said.

"Here's to you kicking much ass and living phat, my nigga," Dee yelled. He was already tipsy when he climbed out of the limo.

"Here's to my new lady, my future," I said with a smile. Then I reached into my blazer pocket and pulled out the blue Tiffany box. "I am going to propose to her on Sunday."

"Oh shit," Dee yelled out. I pulled the ring from the box. It was four carats set in white gold. "Do the damn thing."

"That's all right," Brendan said.

Nate just smiled. He already knew. As a matter of fact he had helped me set up the proposal. Game four of the Heat play-off game was Sunday afternoon and right before the end of the first half, Faith would look up and see the proposal on the Jumbotron, then she would look over and see me on one knee.

"Listen up," Brendan said. "I want to make a toast to you three. You are three of the best friends that anyone could hope for. I just want to toast you three—"

Nate tried to cut him off. "C'mon, man, it ain't about that, we're family—"

"Nah, forget that," Brendan said. "Let me finish."

"Go ahead," Nate said.

"I want to say thanks to each of you. You each did some tremendous things to show your support for me in the last year. Nate, I never apologized for leaving Vegas before your big fight and for missing the rematch, but what can I say?"

He leaned in and they shook hands. He went on, "But I want to say that I couldn't have made it through all of the shit I went through with Trina without your support. I love you all like brothers."

Brendan had caught the first flight out of Vegas when Trina called his phone and told him the news. Khalil was not his son. By the time Nate entered the ring to fight the Horse that night at the MGM, Brendan was in custody. He had dished out more punishment than Nate and the Horse combined. He had been locked up for assault and battery. After drinking himself into a stupor, he had surprised Trina by popping up at her house and finally kicking her ass for all of the hurt and embarrassment she'd caused him.

At one point he thought about putting a pillow over her head. Khalil's screams had gone unheard until that point. Moments before it would have been too late, Brendan looked into Khalil's face and saw an innocent child who didn't ask for the hand he was about to be dealt.

In that moment he knew he could not make the child an orphan, no matter how far Trina had pushed him. He climbed off of her and called the ambulance and the police. He turned himself in right then and there.

Nate, for his part, had gotten him the best legal defense team money could buy. Dee had convinced Trina not to press charges or show up in court. The state picked up the charges and did their best to stick it to Brendan. In the end, Nate's money talked and Brendan served only thirty days of a ninety-day sentence and left with no criminal record. He was ordered to go to counseling. He was Faith's first client.

The year had brought much change. We had all grown as men. Most of the foolish things we had done, and enjoyed doing in our twenties, were all habits of the past. At least most of them.

Brendan was finished with his toast and we all took one last swig. "Oh, one more thing."

"What now?" we all said together.

"We were going to wait until the baby shower to tell you all this," he said, unable to keep the grin off of his face. "We just found out last week that we're pregnant."

I was the first to show enthusiasm. "That's great, man. You ready for that?"

"For sure. I mean, I ain't getting any younger."

Nate had nothing but a scowl on his face. He didn't approve.

Dee laughed and said, "Man, you're a nut."

Just then Nate's cell rang. "Yeah," he said, followed by an okay. Then he spoke some more. "We're at Bed. We're leaving shortly. Okay. Okay. I love you too. I will." He hung the phone up and said, "Brendan, your wife said she's been trying to dial your cell but you haven't picked up."

Brendan looked down at his phone and sure enough he saw six missed calls. He hit the dial button and called her back.

Trina answered on the first ring.

Don't Ever Wonder

Reading Group Guide

We hope that you enjoyed Darren Coleman's *Don't Ever Wonder*. The following questions are intended to facilitate your group's discussion of this engaging and provocative book.

Questions for Discussion

1. As the title suggests, many of the characters in *Don't Ever Wonder* are consumed with questions about the alternate paths their lives could have taken had they made different decisions. What are the decisions for Nate, Brendan, and Cory that could have made a difference? Have they satisfied their curiosity by the end of the book, or are there still questions left unanswered?

2. Why in the world would Brendan make the decision to take Trina back? Will he be able to raise the child as his own? Is there any circumstance when cheating is forgivable, and, if so, how many times before enough is enough?

3. While proclaiming to be a Christian, Nate allows either his temper or his pride to take control of him, and he beats a man, cheats on Anita, and breaks his reverend's finger. Was he justified in any of these actions? How genuine is his newfound spirituality? Will it last?

4. Throughout the novel, Cory and Brendan play women left and right, and it's all good. But when Cory sleeps with Renée, Brendan can't take it and ends the friendship. Was this a genuine betrayal on Cory's part, or is Brendan overreacting? Is it ever okay to sleep with your best friend's exes?

5. Why is it so important to Nate that he regain his belt? What does he risk to attain this goal? How would Nate have reacted if he had lost the championship fight? Is it ever worth risking it all to achieve what one believes to be his or her purpose?

6. Cory breaks his promises and abruptly walks out on Shelly, leaving her a single mother. He is upset with himself for these selfish actions, but he is able to move on. But when he betrays Brendan, it causes major turmoil in his life, and he is barely able to function from the guilt he carries. Does he have his emotional priorities straight? Is he wrong for having more loyalty to his best friend than to his baby's mother? At what point do lovers become more important than best friends?

7. Renée leaves her fiancé when she finds out he has been sleeping with men on the down low. How much of a problem are black men on the down low and how much of an impact do they have on African American women?

Acknowledgments

First off I have to give thanks to the Almighty. We all should, right? I've been through a lot since my career as a writer has taken off, some great and some not so great things. Through it all I've learned that you have to take the bitter with the sweet and most of all you have to stay in prayer. To whom much is given, much is expected, and to fully understand that *is* to have some degree of peace.

The first person I want to thank is my mother, Doris Patrick. Oh, how we have had it out, but no matter what, I know you have my back and I have yours. Thanks for all you've done and continue to do for me. All the days you were tired or sick but still had the time to make sure Tanya and I were well fed, clothed, and educated and for keeping books in my hands. You didn't care if it was a comic book or a *Sports Illustrated*, you just wanted me to read. It paid off.

Family first, so I also want to thank my aunts, Nancy, Esther, Florence . . . all like mothers to me, guiding and encouraging me as well. To my uncles, thanks for being there and taking up the slack of a father who wasn't, Ed, Pee Wee, and Ren, I love you and thanks. To my extended family, aunts, uncles, cousins, friends . . . thank you so much for all the love and well wishes.

To be specific . . . this part is so scary because it's too easy to forget a name even if you don't forget a person.

Michael Morrison, Dawn Davis, Rockelle Henderson, Gilda Squire, Laura Blost, Stacey Barney, Donovan Baddley, Mary Keane, and the rest of the Harper/Amistad family: thanks a million for the confidence and support. Jimmy Vines, you're a great agent, much success to you. Nina Graybill, my lawyer . . . thanks for everything.

Once again to the talented Anthony Carr, man, you never cease to amaze me with your art . . . thanks once again on a fabulous cover. Congrats to you and Renée on your beautiful baby girl. Les Green, thanks for the work on the website as always.

Thanks also to Lynn Hobson, Tressa Smallwood, Tamika Diaz at Culture Plus; Rico Douglass, Trina Holt, and the entire Karibu Books Team and all of the other store owners and vendors out there doing it for me. To Tamara Cooke, my accountant. Thanks also to Sheryl Hicks, Yolanda Marie J., Lynn Thomas, Deena Myles, and S.O.A.R, Kimberly Jones from *superstar.* Lori Carter at 4 Star's Hair Salon in Suitland, Maryland . . . check her out. Special thanks to Tracye Stafford and IKON Entertainment. Tray, I truly appreciate all you do that you *don't* have to. We will slice through the fakes and get the movie done. You are a gem. To Lisa Richardson and Angela Oates . . . you two still have the Write Touch. Thanks also to Leslie German.

My dawgs and homeys, thanks for all the support. It's so good to get the love from your peers. In a world where a brother would sooner hate on you than give you your props, I keep running into positive brothers who lift me up and remind me what real men are supposed to do. First off, I want to thank my fellow mentors, Carl Green, Daren Browning, Daryle Brooks, Dennis, and all the brothers across the land who reach back to the youth by giving their time, energy, and money to help the lil' dudes find their way before they get lost. Ron Brown, stay positive and thanks for having me come down to talk to the youths. I enjoyed that. To Mike Davis and all my crew from the Barbershop, Always. My barber Eric Carter . . . the party starter. Pierre Fletcher and Radical Art Clothing. Curtis Kittrell and Jessica Smith at Emagine Studios in Forestville. Dr. David Harmon, the best orthodontist in Maryland. To the people I run into: Dondre Owens, who always has a good word for me about my work, thank you.

Hey Shaka . . . never forget it's a celebration, nigga. Miami, New Orleans, L.A., Rio de Janeiro, like the ol' boy Rick James would say, *We just getting starting bitches . . . we're just unwinding.*

DeWright Johnson . . . hold on up top, K'wan, I'm waiting for you. Tyrone Wallace, Wahida Clark, Crystal Winslow, William Fredrick Cooper, it's a pleasure knowing you all. Most of all to my man Zach Tate, Eyone Williams, Danette Majette, and the Nvision Publishing family, thanks so much for stepping up the game. To the very special Joy King.

Shout to my brother Jim and the entire Chaney family. Kenny Lattimore and the lovely Chanté Moore. My homey, Ted in Brooklyn at Assorted Flavors Entertainment. Nancy Flowers, you are the bomb, sistah. To my Vickie Stringer . . . I'll always be your baby's daddy. Shannon Holmes . . . I'll roll with you always. Don't trip off the snakes and snitches, their time is short like leprechauns.

Thanks to Community Books in New Orleans. To Victoria Christopher Murray, you are the realest and most genuine author out there. Much success to you. Patty Rice, as always, I'll never forget. Natti at Afrikan World . . . much respect. Karen at A&B, you are my doll baby. Thanks to Eric and Gail for the support. Kevon Thomas, stay real, the future for you is bright. Thanks to everyone at Culture Plus for the support. To my man Massamba Amar, the king of Jamaica Ave. . . . much success, in cha Allah.

Enid, in Charlotte . . . you've been so helpful. I hope to return the favor one day. Twala McCain, thanks for the support, stay up. Theresa in Ft. Lauderdale, Shalisa in Dayton, Tenia in the ATL, Tecia from NY, Demi from all over, Bella in L.A., it's all love. To Lea Williams, the most beautiful future attorney in Carolina . . . Georgetown. IJR, I wished the best for you but sometimes we can't see the forest for the trees, though time will fix that. Keep your eyes and your mind open. Iyauta Moore, I can't wait to read your acknowledgments, you got mad talent. Damien Lyles, *Crocodile Tears,* finally finished. Big cuz is going to walk you through to the promised land.

Thanks so much to Justine Love and Todd B on *Lovetalk and Slowjams* at WPGC. Thanks also to the WHUR morning crew. My peeps at WKYS . . . thanks for the shouts. And to Natalie Case at Magic 102.3. Thanks in advance to all the air across the land for having me. Michael Baisden for the shout and for blazing the path. V103 in Chicago and 92Q in Baltimore.

To Al in Dallas, if that's even your name. You know who I'm talking about. Man, you are sick and the biggest clown I have ever met. But, God bless you anyway.

I never said thanks to Dr. Sydney Walker, my English professor at Bowie State University, for telling me that I was indeed, a writer. At that time I didn't even have my own computer, but I just want you to know that sometimes we plant seeds and have no clue what will come forth from that effort. Keep blessing your students.

Lastly, I just want to say thanks to you, the readers, for the support. If you purchased a book, told someone about me . . . I thank you from the bottom of my heart. I've said it before, without you, there is no me. I hope that I am able to inspire someone to take a chance and follow a dream. It's never easy, but usually worth it.

It's been said that a dream deferred is a dream denied. Who wants to sit around wondering what could have been? Don't Ever Wonder . . .

One,

Darren Coleman